No Bottom

No Bottom

James D. Brewer

Walker and Company
New York

First published in the United States of America in 1994
by Walker Publishing Company, Inc.

Published simultaneously in Canada by Thomas Allen & Son
Canada, Limited, Markham, Ontario

Library of Congress Cataloging-in-Publication Data
Brewer, James D.
No bottom / James D. Brewer.
p.   cm.
ISBN 0-8027-3178-3
I. Title.
PS3552.R418N6   1994
813'.54—dc20   93-23341
CIP

Printed in the United States of America
2 4 6 8 10 9 7 5 3 1

To my daughters . . . who taught me of life
To my wife . . . who taught me of love
To my mother . . . who taught me of life, love,
and the River.

▽

1

Wednesday, October 23, 1872

ALONG THE ST. LOUIS wharf, the *Paragon*'s smokestacks belched a black cloud into the cool October breeze as Captain Luke Williamson lifted a gold watch from his vest pocket and examined it for the fifth time in as many minutes. The loading was horribly slow today. Perhaps he should speak to Jacob. Leaning over the rail, he searched the foredeck until he spotted a large, muscular Negro man yelling and pointing at the dozen roustabouts hauling cotton and wheat aboard the landing stage. Luke was about to call down to him, but thought better of it, closed his watch, and stood erect. It wasn't Jacob's fault. It was all those damned slow-ass passengers. Luke again leaned over the rail and called down to the deck.

"Steven! Steven!"

A skinny man holding a ledger book looked up.

"Captain, did you call me?"

"Get'em moving. We're burning daylight," Luke said. As the man returned a helpless shrug, Luke saw one of the roustabouts mishandling a trunk before the eyes of its owner.

"Careful there! That's not a barrel of flour!"

On his way to the stairwell Luke caught himself reaching for his watch again and forced his hand away from the pocket. They'd be off soon enough. The crew were doing their best, he assured himself. He was being unrealistic. But then, this wasn't just another run. The sooner he was under way, the sooner he'd reach Natchez, and the sooner he'd be able to get some answers.

It had been more than a week since the telegraph brought the stunning news, and not a day had passed that Luke didn't see those horrible words a hundred times.

OCTOBER 14 1872
NATCHEZ MISSISSIPPI

CAPTAIN CHARLES L WILLIAMSON

AT 8:30 PM MARY JUSTICE DOWN EIGHT MILES NORTH OF NATCHEZ JUST OFF RIFLE POINT STOP FIFTY DROWNED STOP THIRTY-FIVE MISSING, SHIP DOWN IN DEEP WATER STOP CAPTAIN LOST STOP

V MATTHEWS

WHARFMASTER NATCHEZ

Ed Smythe had gone down with his ship, and it seemed to Luke like a bad dream. They had been together since March of 1861, seeing each other through the war and into a successful packet service. Now it had all come down to two words: "captain lost." Just like that.

Luke stared along the dock at the steamboats that lay nearby and thought of another morning in New Albany, Indiana, only a few months after the war. Ed had stood beside him as they surveyed a row of government surplus riverboats, all secured to the dock and awaiting sale, their boilers cold and their smokestacks quiet.

"One day all these ships will be under steam," Ed said, "and ours will be right there in the middle of them."

If it hadn't been for Ed, Luke would probably have become a contract pilot, working for one of the many shipping lines that sprang up with the return of peace. But Ed had seen more. He had always seen more, Luke thought. Ed was the dreamer. Luke the doer. But together . . .

Luke smiled. He could still remember the smell of the

boats—like old, dirty clothes—as he crawled through the engine rooms, inspected the quarters, and reviewed every inch of more than fifteen vessels. Using the knowledge he gained working in the Warsaw Shipyard in southern Illinois before the war, Luke selected two former troopships. With financing Ed had arranged, they bought the two stern-wheelers, sailed them to Luke's old shipyard, and had them reworked to Luke's specifications. The result was the *Mary Justice* and the *Paragon*, two of the finest packets to grace the Mississippi. Each ship was outfitted with twin high-pressure steam engines with a twenty-two-inch bore and an eight-foot stroke. They handled 140 pounds of pressure from five boilers, each containing two flues. Those engines made the *Mary Justice* and the *Paragon* among the fastest boats on the water.

Ed arranged the investors, planned the routes, and courted the business. They started slow, each man piloting his own boat and handling the duties of captain as well. But as they became more successful, they hired other pilots and turned more of the navigation over to them. Ed found himself more involved in the business end of the operation, and Luke was glad. The pilothouse was where he felt most comfortable, and the hours of paperwork and nursemaiding guests just bored him. They made a good team—going from running a few thousand tons of cargo and a few hundred passengers in 1866 and 1867 to being one of the busiest small packet services on the Mississippi.

The idea that the *Mary Justice* was gone gnawed at Luke as he gazed down the length of the *Paragon*. She was 260 feet long and 48 feet across the beam, only slightly larger than the *Mary Justice* had been. It was strange, thinking of the sister ship in the past tense, and seemed somehow profane. Perhaps if he had made the run instead of Ed . . . yet he felt ashamed of such a thought. Ed was a good pilot. In fact, apart from himself and one or two others, Ed was the best pilot Luke had ever known. That he could go down just seemed impossible.

"Captain Williamson!" Captain, can you come down here a moment, please?"

Steven Tibedeau's voice shook him to the business at hand; Luke walked over to the center of the deck and down the stairs. On the cargo level he found his clerk conversing in French with a finely dressed gentleman who clutched a carpetbag in one hand and held a hand-carved baton under the other. Luke halted in mid-stride when he heard the words *"Mary Justice."*

"What's the problem?" Luke said.

"Captain, uh, Mr. Brevalier is concerned about the safety of traveling with us." Luke gave the Frenchman a doubtful stare as the clerk continued. "He uh, wants—"

The gentleman again spoke to Steven, alternately glancing toward Luke. The captain's face grew stern as he heard the Frenchman mention Captain Smythe.

"What did he say?" Luke asked the clerk.

Steven looked uneasy. "Uh, Captain, the gentleman, uh—"

"Well get on with it," Luke snapped. "I haven't got all day."

"He wants your personal guarantee that the boat won't sink."

"He wants what?" Luke didn't like the looks of this man to begin with, standing there with his chin in the air and fingering that ridiculous baton as if he were Napoleon. "What's he saying about Ed Smythe?"

Glancing down at the deck, Steven shifted his weight on to one leg and spoke softly, as if trying to take some of the edge off his words.

"He said that Captain Smythe . . . uh . . . He wants you to tell him that the pilot is not an incompetent," Steven said, pausing for a moment, "like Captain Smythe."

Luke ran his tongue over his lips and pressed them together hard. "You tell that sissy-lookin' son of a bitch to go to hell. And if he ever says another word about Ed Smythe I'll personally throw his puny ass in the river and leave him in the backwash."

The clerk took the Frenchman by the arm and began to escort him up the stairs, with Luke's eyes burning a hole in him with every step.

"The captain says we have a very fine pilot," Steven said, ushering the passenger quickly away from Luke.

"Just as pleasant with the passengers as ever," said a tall, dark-haired woman moving toward Luke. She was closely followed by a roustabout shouldering a trunk; he seemed entranced by the way her ass bounced as she walked along in her pink ruffled dress.

"Miss Tyner," Luke said with a nod, his gaze dancing off her milky white breasts, then passing quickly to look into her dark eyes.

She extended her hand, which he took and caressed lightly. "He didn't say what you told him to, you know," she observed.

"Who?"

"The clerk."

"You speak French, do you?"

"Enough to know that he's a lot nicer than you are."

"He gets paid to be nice."

"And you don't?"

Luke shook his head. "I get paid to get you where you're going."

"It's always business with you, isn't it, Captain?"

"Not always."

"Just around me, right?" she said, her smile disappearing.

"Something like that."

She stared at him momentarily as the roustabout shifted her trunk to his other shoulder.

"Well, anyway," she said, "I'm sorry to hear about your friend." Luke nodded. "You and that Captain Smythe were pretty close, weren't you?"

"Yes, we were."

"Too bad," she said, continuing past him and starting up the stairs.

"Traveling alone this trip?" Luke called after her.

Miss Tyner stopped abruptly in the middle of the stairs, causing the roustabout to momentarily juggle her trunk. He recovered and tossed her an angry look, but she glared right back at him, then looked down at the captain.

"Not for long," she said with a wink, then disappeared up to the passenger deck.

Salina Tyner had traveled on the *Paragon* at least a dozen times before, and she'd been on most of the other major St.-Louis-to-New-Orleans packets, too. It was no surprise that businessmen and travelers desired her company, for she was free with the praise and easy with the hugs. Luke figured that was about all that was free, however.

"I entertain gentlemen," she'd confessed to him over a brandy one night a few miles north of Memphis. "I appreciate their company and they appreciate mine."

From the way she dressed and the frequency of her travel, Luke figured they must appreciate her at a rather hefty rate. But he didn't care. She paid her passage, kept her business discreet, and never caused a problem. There was even a certain advantage, Luke figured, to having someone like her on board; and as long as she stayed out of his way, he could care less what she did in her bunk at night.

Salina Tyner had been gone scarcely a moment when a rotund woman in a ridiculously large, feathered hat came tramping down the stairs.

"I'm just not going to have it, that's all. I'm just not going to have it. Captain, they gave me a room that's all darked-in."

"I beg your pardon?" Luke said, forcing a smile. Steven Tibedeau was hustling down the stairs after her as she continued.

"Someone has stacked cotton all along the wall outside my cabin," she complained, shaking her finger at Luke. "Why, it's dark as night in there. How am I supposed to see to get dressed? I've paid too much money to—"

Luke walked away in the middle of the woman's sentence, leaving her mouth agape. Motioning over his shoulder with his thumb, he told Tibedeau, "Take care of this. I'm going to see Jacob."

Standing on a crate near where the gangway extended from the bow to the pier was a tall, husky black man, his biceps peeking from beneath rolled-up sleeves. Jacob Lusk, Luke's first mate, shouted orders to the lines of roustabouts, moving like so many ants in opposite directions along the gangway. His loud, deep voice was a familiar and comforting sound to Luke. Jacob had been with him since he and Ed first started, and he'd dared to entrust to Jacob responsibilities that no Negro working the Mississippi had ever seen. As first mate, he managed the cargo loading and supervised the deckhands. A lifelong riverman, Jacob had worked as a fireman, a sounder, a boiler man; in fact, he'd held just about every deck job a steamboat had to offer. At first Luke had taken him on as an assistant deck chief, running the night shift. He'd been impressed with Jacob's knowledge, so after six months of seeing how the other hands looked up to him, and after an ugly incident with a tipsy first mate, Luke had the drunken employee put ashore just north of Vicksburg and immediately assigned his duties to Jacob.

Giving such a position to a Negro upset some of the crew and shocked the passengers. His actions drew ridicule and predictions that it would never work out.

"A nigger ain't got sense enough to be a deck foreman," they'd said. "Why, he'll be stealin' cargo and runnin' you aground in less than a month."

That was almost seven years ago.

"Are we goin' downriver soon, or should I have the cooks plan Christmas dinner here in St. Louis?" Luke said, stepping up beside the wooden crate where Jacob stood.

Jacob made another entry in the ledger.

"Ain't nothin' to it, Cap'n." His eyes bounced back and forth between his notations and the line of roustabouts hauling cargo.

Whether they were feeling their way along the river in a choking fog, or digging some departing passenger's trunk from underneath fifteen cotton bales, Jacob's answer was always the same: "Ain't nothin' to it."

"How much longer?"

"I figure twenty, twenty-five minutes at the most, Cap'n. Ham be bringin' the steam up anytime now. I done told him."

Ham was the Irish-born chief engineer who ran the boilers and maintained the *Paragon's* engine room; and he was the one man on the boat who could outcuss Jacob Lusk. Their loud exchanges had stung the ears of a number of the more genteel passengers over the past two years. But for all their disagreements about how to run the river, they seemed to hold a certain respect for each other, and both were loyal to Luke.

"I wish you'd look a-here, Cap'n Luke," Jacob said disgustedly. He pointed toward four roustabouts manhandling a large cage. "This right here ain't gonna be nothin' but trouble."

The four men were struggling to haul the cage, containing three bluetick hounds, while each dog was doing his best to relieve the workers of their fingers. The men constantly cussed the animals and changed their grip on their load.

"Careful there, careful now," instructed a rather portly gentleman in a waistcoat.

"Who is that guy, Jacob?"

Jacob checked his list. "That'd probably be a Mr. Caldwell. He wants us to take these here coon dogs to Natchez."

"Is he going with them?"

"No sir."

"Good."

Jacob shouted at the roustabouts who'd placed the cage at the first open spot they could find.

"Not up front, you don't. I ain't havin' them dogs up here. Take 'em on back." The crewmen stared at him in disgust, but they'd learned that look in Jacob's eye, and when he gave an order, smart men followed. So they again grasped the cage, and disappeared along the side of the boat with the dogs snarling and nipping at their hands.

"I'm going to the wheelhouse. Keep 'em moving," Luke said.

"Yes, sir, we'll be under way directly."

Luke had reached the texas and was near the foot of the ladder up to the pilothouse when he heard Steven Tibedeau calling him. Two men from the St. Louis Mercantile Bank had insisted on seeing Luke before he got under way; and rather than leaving them to roam the decks, Steven had taken them to Luke's cabin and had the steward bring them each a drink. Ed had always handled the bank. He'd been the glad-hand man when it came to putting together deals and stroking the feathers on all the right people. Luke hated financial dealings. The river was enough for him, and thanks to Ed and the success of the business, he'd been able to hire people like Jacob and Ham and Steven so he could avoid the unenjoyable parts of being a captain. When he stepped in the door of his cabin, the two were waiting.

"Captain Williamson," said one of the gentlemen, extending his hand, "Jack Aubrey, Mercantile Bank."

"Jeremiah Palmer," the other added. "I think we met last year."

"Yes, yes we did. What can I do for you?"

"Well, Captain, we just wanted to let you know how sorry we are about Mr. Smythe," Aubrey said. "He was a good customer."

"You mean, *Captain* Smythe."

"Oh yes, certainly, certainly." Aubrey shook his head, looking sorrowful. "It's a tragedy, that's what it is, a real tragedy."

"Have you heard any details?" Palmer asked. "I mean, do they know any more about how it happened?"

"Not much so far, but I plan to find out. We're leaving for New Orleans in just a few minutes. I'll be talking to some people and stopping at the site on the way down."

"I see," Palmer said, rubbing his chin. "And do you think

there's much chance of salvage? Do you think we can save any of the boat or the cargo?"

"I wouldn't know, Mr. Palmer. She went down in over a hundred feet of water."

"Of course, I understand, it's just that . . . " He looked uncomfortable and glanced at Aubrey, apparently for support. "Captain Williamson, the bank is, well, on the line for the *Mary Justice.*" He paused, as if waiting for Luke to say something. "The boat was insured, and there will be a settlement, I'm certain."

"But whatever we could salvage would certainly need to be put against your account," Aubrey said. "Even with the insurance, it's not going to cover the loss."

"What you are trying to say?"

The two bankers looked at each other and Aubrey spoke. "There's the matter of the eight-thousand-dollar note—"

"Eight thousand dollars? I don't remember signing any papers for a loan."

"You didn't, Captain Williamson. Captain Smythe did. But he was committing your company. He had the authority to do that, of course."

"But he didn't tell me anything about a new loan."

Aubrey cleared his throat. "Well, I'm sure I wouldn't know about that. We just came by to tell you we're concerned about the future of your packet service. The bank will be looking for you to make up the loss. Wouldn't want to see you lose your boat."

"And you think I would?"

"Well, of course not, Captain. We just wanted to see—"

"You just wanted to look out for your interests."

"Yes, in a manner of speaking. It's just that with the season coming to an end, and bad weather due anytime—"

"Don't you worry about the weather," Luke said. He pointed sharply at himself. "I'll worry about the goddamned weather. Your interests are safe. You'll get your money. At least if I ever get away from this dock. I've got a run to make. If you'll excuse me, I'd like to get under way."

"Well, we . . . uh . . ."

"Steven!"

The clerk, who had been standing outside the door, quickly stepped in.

"Yes, Captain."

"These gentlemen were just leaving. Mr. Tibedeau will show you off the boat."

"Now, Captain Williamson," Aubrey said, "you've got no call to take a tone with us. We're just doing our job."

Luke had disappeared down the side of the hurricane deck and out of sight, so Steven led the bankers out of the cabin. They were barely off the landing stage when the steam whistle signaled departure. Two roustabouts hauled the stage to a forty-five-degree angle and lashed it securely as the riverboat backed away from the dock. Once clear of the other steamers, the huge paddle wheel spanked the muddy water in the opposite direction and gradually pushed the *Paragon* toward the channel. The passengers huddled along the banister and waved toward the shore, while the deckhands wrapped the mooring ropes and completed preparations for the run.

In the engine room, Ham was monitoring the pressure gauges and barking orders to his men. The fire tenders were rapidly thrusting four-foot cordwood into the boiler. On the foredeck, Jacob Lusk was talking to Steven Tibedeau and cross-checking the cargo list to make sure the number of cotton bales he listed matched Jacob's count. Each bale was insured, so an accurate count was critical should something happen. Jacob seldom worried about such things, but Steven did and always had. Worrying was his job. But with the loss of the *Mary Justice*, he was beginning to get some help.

Once he'd satisfied himself with the count, Steven made his way up to the pilothouse to report to Luke. He was always there when you couldn't find him anywhere else. Even though he'd hired Martin Cummings, and personally turned him into a competent pilot, Luke was still there, talking about the currents, pointing out changes in the channel, and offering suggestions.

"Sir, the list checks off. It's all accounted for," Steven said.

"Fine," Luke said, never taking his eyes off the channel. "Martin, swing to port." He pointed at another boat slightly ahead of them. "I don't trust him."

"Is that one of Van Geer's?" Martin asked.

Luke shook his head and leaned over to pick up the voice tube.

"Ham! Bring up the steam. Let's kick it in the ass." He glanced back up at the other boat, which was now moving from his right at an angle that threatened to cut him off from the heart of the channel. "A whole damned river out here and he's got to run on my half."

"Who is that?" Steven asked, straining to make out the name painted across the housing of the side-wheeler. "The *Princess*."

"Well, it's not Haskins," Luke said. "He's too timid to be Haskins. Anyway, I heard he was running the lower river."

Martin moved the wheel hand-over-hand to take them farther left. "I thought he was still on the *Tigress*."

"Who the hell knows? They got fifteen boats."

"Sixteen, Captain," Steven Tibedeau said.

"Sixteen, then."

"They just bought the last of the Sunflower Line," Steven added.

"Where'd you hear that?"

"On the dock this morning."

"Sunflower went bust?"

"Yes sir."

"That's Vince Cawley's outfit. I've known Vince since the war."

"Ever since his big boat ran aground last month, he'd been trying to double up his runs. It just got to be too much, they say."

"Who says?"

"His chief clerk. He was asking me this morning if we had a spot for him," Steven explained.

Luke felt for the speaking tube. "Goddamn it, Ham,

give me some steam? I've got some fool trying to cut me off up here."

The *Princess* was now within a hundred yards of the *Paragon*. If Luke continued on course, he would ram squarely into her port paddle wheel, so Martin began to take them farther left.

"Keep her steady," Luke said quietly.

"Captain?"

"Keep her steady, Martin."

Martin reversed his action on the pilot's wheel and watched as the two boats neared one another.

Luke sounded the whistle when they were less than fifty yards apart. At any moment, the *Princess* should give right rudder and allow the *Paragon* to pass on the left. But the boat showed no sign of recognizing Luke's approach. Luke could see Jacob standing on the nose of the boat, with his hands on his hips, watching the whole affair unfold the way a cat watches a field mouse. Again Luke pulled the lanyard on the steam whistle, this time holding it for several seconds. By now, a number of the passengers were stirring nervously on the deck, some looking up at the pilothouse and talking excitedly, and others moving back toward the rear of the boat.

On the deck of the *Princess*, passengers stood aghast at the sight of Luke's boat speeding toward their flank. The two vessels were now no more than ten feet apart, and the passengers on the *Princess* had already begun to flee that side of the deck. Jacob still stood on the bow, near the spot that seemed almost certain to impact. Then Luke saw the sidewash from the left paddle wheel of the *Princess*, as the foamy water came spitting up to the surface.

"Steady as she goes," Luke said, his voice never rising, his eyes never leaving the other ship.

The *Princess* was turning; her crew dashed about, shaking their fists, cussing loudly enough for Luke to hear them in the pilothouse. As the *Paragon* swept past, she missed hull-to-hull contact by less than a foot, and the suddenness of the *Princess*'s turn threatened to swing her aft section into the side of the *Paragon*.

"Hard right, Martin."

On Luke's command, Martin moved them momentarily parallel to the fleeing boat, and once their speed had propelled them safely past, he resumed their course in the channel.

"Crazy son of a bitch!" someone yelled from the deck of the other ship. But the curses were overwhelmed by a cheer that rose up from the passengers who'd remained on the texas to watch the confrontation.

Luke looked over at Steven, his face unconcerned and his voice calm. "What'd you tell him?"

Steven was slowly releasing his death grip on a brass bar above the pilothouse door. "Tell who?"

"The clerk. The one from Sunflower."

"I told him we didn't have anything."

"You know where to find him?"

"He lives in St. Louis," Steven said, still breathing hard.

"Is he any good?"

"Yes, sir, he knows his stuff."

Luke took an ivory pipe from his pocket and began stuffing it with tobacco. "Well, when we get another boat, we may be able to use him."

When Steven left the pilothouse, Luke began to go over a litany of possible problems Martin should look out for. It wasn't that he didn't trust Martin, for he'd seen the pilot come into his own in the past six months. This listing of what lay ahead was just something Luke always did, and Martin had come to expect it.

"I heard yesterday that they cleared some of the snags from the north side of Piper Island, so you can cut her close and hold near to the east side. But keep your eyes open," he added, lifting a finger in the air. "With the water falling like it is, there's liable to be others popping up."

"Should I stay to the left of the channel?"

"At first. But see what you think when you get there."

Martin was a bright young man, and Luke felt lucky to have him on board. He'd joined the *Paragon* eighteen months ago to study the river with Luke. Since there was no formal school for pilots on the Mississippi, studying with an experienced river pilot was the only way to learn. And of all the pilots running the St.-Louis-to-New-Orleans route, he had chosen Luke because of his reputation for going faster and farther in more difficult water than any man on the river. Luke smiled as he watched Martin whip the wheel back and forth in his hands. He reminded Luke of himself a few years ago—young, brash, and full of himself, just as Luke had been when he started as an assistant mate on board a troop transport called the *Cincinnati*. Luke had learned the basics of being a pilot by running Union troops down the Ohio River to Paducah, Kentucky. As the war progressed and the Federals moved further south, he received a commission as an ensign and was transferred to a gunboat running the Tennessee River. It was there he met Ed Smythe, a pilot-in-training on another gunboat.

"At least we won't have to worry about traffic," Martin said.

Luke nodded. Unless they lucked out and got about a week-long rain, the season was almost shot. Some years the water stayed high enough to run to the first of December, but that was rare. This year the dry spell had come early, and most shipping lines had already suspended operations until the water came up. But not Luke. Not with the *Mary Justice* gone and only one boat left to meet the payroll and pay the bills. Luke peered out at the afternoon sky. Clear again. He wouldn't be able to count on any rises this trip. As he watched Martin, he sensed the young man was edgy.

"Something wrong, Martin?"

"No, Captain, I don't reckon so."

"You worried about the water?"

He slowly shook his head. "It's just that, well . . . with what happened to Captain Smythe and all—"

"It wasn't low water that got Ed."

"You don't think so?"

"No way. Ed Smythe was too good."

"Well, what you reckon it was?"

Luke looked out over the bow and his eyes fixed on the wake edging from the front of the boat. Almost hypnotized, he stood watching each ripple of water emerge from the side of the boat and crawl after the one before it.

"I don't know, Martin. I wish I did." He looked back at the younger man. "It just doesn't make sense. The water is plenty deep where they say he went down, and Ed's been over that stretch hundreds of times."

"Maybe a sandbar came up."

"Not in that water. It's too deep even this time of year."

"Do you know exactly where she went down?"

"No, and I won't till after I talk to the wharfmaster at Natchez. For the life of me I can't see how Ed would have lost it along there." Luke watched Martin's eyes and for the first time in months he sensed doubt in them.

"Martin, you're going to do all right." Martin glanced at him as if looking at Luke would make it true. "No, I mean it. You're becoming a good pilot. Just because the water's down, doesn't mean you can't handle it. Everything I've taught you is still true. You've just got to remain more alert than ever. Remember what I said. High water's got its own troubles, just the same as low water. In fact, I'd rather run low than high."

"Why?"

"Because high water can throw things at you out of nowhere—stumps, new channels, shoals, there's no telling what's waiting out there. But low water is just that. It's low and that's all. Sure, you can have a sandbar pop up at you, but if you watch the eddies like I showed you, you'll do all right." He studied Martin's face again. "The main thing is, you can't let her know you're afraid. Like any woman, if she senses you're scared, or if she thinks you'll hesitate, then she's got you. Understand?"

"Yes, sir."

Luke had seen that look before. Ed Smythe had it on his face a few hours before they began shelling Fort Donelson in February of 1862. When the regular pilot took sick the previous day, Ed had been moved into the pilot's chair. Luke recalled how nervous he'd seemed during a halt of the flotilla during the early-morning hours along the Cumberland River.

"What if I mess up, Luke?" Ed had said.

"Hey, if you don't want the job, I'll take it."

"Part of me would like to give it to you."

"Well, tell the rest of you and let me have it."

Ed laughed. "You'll get a chance, just as soon as they find out how crazy you are. They want crazy men, you know? A crazy man's the only person that would sail this tin heap under those Reb coastal batteries."

"Guess that makes you crazy then, huh?" Luke slapped him on the back and he stepped into a skiff to return to his own gunboat. "Besides, I'll be covering your ass the whole time."

"Yea, that's what makes me nervous."

"Back her down a little," Martin called into the speaking tube. His words shook Luke back to the sad reality that Ed Smythe was gone.

"Why are you slowing?"

"I don't like the looks of that stretch in the main channel," Martin said, pointing ahead. "I'm going to move her over a bit."

As Luke checked out Martin's observation, he smiled. The boy was good. He'd spotted an irregularity in the surface flow that probably meant a huge piece of driftwood floating along concealed just below the surface. While it probably wouldn't have threatened the boat, it would have provided one of those bump-and-shudder situations that a good pilot kept his passengers from having to endure.

"You don't need me up here," Luke said. "I'm going below to smile and be friendly now."

"Don't hurt yourself," Martin said.

As he moved down the stairwell to the cabin level, he could hear Jacob Lusk in an animated conversation with one of the roustabouts, so he paused a few steps before the bottom to listen. From the rear of the boat he could hear the faint sound of dogs barking.

"Go down there and see Anabel and—"

"She'll throw me out for sure, Jacob."

"No, she won't."

"I know damned well she will! She don't allow no deck-hands around the kitchen this close to mealtime."

Jacob lowered his voice. "You just tell her I sent you down there for a piece of meat."

"She ain't gonna give it to me."

"She's gonna give it to you."

"No, she won't, Jacob—"

"You tell her I said you had to have some meat," Jacob said. "And that you won't bother her again. Then take it back there to them damned dogs and feed it to 'em."

"But—"

"Just do it, O'Donnell. Do it right now!"

Luke continued down the stairs and approached Jacob. The roustabout had left, and Jacob was standing beside a mooring rope scratching his head.

"What's the problem, Jacob?"

"No problem, Cap'n, we got it under control."

Luke smiled. "Good."

"Yes, sir, everything's all right, Cap'n."

"Any problems with the cargo?"

"No, sir, it's all secured." Jacob put his hands on his hips and surveyed the bales of cotton lined along the center of the foredeck. "That cotton ought to bring somebody a pretty penny with it bein' this late in the year."

"You're surprised we're making this run, aren't you?"

"Well, sir, I am . . . kindly surprised, what with Cap'n Smythe havin' just . . . what with the accident and all." He didn't look directly at Luke. "I sho' hate it about the cap'n. He was a good man."

"Yes, he was, Jacob," Luke said, trying to change the subject. "Make sure the crew has plenty of blankets tonight. It's going to get chilly out here on this deck." He turned to leave, but paused momentarily. "How many deck passengers we got?"

"Twenty-five," Jacob said. "Most of 'em be gettin' off at Memphis, but I 'spect we'll take more aboard."

Deck passengers were the lowest class of paying customers on a steamboat. Each paid eight dollars and furnished his own food and blanket for the chance to catch a hop down the river. They were a sad bunch, and it often bothered Luke to see women and small children riding with the cargo. He would have liked to offer blankets to them, but there was no sense starting something he couldn't finish. After all, they'd paid their money and taken their choice. He hadn't made them ride with the cargo. He couldn't take care of everybody, even if he wanted. Looking out for the deckhands made more sense. Without them to handle the cargo, the fireman duties, the boiler room, and the soundings, he'd be finished. It was a tough life the roustabouts faced and they were a rough lot, moving from job to job along the river, never staying more than a few months. They were a hardworking, yet generally nasty lot of characters that no boat could survive without. When they weren't working, they spent their spare time taking each other's money in card games or fighting over matters most men would not have given a second thought. It was a tribute to Jacob that he controlled them as well as he did, given the fact that from year to year he never knew who would sign on. Most were poor Irish and blacks, at least on the *Paragon;* Jacob's size, as well as his manner, let them know very quickly who was boss. And while many of them were probably criminals hiding from the law—men who might just as soon cut your throat as speak to you—Luke couldn't help feeling sorry for them at times, particularly during these late-fall months. Still, he kept them restricted to the lower decks and away from the first-class passengers. Paying customers didn't need to fear for their safety or doubt that they would be treated with polish. That was one of the trademarks of the *Paragon*, and Luke wasn't about to see it compromised.

Satisfied that all was well with the lower deck, Luke made his way up to the grand room as many of the passengers began to file in for the evening meal. As it grew darker and an evening chill began to descend, the lamps from the dining room glowed warmly and seemed to invite people in. Dinner on a steamboat was one of the highlights of the day, and the *Paragon* boasted one of the finest menus and most elegantly decorated rooms on the river: 120 feet long, with soft, thick oriental carpeting stretching the full length. Intricately carved woodwork adorned the walls, and immense oil-lamp chandeliers hung in a line along the center of the ceiling. In the fine glass of lamp globes was etched in fancy lettering the phrase "Paragon of the Mississippi." Near the windows, a line of attractive, heavy tables extended down both sides of the room, with filigree and gilded iron traveling up the walls at regular intervals.

At the far end of the room, toward the rear of the boat, was the saloon, operated as a concession by a company in St. Louis. Luke would rather have had his own barkeep run the operation, but he'd long since discovered it wasn't worth it. The concession, which operated bars on more than a dozen different riverboats, could offer the customer a wider selection of drinks than Luke could ever hope to stock; and it was considered a mark of elegance if a customer could be sure his drink was never out of stock on a riverboat bar.

Not far from the bar was a raised platform where the string band would play after dinner. Musical entertainment was a courtesy any boat worth riding would offer its customers, and one that Luke insisted would remain no matter how much he had to cut costs. Since first-class passengers from St. Louis to New Orleans paid plenty for the privilege of riding on the *Paragon*, Luke was determined to see to it they got their money's worth.

Luke walked into the grand room and shook hands with several of his regular passengers, made some small talk, met some new people, and generally worked his way through the room. Ed had always been so much better at this than he was. He hated smiling and shaking hands with people he couldn't care less about; but he knew that keeping them happy was the key to getting them back, and after the disaster of the *Mary Justice*, he figured he had better put a little extra effort into it. If talking to the captain made the passengers feel important, he would give them the chance. But the wreck was all people—at least the regular customers—wanted to talk about and everybody had ideas about what happened, most of them harebrained. Luke was amazed at how ignorance of the facts did not stop most of them from coming to a conclusion.

Strolling through the dining area, Luke observed the white-uniformed attendants hurrying between the tables to take orders and refresh the customers' glasses. Each table was set with monogrammed linen and elegant china, and the guests dressed in their best clothes for the evening meal. Two ladies sitting alone at a table were looking at him admiringly; one dared to gaze a bit longer than was socially acceptable. Luke knew what she meant. He had seen it a lot over the years. If he tarried long, she would be over speaking to him, asking him about his business, talking of people she knew all along the river. And then she would casually mention which cabin she occupied for the trip—a bit of information that Luke might have paid more attention to at one time. More than once a tight-lipped Jacob had encountered Luke during the early-morning hours, his shoes in his hand, silently stepping his way back to his cabin. But not on this trip. Not with all that had happened.

At about seven, Luke moved toward the saloon end of the room and, picking up a menu from one of the attendants, looked it over as he headed for his own table.

BILL OF FARE

Steamer *Paragon*, St. Louis–New Orleans
Charles Luther Williamson, Captain
Steven Tibedeau, Clerk

Dinner on Board the Steamer *Paragon*, October 23, 1872

SOUP
Green Pea   Oyster à la Plessey

FISH
Catfish à la maltre Decate
Trout à la Vortore

ROAST
Beef   Pork   Turkey   Chicken

HOT ENTRÉES
Tendons of Chicken with Dumplings and Green Peas
Fillet of Catfish
Vegetables of the Season

COLD DISH
Cream with Apple Jelly

CONDIMENTS
Lettuce   Green Onion   Pickled Cucumbers
Raw Tomatoes   Chives   John Bull Sauce   Radishes
Spanish Olives

PASTRY AND DESSERTS
Pies: Peach   Apple   Cherry   Gooseberry
Cakes: Pound   Fruit   Cloud   Jelly   Chocolate

NUTS AND FRUITS
Raisins   Almonds   Prunes   Figs   Apples   Pecans

Anabel McBree, Steward

Luke could always count on Anabel and her cooks to keep
the customers coming back; her reputation kept the competition busy trying to hire her away from him. When the
weather didn't cooperate, or the river became ornery, knowing that Anabel would keep the customers' palates comfort-

able was worth seven or eight more deckhands. Luke took a seat at his table and gave his order to one of the attendants. He was sipping coffee when Martin walked up.

"Thomas is at the wheel, Captain. I briefed him like you told me. He's all set for the night. I told him you'd be up to check on him in a little bit."

"Good. Sit down and get yourself some supper."

Thomas Neely was Luke's night pilot, an experienced riverman whom Luke had coached into a solid, dependable boatman. When Luke slept, which was precious little during a voyage, he could sleep comfortably knowing that a man like Thomas was behind the wheel.

"No guests at the table tonight?" Martin asked.

"Not tonight."

Martin nodded and returned to the menu. "What are you having?"

"Chicken. I'm not too hungry for some reason."

Martin ordered and spent his meal talking with Luke about the accident—a conversation the captain could have done without; he even considered taking his meal back to his cabin to finish it, but he didn't want to offend Martin. The young pilot was just curious, and to be honest with himself, so was Luke. He was more than curious. The questions were driving him crazy, and he couldn't wait to talk to somebody who knew something. All the speculation was getting to be too much.

After dinner, the band began to play and the stewards cleared away several tables near the bar for the nightly card games. Martin left and Luke pulled out his pipe and lit it, an indulgence he always allowed himself after dinner; he sat at his table watching the crowd and tried to take his mind off Ed.

$\triangledown$

2

THE WOMAN BEHIND the desk gave Masey Baldridge a hard look, so he lifted his foot from the seat of the chair across from him and placed it on the floor. His knee was already stiffening up, and it was only nine o'clock. He needed a drink. In a few moments she looked at him again, as a schoolteacher might check on a mischievous child, and Baldridge resented it. But he kept his foot on the floor while he waited for Robert Ferguson, president of the Mid-South Insurance Company. Six months ago Ferguson had hired him to investigate a railroad accident in west Tennessee. Using his knowledge of the people and the country, Baldridge saved the company several thousand dollars in false claims. Ferguson decided to keep in touch and to throw an occasional investigation his way.

While he never particularly liked Ferguson, Baldridge kept his mouth shut about it. With money so tight in Memphis these days, he figured a thirty-five-year-old former Confederate soldier was lucky just to have work—particularly with his brand of luck. Three days before Forrest's cavalry surrendered, a Yankee sharpshooter near Selma, Alabama, put a Minié ball in his knee. It was six months before he could walk again and a year before he could ride, and his "souvenir," as he called it, kept him in too much pain to return to his former occupation as a blacksmith. He tried horse trading for a while, but a rash of grease heel and a run of bad luck left him looking for another job. Baldridge had wanted to work for his former commander, General Nathan Bedford Forrest, who was building a new railroad in Mississippi and Alabama; but Forrest took one look at him and knew he wouldn't be able to stand the strain. He contacted Ferguson, one of his former staff officers, and helped Baldridge get a job.

Baldridge tapped his foot and kept watching the front door. He hated sitting in offices—he felt as though the walls were going to crush him—but he eventually leaned back and tried to think of something else. Finally, Robert Ferguson came in. "Mornin', Louise." Seeing Baldridge in the corner, he walked over and extended his hand. "How you doin', Masey?"

Baldridge bent his stiff left leg as far as it would go and rose to his feet.

"Good morning, Mr. Ferguson," he said, shaking his hand.

"Let's go in the office, Masey." Ferguson waved his hand at Louise. "I don't want to be interrupted, Louise. If anybody comes by, either have them wait or tell them to come back later."

"Yes, Mr. Ferguson."

"How's the leg, Masey?" Ferguson said, closing the office door behind them.

"It's tellin' me that cold weather's on its way."

Ferguson laughed. "Is that right?" He opened a box on his desk and offered Baldridge a cigar.

"No thanks." Taking a seat in front of the desk, Baldridge eyed the liquor cabinet in the corner, wishing Ferguson had offered him a shot of brandy. Ferguson lifted a cigar from the box, lit it, and strolled over to the window.

"Looks like we've got another one, Masey."

"Riverboat?"

"Yep. The *Mary Justice*. She went down north of Natchez a few days ago. You might have heard about it."

"Yeah, I heard some talk." Baldridge ran his tongue across his lips and glanced at the liquor cabinet again.

"Now I know you're already working on the *Mercury* case," Ferguson said, taking a puff on his cigar and blowing the smoke out slowly, "but this takes priority." He looked over at him. "I'll be straight with you, Masey. I don't know how much more we can afford to pay out." He pointed the cigar at him to emphasize each word. "Over four hundred thousand dollars in claims in the past year. That's what Mid-South has paid on these riverboat accidents. The *Mary Justice* is the fourth boat we insure that's gone down." He sat on the corner of his desk and tapped the ashes from his cigar into a porcelain ashtray. "It's as if someone had declared war on steamboats."

Something was going on all right—that much Baldridge knew—but three weeks of investigating the *Mercury* accident had turned up nothing solid. It wasn't just Mid-South clients that were suffering; several other insurance companies were falling on hard times as they tried to make up the losses on ships they insured. It had been one of the worst years for river disasters in recent memory, and Baldridge agreed with Ferguson—it didn't make sense. There were too many instances of solid ships, operated by competent pilots, encountering all manner of problems—boiler explosions, snags, or as was the case with the *Mercury*, collisions with other boats when there was plenty of room to pass and reasonably clear weather.

"Who was the pilot?" Baldridge asked.

"A man named Edward Smythe." Ferguson worked a tiny piece of cigar wrapping from between his teeth and plucked it out with his fingernail. "A good man. Experienced man. Knew the river well."

"And the line?"

"Small packet service out of St. Louis. They have . . . well, they *had* two nice boats. We insure both. The other one is the *Paragon*."

"I've heard of it," Baldridge said with a nod. "Supposed to be one of the best boats on the river."

"So was the *Mary Justice*. But now it's lying in over a hundred feet of water, and we stand to be out plenty." Ferguson stood up. "Masey, we've got to find out what happened. Whatever is going on, we've got to put a stop to it—otherwise we're broke. It's that simple. This *Paragon* is now the biggest riverboat we handle, and if it should go down . . . well, I don't even want to think about it."

"At least the season's about over. I mean, they can't run much longer with the water getting as low as it is."

"Most boats won't," Ferguson said, "but I suspect the *Paragon* will."

"How's that?"

"Well, they're down to one boat, they've got a note to pay off . . . you figure it out."

"You raised the rates on his cargo, didn't you?"

"Oh yeah, but that won't stop this boat."

"Why not?"

"The captain. It's Luke Williamson."

Baldridge didn't recognize the name. "Kinda reckless, is he?"

"I'm afraid so. I threatened to cancel them over a year ago when I found out how Williamson made it to Vicksburg in record time."

"Seems like I remember something about that. It was during high water, wasn't it?"

"Yeah. Seems Williamson took out across what used to be open fields, running in not more than seven feet of backwater, for some nine miles. Completely bypassed Turtle Neck Bend. He could've lost the whole boat."

"Instead he set a new record."

"Yeah."

"So, you could still cancel him, couldn't you?"

Ferguson shook his head. "Not now. Not with his other boat having just gone down. It would look bad. It would look as if we were bailing out on one of our customers. With money as scarce as it is right now, we can't afford to run off any new business."

"I see."

Cigar smoke burned Baldridge's eyes as Ferguson came closer. "See what you can find out, Masey. Main thing is, keep an eye on this other boat. I understand the *Paragon* stops here tomorrow on the way to New Orleans. Might be a good place to start checking around. I'm not going to tell you how to do that, but I just can't afford to lose the *Paragon*. Understand?"

Baldridge stood up. "Yes, sir, I do."

The two men shook hands and walked out of the office to the front door.

"Keep me posted on where you are. I'll send a telegram if I hear anything that might help. You do the same."

"Uh, Mr. Ferguson, there is the matter of expenses."

"Oh yes," he said, signaling Louise, who produced a packet from the desk drawer. "That ought to get you started. Now, be frugal, but I think you know how important this is."

"All right, sir."

As Baldridge started out the door, Ferguson leaned close to him and whispered: "And watch the liquor."

Baldridge hesitated a moment. He wanted to tell Ferguson it was none of his damned business, but he knew it was, so he just nodded and started down the street.

As Baldridge walked toward the center of town, a chilly breeze sent reddish-yellow maple leaves cartwheeling across the wooden planks of the sidewalk on Front Street. Over the years he'd worked to make his limp less noticeable, but he had been unable to lose it entirely. He moved along with a rhythmic gait, still angry about Ferguson's comment. Only twice—two times in six months—had he let the liquor get in the way of his work. He'd sworn to Ferguson that it wouldn't happen again. It wasn't like he tried to get drunk, it was just that sometimes the pain got so bad that only spirits—and plenty of them—could make it go away. This time would be different. Ferguson was counting on him, and he'd find a way to get past the pain . . . if the weather didn't get too bad. He slipped a silver flask from his inside coat pocket, twisted the cap off, and took a sip that burned his throat in the crisp morning air.

That night about eight o'clock, Masey Baldridge left his room at the Crestview Gentlemen's Boarding House and walked ten blocks to a Memphis riverfront area known as Whiskey Chute. An alley between Main and Front streets, Whiskey Chute was a wall-to-wall row of some fourteen saloons, all doing a bustling business in liquor and good times. He knew the area well, having spent time in most of the establishments. Although he preferred Pete Flanagan's, most of the rivermen in town hung out at the Eddy or at the Fireman's House. They seemed to be the best places to start looking for answers if he wanted to talk to rivermen; besides, it wouldn't hurt to warm his soul on such a chilly night. He reluctantly passed Flanagan's and went directly to the Eddy, where he slapped down some coins for a bottle of whiskey and took a spot near the end of the bar. The place was busy, with most of the tables handling card games and the rear corner of the building hosting three billiard tables. He noticed deckhands laughing it up at a couple of the tables, and three or four tables from the door he saw what appeared to be several officers passing around a bottle of wine. Beside him at the bar stood a stocky man, wearing a frayed green scarf and an overshirt of a type common among the crewmen who ran the river. The man, four or five inches shorter than Baldridge, had been trying for several minutes to signal an overworked bartender for a refill.

"Have a shot till he comes this way," Baldridge said, sliding his bottle over.

"Thanks." He poured himself a shot and lifted the glass toward Baldridge, then took it down in one swig, smiled, and nodded.

"Cuts the chill, don't it?"

"Sure does."

"What boat you work on?"

"*River Messenger*," the man said. "Headed up to Louisville."

"That's a long haul."

"Don't I know it. We're stacked to our eyeballs in shit all over the deck. I don't know where they're gonna put what they pick up here."

"Where'd you come out of?"

"Vicksburg. Been stuck here two days while they fix one of the boilers. Probably be stuck here for two months the way the water's dropping."

"So you didn't go by the wreck, huh?"

"What wreck?"

"Big boat that went down near Natchez."

"Oh, yeah. I heard somethin' 'bout that."

"*Mary Justice.*"

"Yeah, somethin' like that."

Baldridge refilled the man's glass. "What'd you hear?"

"Not much," said the *River Messenger*'s man, lifting the glass again. "Ain't many boats comin' in with the water this low." He looked around the room. "That's why all these fellas are here. Just killin' time till next season."

"What did you hear about the wreck?"

"Just that she went down in deep water, that's all I know. Wasn't much left, they said."

"Who said?"

The man pointed his empty glass across the room. "The pilot at that table over there, the second from the left. He's about the last to come in." He polished off his second glass. "You headin' down that way?"

"Yeah, tomorrow."

"Huh." He shook his head. "Better you than me."

Baldridge continued sharing his bottle and talking to the man for another half hour, until several of his fellow crewmen came in; and although the *River Messenger* man invited Baldridge to join them, he declined and waited at the bar. When a seat opened up at the pilot's table, he shelled out some of Ferguson's money for another bottle of Kentucky whiskey and strolled over.

"Mind if I join you?"

The three men looked up at him almost in unison; though they said nothing, they managed to make him feel unwelcome. He pulled out the chair anyway and eased down in it, placing his bottle on the table. He poured himself another shot, picked up the glass, and leaned back in the chair, his bad leg extended out to the side of the table.

"I understand you were one of the last to come up from New Orleans," he said to the man identified as a pilot.

"Two or three days ago," the officer said.

"You didn't happen to see where that big boat went down, did you?"

The man nodded. "Saw the spot. Sure didn't see the boat."

"Yeah, I understand it's pretty deep there."

The pilot laughed and exchanged a glance with his comrades.

"I'd say a little bit, yeah. You ain't a riverman, are you?"

"Passenger," Baldridge said with a smile.

"On what? Ain't nothin' running out there now."

"That's not what I hear. I'm planning on picking up the *Paragon* here tomorrow morning." The men again looked at one another.

"Williamson," the pilot grunted, shaking his head. "That's one crazy son of a bitch you're ridin' with."

One of the others laughed. "Ain't but about three or four men I know that would even think about making a run under these conditions."

"And this Williamson's one of 'em?"

"Afraid so," the pilot said. "Why you askin' all these questions anyway?"

"I hear traveling this late in the year is risky. I'm just trying to find out as much as I can." He offered to refill his glass, but the pilot declined. Glancing at the clock over the bar, he grasped the neck of his bottle between his first two fingers and stood up. He eyed first the pilot and then the other officers, then offered a nod.

"You gentlemen have a good evenin'. I got an early day tomorrow."

Baldridge's insides felt warm and his knee didn't seem as tight as he walked along Front Street. Drinking with rivermen was a sacrifice he would make anytime for the job, and he chose not to dwell on what Ferguson would have thought about it. This was his investigation and he would do it the way he pleased; he just wished he could have found out a little more. Either those pilots didn't know much about the *Mary Justice* or they weren't talking. Perhaps it was the slowdown in traffic. With more and more boats stopping their service, maybe news just wasn't traveling as fast as it usually did.

Baldridge was within three blocks of the boardinghouse when he caught the smell of the river on the cool night air; he couldn't resist the urge to walk over to the top of the bluff and look out on it. He'd always been a woodsman, preferring the countryside and a thick stretch of forest to any river. During the war, rivers were just obstacles for the cavalry to cross; but the trip he'd taken down to Vicksburg two weeks earlier to look into the *Mercury* wreck had given him a new curiosity about this long, winding beast, the Mississippi. As he gazed down on the Memphis wharf, he was intrigued by the many lights that seemed to dance by the waterside, and by now even at night, and even in this slow time for river traffic, there seemed to be so much action in and around the boats. The wind was picking up now, and he pulled his collar close up around his neck to ward off a chill. Looking out across the blackness, occasionally shimmering in the coastal light, he could see only a few tiny flickers from the Arkansas side. He began to wonder how it might have felt to the captain of the *Mary Justice* that night, hearing his boat come apart beneath him, feeling her list as she began to sink, knowing that he would soon be surrounded by that cold, black, merciless water. He could almost feel the river engulfing him, closing over him as he sank in the darkness. He would struggle for breath as the cold liquid filled his lungs and robbed him of his strength and pulled him farther and farther down.

Shivering again, he lifted the bottle and, after briefly examining the two fingers of whiskey that played about in the bottom, he finished it off, following the last swallow with a wipe of his sleeve.

"A helluva way to die," he mumbled, tossing the empty bottle into the dirt. He buttoned the top button on his jacket and headed for the boardinghouse.

$\triangledown$

3

T HE STOP IN Memphis took less time than first mate Jacob Lusk had expected, and he was mad enough to spit nails. As he ordered the last of the cargo stowed, he gazed toward the city and resigned himself to remaining aboard the *Paragon*. He had toyed with the idea of trying to get to a bar for a quick drink before they left, but the nearest colored saloon was five blocks away and he dared not risk it. He wouldn't disappoint Luke Williamson—the man had risked his reputation on him, and Jacob wasn't about to let him down. As first mate, he was the lowest-paid officer on the boat, but Jacob figured his $130 a month made him about the highest-paid Negro on the river. It had been six years since Luke gave him the job, and some of the passengers still mistook him for a roustabout or a dining room steward. But Jacob took that in stride as he kept Captain Luke's cargo secure and the roustabouts in line.

They were out of Memphis a little more than two hours, making good time, when Jacob saw the landing at Commerce, Mississippi, up ahead. It was the first of some ten stops before Vicksburg, and like many of the others was little more than a cleared spot in the forest. The routine was second nature to Jacob: Pull close enough to the landing to extend the stage; have Ham hold her in position long enough to spit the cargo and passengers ashore; take on anybody or anything waiting; and then move on fast. Tiny stops like Commerce, Tunica, and Sterling were minor annoyances for the crew, but a good boat was expected to stop, and eventually all the little stops added up to a profit—or at least, that was the way it was supposed to work. At Helena they would tarry for a couple of hours, take on fuel, then proceed to more brief stops at Friar's Point, Old Town, Australia, Victoria, and Napoleon. If Jacob knew Luke Williamson, they would run through the night, even with the water this low, and it would be Saturday morning before they reached Vicksburg. If he was lucky, he could get the cargo ashore, have the waiting baggage loaded and still have several hours to entertain himself before it was time to ship out for New Orleans.

At Commerce the *Paragon* discharged several deck passengers in exchange for about as many new ones, and Jacob supervised the roustabouts as they took on twenty-seven more bales of cotton. The *Paragon* would be loaded to the waterline on this trip; with most boats shutting down for the season, she was a businessman's last shot at running cargo before spring. Sensing that this was probably their last chance to go south for the winter, deck passengers were already crowding the boat. They kept getting under Jacob's feet and in the way of the cargo. If there was one thing about running the river that Jacob hated, it was deck passengers. They caused more trouble than they were worth for the pittance it cost them to ride. But Captain Luke would not even consider limiting their numbers until he was full up, and even then he would try to get Jacob to find more room. Jacob never understood what it was that the captain liked so much about these people. Carrying them just didn't seem to make good business sense.

Once away from Commerce, the boat picked up speed; it rounded Council Bend and stopped off at Tunica and Dunn's Landing. If the water had been up, they would have used the cut-off behind Ship Island, but this time of year Jacob figured his captain wouldn't risk it. He was right. They rounded the bend, bypassed Austin, and landed at Sterling, where again they gathered some twenty or thirty more deck passengers. Eight miles farther downriver, and almost seven hours out of Memphis, the *Paragon* eased toward the dock at Helena, Arkansas. Standing near the capstan, directing the deck hands, Jacob shielded his eyes as the low afternoon sun sent its shadowline over him and gradually up the face of the pilothouse. When the boat slowed even more, he knew Martin was struggling to see.

"Twenty feet, Mr. Martin," he shouted toward the pilot-house; then, turning toward a skinny black man near the bow, he called out, "Stand by with the lead line." The shade from the bank chased the afternoon sun from the pilothouse; Jacob nearly lost his balance when the ship lurched forward and heaved to the right to come alongside the dock. "Damned cub pilot."

With the water this low, the boys would have a slightly uphill hump from the deck to the loading dock, so he wanted to be sure he got the landing stage positioned properly.

"Steady there, Bonson. Keep that stage lifted till I tell you to let it go." With a nod from the crewman, he stepped from the capstan and walked to the starboard side and leaned over toward the dock. Lifting one arm, he motioned for Martin in the pilothouse to ease her in, and with the other arm he pointed to Bonson on the rope for the landing stage.

"Not yet, not yet," he called to Bonson, and waved his hand again toward the pilothouse. Then when he was satisfied with the position, he closed his hand into a tight fist and brought it to the top of his head several times. Once the boat began to court the edge of the dock, Jacob signaled the men to secure the mooring lines and Bonson to lower the stage.

"The bottom of Helena's dock is one view I'm not used to seeing," Luke Williamson said as he walked up behind Jacob.

Jacob shook his head. "Water sho' is down, Cap'n."

"Sure is, Jacob." Luke looked up at the pilothouse. "How you think Martin's doin'?"

Jacob was surprised by the question. "How *I* think Mr. Martin's doin'? Is that what you asked me, Cap'n?"

"Yeah."

"Well, sir," Jacob said, looking up at the pilothouse and then back toward the dock, "this here was a tricky landin', yessir, sho' was. But I reckon Mr. Martin's doin' all right. 'Course, I wouldn't know that much about it."

Luke grinned. "Yeah, you would. I figure you'd know better than just about anybody."

"Well, sir, I'd have to say I think he goes a little too fast sometimes, but then—"

"Goes too fast?"

"Well, yessir, Cap'n, sometimes . . . when he's roundin' a point, or when he's comin' alongside the dock . . . maybe a little."

Luke laughed out loud and slapped Jacob on the shoulder. It was the first time the mate had heard Luke laugh since word came about Captain Smythe.

"That's funny, Jacob. I told him I thought he was dragging ass." Luke turned and started down the side of the boat, still laughing at Jacob's comment. Watching him as he disappeared between the cotton bales, Jacob wondered if the captain didn't expect too much from his cub pilot. Just because Luke seemed to lead a charmed life in the pilothouse, didn't mean this youngster would. Jacob had always been amazed at the way Luke handled his boat. It seemed as if he was always on the edge, always doing something that would have horrified any other pilot. Jacob was afraid that Luke expected Martin to work the same kind of magic with a boat; but the intricate maneuvers that Luke Williamson pulled off daily would have given other pilots stories for their grandchildren. Jacob remembered how well they had worked together as a team, navigating dangerous bends and handling tricky undercurrents in all kinds of weather. He knew how important his soundings and signals were to Luke, and he took pride in their teamwork. It hadn't been as much fun since Luke stepped from behind the wheel. It wasn't that the men he hired and trained were not good—Martin and Thomas were safe, conscientious rivermen—but when Luke was up there, Jacob felt more comfortable. He sensed that

Luke was not as satisfied either now, since taking on more of the duties as captain. Sometimes Jacob thought he could see a longing in his eyes.

The loading at Helena was moving along smoothly, and Jacob had just returned from warning Ham in the engine room to bring up the steam pressure, when he noticed a commotion on deck. By lantern and torchlight, the roustabouts had been loading hundred-pound wheat sacks aboard when Jacob discovered several of the men on their hands and knees near the edge of the landing stage. They appeared to be searching the deck for something, and Jacob was about to confront them when he heard a metallic clink and caught the flash of a coin caroming off the mooring post and rolling across the deck. Slowly lifting his head, Jacob saw two finely-dressed ladies and their gentlemen laughing and cutting up along the deck rail above him. As he watched, the women each tossed a coin near the mouth of the landing stage on the deck below. Instantly, the roustabouts, who were already on their knees, began tracking the course of the coins much as a cat would watch a June bug. Two more deckhands, who had just stepped on the boat, lowered their sacks and joined them in the hunt. The commotion quickly lured five or six others to the scene, as more coins came tumbling from above, the roustabouts began to struggle with one another for position. Jacob stepped from under the overhang and looked up at the passengers. Both ladies wore expensive dresses and wide, elegant hats, and Jacob recognized one of the men as the gambler Victor Burl. They seemed to be thoroughly enjoying the confusion on the lower deck, laughing and pointing at the deckhands scurrying about.

"You men get up off the deck," Jacob barked, "and finish loadin' that wheat."

Normally Jacob's command was enough to get the men moving, but faced with a shower of money right in front of them, the deckhands chose not to listen. So Jacob walked over to the man nearest him, grabbed his collar, and lifted him with one hand.

"I told you to get back to work."

"He's just havin' a little fun there, darky," shouted one of the women. "Leave him be."

Jacob cut his eyes to the crowd above, then back at the man he held before him, and then at the others crawling about on the deck. Suddenly, another coin came bouncing across the wooden flooring and started rolling toward Jacob. Rocking his foot on to his heel, he rotated his leg and with a snap he pinned the coin beneath his shoe, narrowly missing the outstretched fingers of the Irishman Devin Hurley.

Still holding on to the roustabout, he growled, "Leave it."

"Jacob, I-I-I need to—"

"I said, leave it."

The other roustabout began struggling to free himself from Jacob's grip, and seeing that he was occupied, Hurley grabbed Jacob's leg and tried to lift his foot from the coin. The scene was amusing the passengers above until Jacob let out a yell and sent the first roustabout crashing into the lower deck rail, where he slumped to the floor. Then Jacob lifted his free leg and drove his boot squarely into Hurley's forehead. The blow stunned the Irishman, and he lay staring straight ahead for several seconds until his head began to rotate slowly and he released his grip on Jacob's leg. The violence had not escaped the attention of the other roustabouts, even the ones who were still searching the deck for coins, and when Jacob sent a cold stare in their direction, they jumped to their feet and returned to their sacks. One of the ladies continued to toss coins defiantly to the deck below. Jacob stared up at her. The woman was loudly complaining to her companions about how Jacob was messing in her affairs.

"Please, ma'am, don't be throwin' no more money down here," Jacob called to her, his eyes steady.

The woman stepped back slightly from the railing, her mouth open in surprise. She looked first at Victor Burl, then down at Jacob.

"I'll do as I please," she said. "I'll not have a colored deckhand telling me how to behave." She defiantly tossed another coin, which missed Jacob by no more than a couple of inches. "The very idea! I've half a mind to send Victor down there to give you a good thrashing."

"You're right about one thing," the stinging voice of Salina Tyner offered from a nearby doorway. "You do have half a mind." The angry woman glanced over her shoulder just in time to see Salina step before her, snatch her coin purse from her hand, and in the same motion send it sailing over the railing and into the dark, muddy water below.

The woman's hand came up to her throat in shock. First she glanced at her companions as if they should do something, but they only watched, equally wide-eyed.

Salina glared at the other woman, who pulled her purse close to her body and stepped nearer to Victor Burl.

"How dare you!" the first woman choked out as Salina turned and began walking away. "You—you owe me every penny that was in my purse!"

Without looking back, Salina called out loudly, "Have Mr. Burl come see me tonight. Maybe we can go double or nothing for it."

Jacob allowed himself a short-lived grin as the rowdy group left the deck, consoling one another over the horror they had witnessed. He had work to do.

"Hear we had a little trouble up here," the captain said ten minutes later.

"Ain't nothin' to it, Cap'n."

"Anything I need to get involved in?"

"No, sir, everything's fine now." Jacob related the incident as the deckhands secured the last of the cargo and readied the boat for departure.

"You say Burl was involved, huh?"

"Yes, sir, but just like always, he stands off an' lets others raise the hell. Somethin' about that man bothers me, Cap'n. He's got this grin when he looks at me, that . . . well . . ."

"The man's a troublemaker, Jacob, but he spends a lot of

money on the boat, and until it gets to where we can't handle him . . ."

"I know, Cap'n."

A first mate having to bust heads now and then was a fact of life along the river, and barely caused Luke to raise an eyebrow; but he perked up and listened with interest as Jacob described Miss Tyner's intervention, and the first mate thought he detected a more than professional concern in his captain's eye.

"You go off watch pretty soon, don't you?" Luke asked.

"Yes, sir, soon as I get us outta here."

Luke watched the deckhands as they retrieved the mooring lines, secured the lanterns for nighttime running, and cranked the landing stage to its vertical position. One long and two short blasts from the whistle signaled that Martin was ready in the pilothouse, and Jacob was about to lift his arm and signal him to begin backing her away, when he stopped and turned to Luke.

"Sho do miss you up at the wheel, Cap'n. Course, I'm not saying nothin' bad about Mr. Martin. Like I said, he's doin' a real good job." He gave the signal to the pilothouse and continued talking to Luke. "But me and you, Cap'n, we, uh . . ."

In the flickering light of the lanterns, Jacob saw Luke smile.

"We've had some good times, haven't we?"

Jacob laughed. "Yes, sir, sho' have. And some damned scary ones, too."

"Like the time we crossed Turtle Neck?"

"Yes, sir, that would be one of 'em." Lusk shook his head. "Uhmm, uhmm, uhmm, ain't nobody ever took no riverboat through there like that before, and ain't nobody done it since. Set us a speed record, we sho' did."

Luke laughed with him. "I'm not so sure I'd want to do it again."

"No, sir. No, sir. Me neither." He spat tobacco juice over the side of the boat and looked down at the deck, then up at Luke. "But it's somethin' to say we did it, ain't it?"

"Yeah, I guess it is."

"Well, anytime you get a chance to get back behind the wheel, it'll be all right with me, Cap'n."

"Well, I do appreciate you approving of me piloting my own boat, Jacob."

"Yes, sir, Cap'n, you has my permission."

"You been on watch too long, today. You better get Davis up here." As he was leaving, Luke called back to Jacob. "I'm going up to the dining room. You takin' supper upstairs?"

"No, sir, I believe not tonight."

"Well, find me before you turn in. I want to know that everything is secure."

"Yes, sir, Cap'n, sho' will."

▽

4

THE DINING HALL of the *Paragon* was crowded with passengers finishing a late supper and waiting for the band to being playing. Masey Baldridge stepped up to the bar.

"I'll have a peach brandy," he said, tossing a coin on the bar.

The affluence of the passengers was apparent from their dress and manner; most of the eligible ladies were escorted by gentlemen, and each was attired in the height of fashion. The room was crawling with white-uniformed attendants catering to the customers' every whim while a piano player, located at the far end of the hall, played dinner music. Baldridge had passed on supper; something about being on a ship always made him lose his appetite the first day. While the string band was tuning up, several porters cleared away an area for dancing, and the five or six game tables located across the room were already hosting some heavy poker action.

He grimaced at the first sip of his brandy and held the glass up toward the chandelier. A bit disappointed at the quality, he took another sip and surveyed the crowd. Those finishing dinner were turning their chairs around to better hear the band, while a dozen or so ladies gathered with their beaux about the edge of the dance area. Shortly the band began a waltz that he didn't recognize, and the floor was soon filled with couples moving to the music.

Watching them reminded him of the grand balls during the war. Forrest's cavalry entering a town was cause for great celebration, particularly in areas that had been occupied by

Federal forces. Whenever time and the tardiness of the enemy would allow it, cavalrymen partook of the hospitality of the community. The wine flowed, the food—carefully hidden from the Yankees—appeared out of basements and cellars, and there was always a fiddler to strike up a tune. Watching a shapely woman glide across the dance floor in front of him, Baldridge smiled as he recalled the feel of a beautiful woman next to him.

"Drinking alone?"

Turning to his left he saw a tall, slender, dark-haired woman with coal-black eyes. He caught himself staring at her exposed shoulders as her perfume drifted about him.

"I was," he said with a smile.

The woman looked at the bartender then back at him.

"Oh, pardon me. I've lost my manners." He motioned for the bartender. "The lady will have . . ."

"Whiskey," she said, leaning back against the bar. Her inviting breasts peeked from her low-cut dress. She offered a hand. "Salina Tyner's my name."

"Nice to meet you, Miss Tyner," he said, taking her hand gently. "My name's Masey Baldridge. Where are you heading?"

"New Orleans. How about you?"

"Natchez," he said, dropping another coin on the bar as Salina picked up her drink.

"Nice town, Natchez. I know some people there."

"I've never been there before."

"You traveling alone?"

"Afraid so."

She looked at him, leaving no doubt of her intent. "So am I, and I find it most discomforting. There's nothing like spending time all alone in that cramped cabin."

Baldridge knew what was coming; he'd encountered her type before. But as he studied her, he wondered what a woman as attractive and desirable as Salina was doing working the boats. Most of the prostitutes were used-up women who showed every mile of the hard road they'd

covered. But this young woman had a fresh face and a spark
in her eye where the others only looked vacant and tired.

"Look, I . . . uh . . . I'm not lookin' for company tonight."

Salina looked at him disgustedly. "Figures. The handful
of single men I'm finding on this boat aren't interested, and
the married ones can't get away from their wives. What are
you? A religious type or something?"

He shook his head. "No. No more so than anybody else."

"Married? Being good to the little woman back home?"

"No, I'm not married."

"You don't like men, do you?"

"No," he said, shifting his weight.

"Good," she said, smiling. "How'd you get that bum leg?"

He took another sip of brandy. This was one pushy
woman. "Jealous husband," he said.

"Sure."

"No, I was just in the wrong place at the wrong time."

"I know what you mean," she said, surveying the crowd
and letting out a long sigh. "I'm beginning to think that's
where I am. Look out there," she said, pointing across the
room. "The ones with any money are hooked up." She
finished off her whiskey. "How's a girl supposed to make a
living? And this is probably the last decent run of the year."

"Is that why you're going to New Orleans?"

She nodded. "That's where the money's at, at least during
low water. Weather's better, too."

"I'm sure it is."

"Where you from?" she asked.

"Just outside of Memphis."

"Maybe that's where I should have gone."

"Looks like some of those fellas aren't accompanied,"
Baldridge said, indicating several tables of cardplayers.

She reviewed the area with a practiced eye and shook her
head. "Nothing worth my time over there. Most of them just
want to drink and gamble. At least Burl's having a good
night."

"Who?"

"Burl. Victor Burl." She pointed at a well-dressed man in a gray hat. "He's a gambler."

"You know him?"

"I've had the pleasure." She offered a wry grin. "Actually, as I recall, *he* had most of the pleasure. Burl runs the river more than I do."

"Knows the river, does he?"

"Next to the pilots, and maybe me, I guess Burl spends more time on the water than anybody." She pointed at the men at the table with Burl. "See those planters?" Baldridge nodded. "They work all year to make their crops, then come aboard with the cash from their sales. And by the time they get off, they're lucky if Burl doesn't own their home and their farm. They don't know who he is. If they did, they wouldn't be playing with him."

"He's that good, is he?"

"Take my word for it. He's a son of a bitch. Besides, he's bad for my business. Once they've lost all their money to him, there's none left to spend on me." She stepped away from the bar and brushed at the front of her dress. "Watch this. I'm going to piss him off."

Prissing across the room, Salina Tyner walked up to the table where Burl was playing seven-card stud.

"Victor! My goodness, I haven't seen you since . . . oh, when was it? The last time the *John Logan* went south?"

Burl looked annoyed and tried to ignore her. She peeked over his shoulder and stepped back in mock horror, her hand over her mouth.

"Oh, my heavens, all those cards of the same kind! That's the same hand you had when you won all that money from those poor farmers in Louisiana, isn't it?"

Burl set his jaw hard as the other cardplayers began looking at one another.

"Why don't you go have a drink, Salina?" Burl said, offering her a forced smile.

"Oh, I think I'd much rather watch the famous Victor Burl play cards."

Two of the other players tossed in their hands and left the table, and the remaining two eyed each other nervously.

"Oh, look! An open chair." Salina took a seat. "You don't mind if I sit in with you, do you, Mr. Burl?"

Burl raked the money from the pot and picked up the cards. He straightened his blue ascot and adjusted his hat, trying to appear unbothered by her presence.

"If you want to play," he said firmly, "let's see some money." He looked at the two remaining players. "You gentlemen don't mind if the lady plays, do you?"

They shook their heads and were anteing into the middle of the table when Salina called across the room.

"Masey, come on over," she said with a wave. She pointed to the empty seat next to Victor Burl. "You look like you've got some money to lose."

He tried unsuccessfully to disguise his limp as he came around the edge of the dance floor and stepped up to the table.

"Victor Burl, this is Mr. Masey Baldridge," Salina said. She looked at the other players, then at Baldridge. "And this is the infamous Victor Burl, cardplayer supreme."

Burl stood up and shook Baldridge's hand. Over six feet tall, he had a firm grip and the appearance of a man of culture and good taste. Returning to his seat, Burl began to shuffle the cards, a large Masonic ring flashing on his left hand.

"You're a Mason?" Baldridge said.

Burl nodded. "And you?"

"Been one for ten years."

Burl smiled. "Always good to see a brother Mason."

As Burl shuffled the cards Baldridge noticed how meticulously his fingernails were manicured and how neatly his money was stacked before him, all in little piles, all of equal height.

"You sound like a southerner," Burl said.

"Tennessee."

"Wounded in the war?"

Baldridge nodded. "Afraid so."

"That's something to be proud of. Suffering for the cause ought not give any man shame."

"Were you a soldier?"

"Victor sat that hand out," Salina sniped from across the table, "didn't you, Victor, honey?"

Burl frowned and looked at Baldridge. "I worked for the Confederate government." He began dealing the cards. "Five-card draw, jacks or better to open, take four to an ace."

They played several hands, with Burl only winning one or two, Salina winning three, and the others each winning one. The whole time they played Burl talked about the war, expressing interest in every aspect of Baldridge's experience. The others at the table listened intently, except for Salina, who never missed an opportunity to tweak Burl. Finally growing tired of both the game on the table and the one with Burl, she left, several dollars ahead.

"At least I made *something*, Victor," she said, winking at Baldridge. She was soon followed by one of the men, leaving only Burl, Baldridge, and one other player. Baldridge ordered a bottle; the three men enjoyed several drinks and were beginning to do more talking than card playing. Because of what Salina had told him, Baldridge had hoped to talk to Burl about the river, but he wasn't having much luck. As the band continued to play for the dancers, the gambler extended his foot into the empty chair, revealing a pair of rattlesnake boots that Baldridge figured must have cost ten dollars; he'd always wanted a pair of boots like that. Leaning over, Burl spoke to Baldridge as if in confidence, the whiskey strong on his breath.

"So what are we going to do about what's happening?"

"Do about what?"

"Why, the country, man! That's what." Masey looked puzzled. "I'm talking about how the federal government is crushing the states," Burl said.

"Oh, well, I don't know." Baldridge laughed. "We already fought that one and lost."

"Lost? What makes you think it's over?"

Baldridge thought Burl was teasing, so he smiled.

"Seems to me we're still fighting Yankees," Burl continued. "You know it's getting bad. Everywhere you look there's some northerner sticking his nose in southerners' business."

"You're right about that."

The other cardplayer, who'd been silent until now, spoke up. "Could be because the South couldn't take care of its own business."

"What's that supposed to mean?" Burl growled.

"Just that the war showed that the South needed somebody to straighten it out."

"Spoken like a true Yankee, eh, Masey?" Burl said. Baldridge didn't respond, but noted the growing impatience in the other player's eyes. "You got your Freedman's Bureau, your military governors . . ."

"Yes, but most states are getting back to normal now," Baldridge said, picking up the hand the northerner dealt him.

"Back to normal? Things'll never be back to normal until . . ." Burl arranged the cards in his hand and tossed a dollar on to the table. "Well, they'll never be the same again."

"Probably not."

"I'm just tired of apologizing for being a southerner, aren't you?" Burl asked.

"I don't," said Baldridge.

"How's that?"

"I don't apologize."

"Sounds like more of that southern arrogance," the other player said. "That's what got you people whipped in the first place."

Baldridge looked at the man. "Whipped?" He shook his head. "We was never whipped."

"Oh, hell, man, don't take it so personal. The South got—"

"Don't take it personal?" Baldridge could sense the whiskey was beginning to talk for him, and though he tried to hold back, he seemed unable to stop the words. "It's personal, all right. When you see your friends die it gets real personal."

"I didn't mean to say that—"

"But you did. And I'll tell you right now, General Forrest was never whipped. Never! You got that?" Baldridge realized he was standing now and shouting, pointing his finger at the man. Victor Burl seemed delighted by the whole scene.

"Okay. Okay," the man said. "Let's just play cards." He paused momentarily. "On second thought," he said, tossing his hand in, "deal me out."

As the man walked away, Burl said, "That's what's wrong with the country. People like him." He lifted his glass. "A toast, Mr. Baldridge. A toast to the gallant General Forrest and his brave men. If we'd just had more, we wouldn't have to listen to the likes of that ignorant fool."

Baldridge met his toast and for the next half hour sat with Burl and talked about the war and Reconstruction. He was an angry man, more angry than Baldridge had seen in years. Still, despite the long conversation he was unable to discover what Burl actually did during the war. Whatever it was, it had soured on his hands. As they spoke, the band had been playing a number of songs popular during the war, and after a while, Burl commented to Baldridge how they all seemed to be Yankee songs. Baldridge hadn't paid much attention, but Burl appeared greatly annoyed. A young girl, not more than fourteen, had taken the stage at the request of some of the passengers and, accompanied by the string band, was singing "Marching Through Georgia." She had a beautiful, clear voice, Baldridge thought; he was enjoying her performance when several men in the dining hall began to sing along with her, agitating Burl.

Three or four years ago Baldridge had stopped being bothered by Federal war songs—in fact, he often enjoyed them as much as those of his own side; but it was apparent that Burl didn't share his view.

" 'The flag that makes you free'?" Burl shouted, quoting

the lyrics of the song. "You mean the flag that condemns southerners to being houseboys for the North, don't you?"

Fortunately, the singing drowned out Burl's comment, but Baldridge was growing increasingly uncomfortable in the man's company. Then Burl stood up and walked up to the band. They had just finished the song, and the crowd was expressing its pleasure with the young girl's performance, when Burl began to talk loudly.

"Young lady! Young lady!" he said, grabbing her by the arm as she stepped off the platform. "Can you sing 'The Southern Soldier Boy'?" The girl looked frightened and glanced toward her parents, who stood in the crowd. A rather short gentleman stepped up beside his daughter.

"Sir, please, my daughter doesn't wish to sing another song."

"Doesn't *wish* to sing? Doesn't want to sing a southern song? Is that it?" His voice was loud and accusatory, though his physical manner remained under control. "The lady, or should I say woman?—we in the South believe there's a difference—doesn't *wish* to sing a southern song." He looked across the room. "Surely there's someone out there who will sing a song for the South!"

The crowd was growing sullen, and the people were mumbling and pointing at Burl. He turned to the bandleader. "Play something for the South, my good man." Reaching in his pocket, he pulled out a gold piece. "You'll do it for money, won't you? This Yankee boat, run by its Yankee captain, will do anything for money, ain't that right? You Yankees'll do anything for money, won't you?" Steven Tibedeau was moving through the crowd as Burl continued, and the bandleader eventually struck up "The Yellow Rose of Texas." Baldridge fully expected Burl to return to his seat; surprisingly, he remained by the platform, staring angrily at the crowd.

"No, no, no," he said, waving his arms at the band and laying his hand across the banjo. "I want to hear 'Homespun Dress.' I want to hear of the gallant sacrifice the ladies of the South made." Reaching out to the young girl again, he tried to take her sleeve, but her father pushed Burl's hand away. As he did so, the gambler reached inside his jacket, produced a two-barrel knuckleduster, and held it up in the man's face.

"I'm going to hear 'Homespun Dress," he said, "and I want your daughter to sing it. It's only fair. We've been subjected to these Yankee songs all evening, and now I want my fair share of southern songs."

The crowd was fully hushed now, watching Burl and waiting to see if the young girl would sing.

"Now, honey, are you going to sing my song?"

The girl was in tears. "I don't know that song, sir. Please let go of my father."

Burl released the man and waved the knuckleduster toward the ceiling. "That what's wrong with this country!" he shouted. "That's what's—"

"Mr. Burl!" someone called from the crowd. Turning, Baldridge saw Captain Luke Williamson parting the onlookers as he made his way to the platform. "Mr. Burl, perhaps I can help."

Burl's eyes were fired with whiskey and hate as he looked at Williamson. "And how are you going to help? Your belly's as blue as these others'."

Luke stepped up to Burl. "You've had a lot to drink, Mr. Burl. Perhaps if you have a seat—"

"I want to hear my song!"

"I'll have to take that weapon, sir," Williamson said. Baldridge was impressed by the calmness in the captain's voice and the quieting effect his presence seemed to have over the crowd. Burl stared at Williamson for a long moment, then lowered the knuckleduster.

The captain surveyed the crowd. "Does anyone here know this gentleman's song?"

No one spoke up until a voice called from the back of the room.

"I know it."

The crowd parted to reveal Salina Tyner strutting toward the band. Luke Williamson smiled.

"Miss Tyner." He helped her onto the platform, then looked at Burl, who relinquished the gun. "Now you've ridden with us enough to know we check weapons on the lower deck." Burl showed not the slightest sign of embarrassment, but met Williamson's eyes squarely.

"Another time, Captain," he said; then he glanced up at Salina Tyner and smiled knowingly. "I might have known," he said in a low voice, then started back to the table where Baldridge stood.

As Luke Williamson and Steven Tibedeau brushed past him on their way out, Baldridge overheard them.

"If that sorry bastard causes one more second of trouble," he whispered, "I want you to throw his ass overboard. You got that?"

"Got it, Captain."

The band played an introduction and Salina Tyner began to sing.

After three verses, the crowd, which had been nearly silent, offered up warm applause. Burl stood and looked at Baldridge.

"You see? I told you it wasn't over." Gathering up his money, he slipped through the crowd and out of the hall.

An hour later, Baldridge found Salina on the starboard deck outside the dining hall. The night breeze was tossing her skirt as she stood staring out over the water.

"Nice job," he said, stepping up beside her, while keeping one hand behind his back.

She smiled. "Somebody had to do something."

"Yeah, but why you?"

"We go back a ways."

"You and Burl?"

"I shared a place with him for a while after the war," she said with a forlorn glance at the ceiling. "You know, livin' in sin and all? But it wasn't to be. We were too much alike. Me, I had to be on the move to be happy, and him . . . well . . . he never got over his wife. Lost her during the war."

"I see."

"Anyway, that's old news. I've hated the son of a bitch ever since."

"Yet you sang for him."

"I guess I felt sorry for him." She turned to face Baldridge. "Burl's so full of hate there's no room for anything or anyone else." She tried to peer around Masey to see what he was holding, but he turned out of her view. "What have you got back there?" she asked with a mischievous grin.

"Oh," he said, looking toward the passenger cabins, "a little something for a bedtime toddy." He looked as pitiful as possible. "Guess I'll have to drink it all by myself."

"That's a real shame."

"And I've got this bad leg, too," he added.

"Oh," said Salina, mocking him, "and I bet you'd like somebody to rub it for you and tuck you in."

"It does cause me a lot of pain."

"Honey, for the right price I'll rub anything you want."

▽

5

OCCASIONALLY JACOB LUSK dressed for dinner and joined Luke in the grand hall, but only after considerable urging. As first mate, he had every right to be at the captain's table, and Luke always tried to make him feel welcome; but too many times he had felt the not-so-subtle stares of the passengers and overheard their comments. He felt more at home eating in the kitchen, where he enjoyed the heftier portions and particularly the company.

Anabel, the chief cook, treated him like a king. As he strolled into the kitchen that evening at nine-thirty, she and her four assistant cooks were pulling chicken off the bone to use in soup the next day.

"You draggin' in here pretty late tonight," she said, smiling broadly as he plopped down in a chair near the door. "You lucky I don't send you out a-beggin'."

"Now, Anabel, you know I can't just up and leave the deck."

"Everybody else done eat," she said, lifting a cloth from a plate she had prepared for him. She walked over to a small table beside him and laid out the plate and some silverware. "Seems like a shame when the big hog at the trough don't get to feed till all the little ones are done."

"Long day, Anabel."

She wiped her hands on her apron. "I know what you mean. Lord, sometimes it seems like I been cookin' for twenty-four hours straight. Got another three or four more before we can get out of here for the night."

He sprinkled some salt on the roast beef and looked up at her. Two days out of St. Louis and already she looked tired. He knew something of what she faced, and though he never admitted it to her, he figured she put in longer hours than he did. Fourteen or fifteen hours a day in this hot kitchen was enough to wear anybody out. Still, whenever he came by, she was always ready for him with a plate and something to drink. And though she was usually working while he was there, she took the time to talk to him. As first mate, he could not sit and talk with the deckhands: He could not very well swap lies and share a bottle with a man one day and take him to task the next. The mud clerk, Steven Tibedeau, seldom sat still long enough to visit with anybody, and the pilots—the pilots lived in their own world and seldom descended to earth long enough to talk to a simple workingman. That was what made Luke Williamson so special. He had gotten to know Jacob and he didn't seem to think he was too good to spend time with him. Yet Jacob never lost sight of the fact that Luke was the captain. It was strange, how he could talk straight to Luke and still respect him. He was just sorry it didn't work that way with the men he supervised.

So Anabel had become his closest friend on the boat— someone he could count on seeing every day, someone he could talk to about most anything. As he tore off a piece of biscuit and sopped it in gravy, he watched her moving about the kitchen, directing her assistants. She was a stocky woman, though not fat, and her face had somehow dodged the aging that had hammered Jacob's. He wasn't sure, and he had never asked, but he figured Anabel to be forty, maybe forty-two; and she had a certain compassion and a genuine love of life in her eyes that had always intrigued him. Her husband had died almost ten years ago, leaving her with four children, of whom all but one were grown and on their own. She loved to talk to him about that "baby" of hers, though, and how much she missed him when they were making a run; and she was constantly quizzing Jacob about bringing the boy on board. Tonight was no exception.

"When you gonna let my baby come to work for you?" she asked, as she refilled his coffee cup.

"He's too young, Anabel."

"Too young, my foot! Why he's a big ol' strappin' young' un."

"He ain't big enough," Jacob added through a mouthful of biscuit.

She set the pot down on the table hard enough to bounce his knife into the air. "You was thirteen when you started on a boat. You told me so."

"That boy needs to be in school, not out here totin' sacks."

"Cap'n Luke would hire him."

"Cap'n Luke won't hire him lessen I say so."

"Oh, you that tight with the cap'n, are you?"

"Me and the cap'n go back a long ways."

"And I don't?" She crossed her arms. "Jacob Lusk, I'll have you know I been cookin' for Cap'n Williamson longer than you been hustlin' yo black ass around these decks."

Experience had taught Jacob that getting Anabel riled up was not the thing to do. He raised his hands. "Okay, okay. You've been here the longest." He took the last bite of roast beef and grinned. "But I still ain't gonna put your boy on. Besides, this'll be the last run of the season."

"So if it wasn't, you sayin' you'd let him work?"

As Jacob started to say no, Anabel reached down and took his cherry pie away from him.

"What you doin'?" he protested.

"And if it wasn't the last run?" she said, holding the pie out of his reach.

"Anabel . . ."

"Would you hire him if it wasn't the last run?" He tried for the pie but she held it out of reach. "Jacob?"

"Oh, Anabel."

"You gonna give my boy a chance next season?"

He let out a long sigh. "Oh, I reckon so." As she handed him the plate, he lifted his finger. "But not as a full deckhand. Not at full pay."

She pulled the plate away again.

"Come on, Anabel! He's not old enough to do a man's work yet. I'll give him a job. It may be emptyin' the sludge pans from the boilers, but I guess I can find something for him."

Anabel smiled broadly. "Well, finally." She placed the pie on the table. "It's a shame I have to starve you to get you to do what you know you ought to."

Jacob was making a last round of the hurricane deck before checking with the captain and turning in for the night, when he came upon a passenger standing in the dark overlooking the paddle wheel. Afraid of startling the man, Jacob slowed as he neared him, but the man never turned around.

"Evenin', sir," Jacob said. "Are you all right, sir?"

As the man turned around, the distant lantern revealed a silver flask in his hand. His shirt was partially unbuttoned, and his hair was disheveled.

"Good evening," he said slowly.

Jacob surveyed the man's face in the poor light. "I saw you back here all by yourself, and I just wanted to be sure you was all right."

"I'm better than all right, my good man. I'm doing just fine." He offered the flask, but Jacob declined, so the man took a quick sip. Jacob was concerned that he might have had a little too much; having some drunk fall over the deck and jam up the paddle wheel was all he needed to keep him up the rest of the night. And it would be one hell of a mess to clean up.

"I'm the first mate, sir," Jacob began, "and I'm just a little worried about you being out here this late by yourself."

The man peered over the deck at the paddle wheel, then looked at Jacob. "Relax, there, chief. I ain't gonna be takin' no dives, if that's what you're thinking." He held up the flask. "And this, well, this here is just medicine." He took another swig, then slapped his pants leg. "Got this bum leg here, see?"

"Yes, sir, I see."

The man squinted at him through whiskey eyes. "Colored mate, huh? Can't say I've ever seen a colored mate before."

"I believe I'm the only one, sir."

"Things is changin'," the man said with a grin. "Like that song they were singing downstairs a while ago. He began to sing slightly off-key. " 'Better times a-comin'. Better times, better times . . .' " He looked at Jacob. "You know that song, don't you?"

"Yes, sir, I know it."

The man lifted his flask in a toast. "Well, I've already had a better time tonight than I've had in a long while," he said, taking another swig.

Jacob quietly watched the man while he tried to come up with a courteous way to get him inside. Again the gentleman spoke.

"You know, you really ought to have a talk with that bartender down there," he said, pointing at the floor with exaggerated emphasis.

"How's that, sir?"

"Name's Baldridge, Masey Baldridge," he said, offering his hand. Jacob shook it and the man continued: "That rascal down there is passin' off some homemade shit as good French brandy."

"Is that right, Mr. Baldridge?"

"Damned straight." Baldridge leaned back as if to get Lusk in focus, and Jacob almost reached for him, fearing he would somersault over the rail. "I know what he's doin'. I know damned well what he's doin'."

Jacob stepped over to the rail more to be in a position to steady Baldridge than to be sociable. "And what's that, sir?"

"See, here's what he's doin'," Baldridge said, leaning close to Jacob and talking with his hands, the smell of bourbon heavy on his breath. "He takes cod-liver oil, you see, and a little nitric acid, and he mixes it with Kentucky bourbon." He looked at Jacob, deadly serious. "You're followin' me, aren't you?"

"Uh, yes, sir, I believe so."

"Well, then he takes some roasted peach pits, and lets 'em sit in that mixture for a couple of days to give it the taste, and there you have it." Jacob offered a vacant nod. "It'll fool a lot of people, I tell you, it will." Baldridge pointed his finger at Jacob. "But he ain't got no business passin' it off as French brandy."

"I see. Well, Mr. Baldrige, I sho' will speak to the cap'n about this here matter."

Baldridge turned and stared out the back of the boat again.

"First mate," he observed again. "Must be a tough job on a big boat like this."

"Yes, sir, it can be."

"Then you'd know about what speed a boat like this will get?"

"Oh, yes, sir. She'll make twelve, sometimes fourteen miles an hour runnin' with the water."

"That fast, huh?"

"Yes, sir."

"Even if she took a snag?"

"How you mean, sir?"

"Well, say if the boat hit a snag, and was taking on some water, could she still make that kind of speed?"

"Well, sir, if the wheel wasn't hurt, I 'spect she could get about that."

"So once a pilot hit a snag, it wouldn't take long for him to turn the boat and head her into the shore, would it?"

"You mean run her nose aground?"

"Yeah. I suppose so."

"Depend upon how far she was from the shore, Mr. Baldridge."

"I see. But isn't that what a pilot's supposed to do?" Baldridge turned to face Jacob again. "Isn't he supposed to try to get to the shore so people can get off?"

"Why you askin' all this, Mr. Baldridge?" Jacob forced a laugh. "The *Paragon* ain't gonna sink, if that's what you're afraid of."

"But isn't that what a pilot's supposed to do?"

"I ain't no pilot—"

"But I bet you know."

Jacob was growing uncomfortable. He also sensed that Mr. Baldridge was not as drunk as he had originally believed.

"Yes, sir," he said softly. "That'd be what a pilot would do."

Eventually the gentleman tired of his perch above the paddle wheel. He accompanied Jacob back to the stairwell, where the first mate bade him good evening as he disappeared toward the passengers' cabins. Minutes later Jacob was knocking on the door of the captain's quarters.

"Come in."

"Cap'n?" When he peeked in, Jacob saw Luke sitting in a cane-bottomed chair, his sleeves rolled up and his suspenders hanging from his waist. Pipe in hand, he sat bent over a tiny desktop that folded out from the wall, his eye busily scanning a map in the weak light.

"Pull up a stool, Jacob," Luke said without looking up from the map. "You want some coffee?"

"No, sir, I believe not." Jacob retrieved a small stool from beside the bed. A man as large as he looked strange perching on a tiny footstool, and he leaned slightly forward to maintain his balance. The cabin was austere compared to some Jacob had seen in his years on the river. The six-by-eight-foot room held a feather mattress stretched across an iron frame which was slightly fancier than those the cabin passengers occupied; a porcelain washbowl and pitcher rested on a modest three-drawer washstand in the far corner. Only one painting, of Canal Street in New Orleans, decorated the walls, and a small velvet drape hung over the window in the cabin door. Jacob had seen other captains' quarters twice this size, but they were occupied twice as much. Captain Williamson spent most of his time on deck, and the rest of the crew knew that they could find him in his cabin only at bedtime. What the rest of the crew didn't know, and Jacob did, was the real reason Luke avoided his cabin.

Late one night about two years ago, during the hottest part of the year, Jacob had stopped by after last watch, very much as he was doing tonight, and Luke had begun talking to him, first about the boat; then about the business in general; and then, surprisingly, about himself. It was then that Jacob learned his captain's greatest fear. It wasn't the river, or anything she might throw at him, and from what Jacob had observed over the years, it wasn't any man he had ever come across. In fact, Jacob had always figured that Luke Williamson had the biggest balls of any man he had ever known. But that night Luke had described to him how as a boy of twelve he watched helplessly as the scourge of yellow fever seemed to clench its unseen hands around first his mother, then his father, and slowly squeeze the very life from them. And it was fear of the disease—of being closed up in a cabin and of breathing what he called "bad air"—that kept Luke circulating about the decks all hours of the day and night. What most of the crew joked about as a man's obsession with his work, Jacob knew to be something else.

"Jacob," Luke asked, lifting his cup to his lips and taking a sip, "how deep would you say the river is off Rifle Point this time of year?"

As he thought about the question, Jacob noticed that the captain was studying *James' River Guide,* a collection of charts and maps of the Mississippi, issued every three years. Luke occasionally consulted one of the guides when information from a wharfmaster or another pilot led him to believe the channel, islands, or principal bars had changed along the route from St. Louis to New Orleans. But Jacob never trusted the guides, primarily because he had trouble reading and interpreting them; he relied entirely upon memory when it came to locations, and upon word-of-mouth about current river conditions. Luke held a map up and pointed to the area, and Jacob leaned forward to get a closer look.

"You talkin' 'bout down there 'round Giles Bend, Cap'n?" Luke ran his finger along the map and nodded his head. "Yes,

sir," Jacob continued, probing his memory for an image of
that stretch of river. He scratched his head and squinted at
Luke's map. "Cap'n, I'd say it'd be anywhere from fifty feet
to . . . to no bottom." He leaned close to the map. "Is this
Rifle Bend right here?"

"Yeah."

"Well, that's your deepest spot." He lifted his hand as if
drawing a picture in the air. "Along the east bank, through
there, is that real high bluff. You know the one I'm talkin'
about, don't you, Cap'n?"

"Yeah. Yeah. I know where you mean."

"Well, anytime you got a bluff that steep, and low ground
on the opposite side, the river, she just dig herself a hole. I've
called 'no bottom' there a few times, yes, sir, I sho' have."

No bottom was the sing-song signal of the sounder, the
crewman on the nose of the boat who was constantly
lowering a lead line into the water to check the depth. Using
a heavily weighted rope knotted at one-fathom intervals, he
would toss the rope alongside the boat and wait for it to hit
bottom. When he felt it go slack he would call the depth up
to the pilothouse and retrieve the rope for the next cast. "No
bottom" meant the rope never went slack. There were
several places along the route to New Orleans where Jacob,
in his earlier days as a sounder, had sung out in his rich bass
voice, "Noooooooo Baaaaaahhhhhaaduuum."

"No bottom, huh?"

"I ain't never slacked rope there, Cap'n. Now, I've heard
it said that stretch along there is more than two hundred
feet deep, but I can't swear to it." He looked intently at Luke
Williamson. "What you studyin' about, Cap'n?"

"The telegram from the wharfmaster at Natchez said the
Mary Justice went down sixteen miles north of Natchez."
He pointed again at the map. "That's got to be river miles,
because as the crow flies, the spot I'm talking about is not
more than four and a half, maybe five miles from Natchez."
He tapped his finger on the map. "See, if it was straight-line
distance, that would put the wreck close to Port Gibson, and

the wharfmaster there would've sent the telegram. Understand?"

"Yes, sir, be river distance. I understand."

"So even if the wharfmaster was off by a mile or two, Ed
had to have gone down somewhere near here." He pointed
at the map again.

"Yes, sir, I reckon so."

Luke turned his head slowly toward Jacob and looked at
him with an odd frown. "But that doesn't make sense, Jacob.
There are no sandbars along that stretch. There haven't been
in five or six years. The last sandbar to come up through
there showed up on the west side of the river right after the
war. You remember that, don't you?"

"That's the one that come up around the gunboat that
sank, ain't it?"

"Yeah. It went down not more than a hundred and fifty
feet from the west bank. The river deposited silt and sludge
all over it, and in a couple of years a sandbar grew up."

"Yes, sir, I know where you talkin' about. They's trees
growin' on that now. That's done turned into an island."

"Sure it has. But everybody knows it. I mean, it's not
something that Ed Smythe wouldn't have known about. And
even if Ed wasn't in the pilothouse, he would have made sure
Eli and Tenny knew about it."

Luke was right. Not only was Ed Smythe a quality pilot
himself, but also, Jacob figured, he always got the best deal
among the hired-ons when he and Luke stepped down from
the pilothouse to become full-time captains. Eli Winston
and Tenny Mays were much more experienced river men
than either Martin or Thomas, though that was due largely
to Luke's reluctance to give up the wheel. He had insisted
on pulling a full night watch in the pilothouse and still
attending to his captain duties during the day up until about
a year ago, when Ed Smythe had said enough was enough.

Jacob recalled their argument—one of the few he had ever
witnessed between the two friends—and the frustration in
Ed Smythe's voice that day in St. Louis when the *Paragon*

docked and he found Luke curled up on the floor of the pilothouse for one of his catnaps. He had gone so long on so little sleep, the landing whistle hadn't even awakened him. Ed had come on board to talk about some deal he was setting up and Jacob was standing near the wheel conferring with young Martin when it happened.

"Good God, Luke. What the hell you doin' on the floor?" Luke sat up with a start.

"Is something wrong? What's wrong?" he said, rushing to his feet. Clearing the sleep from his eyes, he recognized Ed.

"What're you doing here?"

"Luke, you're in St. Louis."

"I knew that," Luke fired back, still looking about in bewilderment.

"The hell you did!" Smythe said, gritting his teeth. "You were on watch again last night, weren't you?"

"Hell, yeah."

"That's what you hired Neely for, Luke."

Luke shook his head as he wiped the sleep from his eyes. "He's not ready for nights yet."

"That's bullshit and you know it. Goddamn it, Luke, that's why we hire pilots!"

"I just don't think he's ready."

"I'll tell you who's not ready. You're the one who's not ready. You're not ready to give up the wheel."

"This is my boat, Ed," Luke said with a half smile. "I'm wild and woolly and full of fleas, and I'll run my boat like I goddamned please."

"Don't give me a bunch of horseshit sayings. It's my boat, too. Remember? Fifty-fifty."

"So?"

"So I don't want to see my half going to the bottom because you're too tired to keep your eyes open."

Luke was getting angry. "I'm wide awake at the wheel, and you know it," he said, pointing his finger at Ed.

"Maybe last night. Yeah, maybe so. But what about next week? Or the week after that? You can't stay up night and day forever. Look at yourself. You look like shit. You need a shave. You need a bath. Hell, Luke, what are the passengers gonna think?"

"I don't give a damn what they think."

"That's the problem. You *don't* care what they think. You're supposed to be the captain of this boat, man!"

"You don't tell me what to do," Luke said, stepping closer to Ed. "You don't *ever* tell me what to do. You got that?"

That was the only time in the years Jacob had known the two men that he thought they might actually resort to fisticuffs over something. And if Luke had been pressed much further, they probably would have fought. But Ed Smythe knew something that Luke didn't—when to quit—and fortunately for their friendship and the business, he did. But something he said must have registered; less than two weeks after the incident, Luke allowed Thomas to handle the night run, and from that time on, he had been the night pilot.

Jacob snapped his attention back to Luke when the captain rose from his chair and walked over to the cabin door. He pulled the curtain and stared out into the night.

"Jacob, I just can't imagine why in the world he would not have beached her, can you?"

"That's funny, Cap'n. You the second man to ask me that tonight."

Luke turned around. "What are you talking about?"

Jacob pointed to the hurricane deck. "Some fella I run into before I come in here asked me the same thing."

"About running the *Mary Justice* to shore?"

"Yes, sir."

"Who was it?"

"Oh, just one of the passengers, Cap'n."

"What was his name?"

"Baldridge, as I recollect."

"Why was he asking about the *Mary Justice*?"

Jacob stood up from his stool, his immense frame nearly filling the room. "Oh, I don't know, Cap'n. He was about half drunk, standing at the back of the boat, sippin' on some whiskey and carryin' on. Ain't no tellin' what he was liable to say. Never did say her name, though, as I recollect. Just asked general-like."

"Baldridge, huh?"

"Yes, sir."

"What else did he ask?"

"Something about how fast she'd go."

"*Mary Justice*?"

"Uh, no, sir. The *Paragon*."

Luke turned and looked back out the window. "If he asks you anything else, you tell me." Jacob nodded. "And I want you to point him out to me tomorrow."

"Yes, sir, I'll do that. Everything's fine on deck, Cap'n, and if you won't be needin' nothin' else, I guess I'll get on to bed."

Luke opened the door to the cabin. Jacob stooped low to avoid the top of the door and stepped out on to the deck. Turning back to Luke, he touched his hat respectfully. "We'll be there soon enough, Cap'n. Then we can see for ourself 'bout what happened."

"That's what I'm counting on."

"Yes, sir. Well, evenin', Cap'n."

"Good night, Jacob."

"Oh . . . uh, Cap'n?"

Luke leaned out of his cabin. "Yes?"

"Cap'n, did you ever taste the brandy that fella's servin' in the bar?"

"The brandy?"

"Yes, sir."

Luke shook his head. "No, why?"

"Oh, nothin', Cap'n. Nothin'. I'll see you in the morning."

$\triangledown$

6

"COME ON . . . COME on, Mama . . . come on one time for me!" someone shouted from a crowded dice table. The air was thick with smoke and smelled like bad perfume and sweat as Luke Williamson pressed through the crowd, occasionally rising to his tiptoes to search the faces around him. A man with his arm encircling a well-traveled, scantily-clad woman bumped into him and shoved off with his elbow. Luke felt a sting in his ribs and moved to retaliate; but considering the looks of the man and the personality of the crowd, he thought better of it.

The wharfmaster had told Luke that Russell Flint, one of the deckhands on the *Mary Justice*, had survived the wreck and was supposedly still in Natchez. If he was, Luke knew he would not be far from a dice game; Ed Smythe had suspended Flint three times in the last two years for gambling on the work deck. If Flint was still around, he would be in Natchez-Under-the-Hill, the biggest gaming spot this side of New Orleans. Silver Street, which led down from the aristocratic bluffs of the city of Natchez, met the river amid a dozen of the raunchiest gambling houses, saloons, and brothels to be found anywhere on the Mississippi. Since the early 1800s, Natchez-Under-the-Hill had offered anything a man could want, legal or illegal. A shorebound parasite, it fed off river traffic, sucking the blood out of wealthy plantation owners and unsuspecting businessmen who dared to drop in for a little game. But there were no little games in

Natchez-Under-the-Hill—only life-and-death games, and mostly death. And a body facedown on muddy Silver Street, with a bullet in the back and pockets inside out, was not an unusual find.

In addition to the tip on Russell Flint, the wharfmaster confirmed that the *Mary Justice* had gone down in deep water just off the bluff where Bisland Bayou empties into the river. That would put it off Rifle Point and slightly north of Giles Bend, not far from where Luke had figured. When they had passed Giles Bend approaching Natchez, Luke had Martin slow the *Paragon* and ease her from one side of the river to the other in hopes of seeing something, anything that might hint of what happened. But except for some debris that had washed ashore, and a handful of locals on the west bank apparently scavenging for salvage, it was as if the river had swallowed the *Mary Justice.*

According to the wharfmaster, she'd gone down somewhere between eight and nine P.M. on Monday, October 14. The first reports, which came downriver about an hour later, indicated she took a snag—probably a large tree, or portion thereof, that had eroded from the banks and worked its way into the channel. The trunk, being heaviest, would have lodged in the river bottom, leaving the branches pointing upward and waiting like so many lances to pierce the hull of an unsuspecting steamboat. At first the wharfmaster didn't figure the incident to be serious. Boats frequently hit snags, especially during low water. Some were more dangerous than others; to hit a snag didn't necessarily mean a boat would sink. It might take on some water, or even have some cargo jolted overboard, but many boats would limp to the nearest bank and hold up for repairs.

About an hour later, another report claimed there had been an explosion on board; perhaps this was one of the boilers. Then, about a half hour after that, word came that the *Mary Justice* was gone, down in deep water, and that only a handful of passengers and crew had escaped. Luke had pressed the wharfmaster for more but there weren't many details he could offer; he suggested Luke find some of the survivors. Fifty or sixty people got off the boat, many of them turning up in Natchez initially. Most had scattered since then, but the wharfmaster named several he thought were still in town and told Luke of about two dozen others who'd gone on to New Orleans. Luke recognized the names of some crewmen; one, Asa Turner, had been a cabin steward on the *Mary Justice* the last three years. When Luke asked about Ed Smythe specifically, the wharfmaster just shook his head and looked down at the floor.

Luke did get two surprises. Apparently, he hadn't been the first person to see the wharfmaster that day. Within an hour after the *Paragon* landed, the wharfmaster said, he had had a visit from another man inquiring about the wreck. When Luke asked the man's name, the wharfmaster could not recall, but he did remember that the man walked with a limp. Luke's biggest surprise, however, was learning that Tenny Mays, the night pilot, was still alive—alive, but in bad shape. He was in the hospital on Franklin Street in Natchez, and the last anybody had heard, he was drifting in and out of consciousness and barely holding on. Luke planned to try and talk to Mays that afternoon, before the *Paragon* set out for New Orleans, but for now he concerned himself with Flint.

This hellhole was Russell Flint's kind of place, so Luke continued to search through the crowd. He slipped his hand inside his waistcoat and touched the navy Colt revolver tucked in his belt to reassure himself as he circled the jammed dice table like a hawk around a potato patch, coming in close to check each face. Finally, at the distant end of the table, he saw him. Flint was slapping down cash on the layout and arguing with the man next to him. Luke moved around behind him and tapped him on the shoulder. At first, Flint didn't look up, so Luke tapped harder.

"What the hell you want?" Flint barked over his shoulder. "Can't you see I'm tryin' to make a bet here?"

"Flint, I want to talk to you."

When he turned around, Flint recognized Luke immediately. "Well, I don't want to talk to you. I'm busy."

"It's about the wreck."

"Leave me be, *Captain*." He said the word as if it disgusted him. "I ain't workin' your boats no more." He tossed two more bills on the table.

"Flint, we're going to talk," Luke said, raising his voice to be heard over the players. "I need to know what happened."

"Damned boat sunk," Flint shouted back, without taking his eyes off the table. "Ain't nothin' to talk about." Some of the players laughed at Flint's comment, but others were getting irritated at Luke interrupting the game, so they squeezed closer to Flint to try and seal him off.

"Your boat just about got my ass drowned," Flint said. "Smythe just lost it, that's all. He just lost it. He wasn't shit anyway. Got his passengers killed and his—"

Flint stopped in mid-sentence as Luke pushed his way closer and pressed against him, his face next to Flint's ear.

"Now what you feel in your back, Mr. Flint, is a thirty-six-caliber navy Colt," Luke whispered. "I ain't playing with you. And unless you want the next bet on that table to be your guts, you'll back off from those dice and give me a few minutes of your precious time."

Flint squeezed his money into his palm and began to move slowly away from the table. Looking around the room, Luke spotted a vacant table in a dark corner nearby. He led Flint toward the spot, never allowing the barrel of his revolver to leave his spine.

"Have a seat, Mr. Flint," Luke said, shoving the man toward a chair.

Flint glared at him. "You got no call to be pullin' a gun on me, Captain. I didn't even work on your boat. You got no—"

Luke put his foot up in the chair opposite Flint and laid the revolver on the table, his palm spread across it. Then he removed his hat and placed it to conceal the weapon.

"I'm going to ask you again, Mr. Flint. Tell me what happened that night."

"I-I-I really can't tell you much, Captain. I was stretched out on my blanket back near the stairwell. I remember feelin' a jolt. It rocked me right off the cotton bale I was sleepin' on. The captain, that is Captain Smythe, sounded a long whistle and I figured we must've hit something. Didn't know what, just knew we must have hit something."

"So Ed Smythe was in the pilothouse?"

"Well, sir, I reckon." Flint kept eyeing Luke's hat.

"What do you mean, you reckon? You didn't see him?"

"No sir, I just heard tell he was up there."

"Heard from who?"

"I don't remember." He glanced around nervously. "Look, Captain, that was a real bad time for me, you understand? I-I don't much like talkin' about it."

"So what happened after you felt the jolt?"

"Well, I jumped up figurin' I'd have to pitch in—"

"Then what happened?"

"Well . . . it was dark and all . . . and I can't really say for sure."

"Think about it, man."

"Well, I was standin' there on the deck when all of a sudden something exploded." He offered a nervous laugh, and his eyes kept darting about the room as if in search of someone. "Next thing I knew I was clutchin' to a piece of the railing and watching her burn right there in the middle of the channel. Weren't nothing I could do, Captain. Weren't nothing."

"Was she aground?"

"Maybe. Yeah, I reckon she was."

"So what did she hit?"

"Hell, I don't know, Captain. I done told you. I was sound asleep when it happened." Again he glanced toward Luke's concealed revolver. "You gonna let me go now? I done told you all I know." Luke motioned with his head for Flint to leave, and as the crewman stood up he looked at him. "Boats go down all the time, Captain. All the time. Just wasn't my day to die. That's all I know to say. Just wasn't my day."

Flint walked back toward his dice table and Luke slipped his revolver in his belt and watched him. He had never liked Flint. Ed said the man was a troublemaker; he only took Flint back on the *Mary Justice* because he felt sorry for him. But something about what he said didn't ring true. Luke wasn't sure what it was, but he didn't think Flint was telling him everything. Boats did go down all the time, but not *his* boats. Not with a man like Ed Smythe on board.

Now Flint began talking excitedly as several men gathered around him, some of them looking in Luke's direction. Rather than rejoining the dice game, Flint spoke to the men for several moments and then disappeared into the crowd.

From the opposite side of the packed room, "Ring, Ring the Banjos" from the piano mixed with loud voices to create a steady roar, and Luke decided he should move on to the hospital to see Tenny Mays. But when he started for the door, three or four men blocked his way, so Luke backed away and moved toward the bar, his eyes searching the room for another exit. Finding none, he chose another route along the bar, but it, too, was suddenly closed off by two large, shabbily attired men. One held a bottle of whiskey in his hand; the other was a broad, muscular fellow wearing a bright red shirt. Luke backed up several feet and tried to use some of the other customers to shield himself from view; but the men moved after him, pushing aside those in the way. Luke found himself back near the table where he had talked to Flint; anxiously searching, he still could find no other window or door. With the two men from the bar moving closer, the three others Flint had spoken to at the dice table began to approach him from the opposite side of the room. In seconds he would be encircled, the reveling crowd oblivious to what was happening, and somehow he felt that even if he started shooting, they would only be distracted long enough to take cover. No one saw anything in Natchez-Under-the-Hill.

The man carrying the whiskey bottle moved in first. "You got no business down here, you understand?" He took the bottleneck in a reverse grip and lifted it, its modest contents gurgling out on to the floor. "You may be Mr. High 'n Mighty on the river . . . big pilot and all . . . but down here," he said with a grin, "down here you ain't shit."

"What you talkin' to Russell Flint about, anyway?" one of the men from the dice table asked.

"I'm just trying to find out what happened to the *Mary Justice.*"

The man in the red shirt glanced at the one holding the whiskey bottle. "Oh, I can tell you that. She sunk," he said with a chuckle. The others joined him in the laugh. "Like a goddamned rock. All flaming and everything!"

Luke grit his teeth. "You saw her go down and . . . you think that's funny?"

The man in red smiled. "When it happens to a Yankee it is. And I 'spect you a Yankee, too, ain't you?"

"Hell, yeah, he's a Yankee. I seen him before. This here's Captain Luke Williamson," one of the others said in an inflated introduction. "Set him a speed record here last year. Supposed to be some kind of highfalutin pilot." The man folded his arms. "He's a bluebelly all right. Got a lot of damned nerve coming in here."

Luke stared at him. "The war's over."

"The hell it is," growled the man with the whiskey bottle as he swung it at Luke's head. Seeing the glass glint in the light, Luke instantly pulled his head to the side, taking the force of the blow on his shoulder. The bottle didn't break, and the man was drawing it back for another try when Luke balled his fist and drove it hammerlike into the man's nose. He felt one of the others grab him by the left shoulder, and when he reached to retrieve his Colt, someone caught his other hand. He struggled against the man's grip and was within inches of the handle of the pistol when one of the others delivered a vicious punch to his left jaw. The force of the blow sent him reeling back, exposing the weapon in his belt. He felt the barrel sliding against his skin and out of his belt, and shaking off the punch, he found himself staring down that same barrel. The red-shirted man held the weapon with both hands—it was only inches from Luke's face—while the others, two on each side, held him bent over backward, his arms and shoulders pinned against the table. Glancing past the gunman, Luke noticed that no one in the room was paying attention to what was happening. It was if they were making every effort to look the other way. This was crazy, he thought. Any moment this man might pull the trigger and blow his head off, and Luke doubted the incident would do more than draw a passing glance before someone ordered the next round.

"Why are you doing this?" Luke asked, still struggling against the hold of the others.

"Yankee son of a bitch got what he deserved, that's what I say," the man with the bottle said.

Luke rolled his head to the side. "What are you talking about? Ed Smythe never did anything to you."

The click of the hammer caught Luke's ear and his eyes darted back to the man before him; then he heard the report of his own revolver being discharged in his face. Every muscle in his body seized in that second as he expected to feel the piercing heat of a .36-caliber round driving into his skull. This was it. It was all over.

But the bullet never came. Instead, his ear aching from the blast, his eyes watering in the smoke of the discharge, he struggled to make out the tall, slim, sandy-haired man now before him. Luke recognized him as the man Jacob had pointed out to him just before they docked: Masey Baldridge. The man in the red shirt who had tried to kill him was now doubled over on the floor, his hand clapped tightly against his head, a dark trail of blood trickling between his fingers as he kicked and screamed on the floor. Suddenly Luke's right arm was freed, as one of his assailants stepped forward to counter Baldridge, who managed to block the attacker's arm and thrust a broad blade into the man's abdomen. There was a muffled groan accompanied by a look of terror as the man kept gripping at Baldridge's clothes and fighting the urge to drop to the floor. He lost, and slumped helplessly beside his companion in the red shirt. Grabbing a handful of curly brown hair, Luke jerked at the man holding his left arm and then drove his right knee into the man's left temple—once, twice, a third time, until the dazed attacker released him and crumpled against the table. Seeing what was happening to their buddies, the other two assailants quickly stepped away from Luke and melted into the crowd. Masey Baldridge moved back and calmly surveyed the two wounded men on the floor before them.

"Goddamn you!" the man in the red shirt shrieked, "you cut my damned ear off!" His hands were scarlet from the deep gash on the side of his face; his associate lay twitching in fetal position, moaning and struggling to hold his intestines in.

"We might ought to get out of here," Baldridge said, leaning over and wiping his knife on the shirt of the man with the stomach wound. "You can bet they've got friends who'll come lookin'."

Luke picked up his revolver from the floor and headed for the front door. At the sight of him waving the Colt around, and of Baldridge walking behind him still cleaning his blade, the crowd parted. Once outside, the two men hurried down Silver Street, making about five hundred yards before ducking into a thick stand of mimosa trees lodged up against the base of the bluffs. Luke got to cover first and watched as his companion limped in behind him.

"You hurt?" Luke asked.

He shook his head, then turned and peeked through the branches to see if they were being followed.

"I don't know why you did it," Luke began, breathing fast and shallow, "but I thank you for what you did."

Masey leaned over, forcing himself to take slow, deep breaths. "Forget it."

"Why'd you get involved?" Luke said.

"Whiskey."

"Whiskey?"

"Yeah. Did you see how much good whiskey that fool

wasted just for the chance to hit you with that bottle? Hell, he deserved to spill his guts."

Luke stared in disbelief. What kind of fool would split a man wide open over a bottle of whiskey? Luke knew Baldridge was studying him and he didn't like it, but felt awkward confronting someone who had just saved his life.

"It was you talking to the wharfmaster about the wreck, wasn't it?"

"How'd you know that?"

"I didn't drift in last night on a flatboat, Mr. Baldridge."

Running the back of his hand across his lips, Baldridge reached in his inside pocket, retrieved his silver flask, and carefully unscrewed the top. Turning the flask all the way up, he raised it a couple of inches from his lips and shook the remaining few drops on to his tongue. His face reflected his disappointment.

"Well, I'd like to talk to you about that, Captain Williamson"—he looked forlornly at the empty flask—"but I seem to have exhausted my supply of Oh-Be-Joyful." Luke was growing impatient as he watched Baldridge meticulously return the container to his pocket and straighten his jacket. "I suggest we go up into town and find a nice spot to refresh ourselves."

"I suggest you tell me what the hell you're doing asking all these questions about the *Mary Justice.*"

"After you, Captain," Baldridge said, motioning toward the incline of Silver Street that led to the city of Natchez. "We might not want to hang around down here much longer."

Luke was tempted not to go. He considered just having it out right on the spot—demanding to know Baldridge's business. But the threat of those thugs bringing their friends after them, and Baldridge's skill with the bowie knife he kept strapped to his side, convinced Luke he should go along.

"So that's what it's all about, is it?" Luke said as he leaned back in his chair. They were the only two customers in a tiny saloon on the corner of South Wall and State Street, just opposite Lawyers' Row. It had taken him the entire walk from the landing to get out of Baldridge what he was doing on the *Paragon*. When he found out the man worked for Mid-South Insurance, Luke became angry.

"You're here to check up on me, aren't you?"

"Not exactly."

"The hell you're not!" Luke jumped to his feet and shoved his chair back away from him. "You think I don't know how you people operate?" He pointed his finger at Baldridge. "You're just looking for a reason to cancel me, that's what you're doing."

"You got it all wrong, Captain."

"No," Luke said, shaking his head vigorously. "I think I got it nailed dead to rights." He looked as if he had just come upon a great truth. "That's why you helped me, isn't it? You're just protecting your investment. You people are just like those worthless bankers in St. Louis. They don't give a woolly rat's ass about me or about the men and women who work on my boat. That's the last thing on their minds. All they give a shit about is their money."

Baldridge sipped on his glass of bourbon, waiting for the storm to blow over, listening to Luke as a father might listen to an angry child.

"Well, say something, man!"

"I'm not here to cancel your insurance."

"Well, I don't give a damn if you do." Luke reached inside his jacket and put his hands on his suspenders, then swaggered across the room. "I'll run without goddamned insurance. The Mid-South Insurance Company can go to hell."

"You can't run without insurance, Captain Williamson." Baldridge took another drink. "You know it and I know it. Nobody's gonna put their goods on a boat with no insurance." He motioned to Luke. "Sit down a minute and listen to me."

Luke reluctantly took a seat, still glaring at Baldridge as if he had been betrayed.

"I want the same thing you want."

"And what's that?"

"I want to find out what happened to the *Mary Justice.*"

Luke kept staring hard. "You know, your company hasn't paid off yet. As of the day we left St. Louis, the Mid-South Insurance Company hadn't delivered one dime against the cargo lost on the *Mary Justice.* Why don't you tell the truth, Mr. Baldridge?"

"I don't take kindly to being called a liar, Captain."

"Then don't lie. Admit it. You're down here looking for a way to avoid paying us what we're due." Baldridge didn't answer, and Luke continued. "Maybe if you find that she went down because of something the pilot did, you don't have to pay off. Maybe you can find some loophole in the contract."

"Captain—"

"Well, I'll tell you right now, Baldridge"—Luke's voice grew sharp—"you ain't gonna find nothing that Ed Smythe did wrong. Not one thing. You can go back to Memphis if that's what you're up to, 'cause you're just pissin' in the wind. Do you understand? Ed Smythe was the best riverman I ever met."

"I think you're right," Baldridge said quietly.

Luke was surprised. He hadn't expected Baldridge to agree so easily.

"Look, Captain, I'm no riverman. Don't claim to be. But even I can see that something ain't right with this wreck."

"What do you mean?"

"Do you know how many boats have gone down this year?"

"A lot."

"Too many. Too many for all of them to be accidents."

Luke leaned back in his chair and shifted his weight. "What are you saying?"

"I'm saying that what happened to your partner's boat just doesn't add up." He lifted his stiff leg and placed it in the chair beside him. "I've been talking to people and I'd have to say you're right. Smythe was a good captain. And he hired good people. The pilots were good. Even if he wasn't in the pilothouse himself, the people Ed Smythe hired knew what they were doing."

"You're damned right they did."

"And the reports about the wreck," Baldridge said, "they don't jive. It's all too much."

"What do you mean?"

"Since when does hitting a snag or running onto a sandbar cause a boiler to explode?"

Luke thought about the question. When he considered what the wharfmaster had said and what Flint had told him, he realized that Baldridge had a point. Such incidents had caused their share of steamboat accidents, but seldom, if ever, did the two occur at the same time. Most boiler explosions resulted from boats racing or trying to push their engines too hard. He'd come close to splitting the cast iron a few times himself, when his pride had outstretched the ability of his engines. But Baldridge was right about snags. There was nothing in the hull catching a snag that would make a boiler explode.

"How did you know about the explosion?"

"The wharfmaster."

"Flint said it, too."

"He did?"

"Yeah."

Baldridge shook his head. "Well, I guess that answers one question."

"What's that?"

"I'd been wondering why the pilot didn't try to get to shore."

"You asked my first mate about that."

Baldridge looked surprised. "News does travel fast on the *Paragon*."

"So what question does that answer for you?"

"Well, if the boiler blew and she caught on fire, that pretty well explains why she didn't make for the bank, doesn't it?"

Luke wanted to agree with Baldridge, and then again he didn't. If he said yes, that would take Ed Smythe off the hook. Ed couldn't have done the right thing, he couldn't have run her to shore, since the engines wouldn't have responded. But agreeing with Baldridge meant accepting the fact that Ed had likely burned to death, and the image of his friend perishing in the flames was more than Luke could stand. If he said no, then the possibility that the pilot had made a deadly error still loomed.

"Ed would have gotten to shore if he could have. He would've run her nozzle against the bank until everyone got off."

Baldridge paused a moment, then continued: "What do you figure she hit? A sandbar?"

Luke shook his head. "Not a chance. The water's way too deep through there."

"A snag, then?"

"It's possible." Luke thumped the table. "I just can't understand the crew of the *Mary Justice* not seeing a snag big enough to do the kind of damage we're talking about. If the pilots hadn't seen it, surely one of the sounders would have."

Luke continued talking with the insurance man for over an hour, until the latter suggested they pay a visit to Tenny Mays. But he still didn't trust Baldridge. For all he knew, the man was just blowing smoke. He could be lying about the insurance company's investigation. He could turn around and use everything Luke said against him. Baldridge was a strange man to send to investigate a river accident. But for all Luke's doubts about him, he had pulled him out of a tough spot, and Luke figured that even if Baldridge wasn't telling the truth, he himself could always use some help in finding out what happened. If Baldridge was lying about the insurance company paying off, Luke figured he would know soon enough, so he decided to play along and see where things went.

When they arrived at the hospital on Franklin Street, they

discovered that Tenny Mays had been moved. The doctor told them that since he wasn't expected to live, and since there was nothing further they could do for him, he had been moved to Cherokee, the home of cousins named Murdoch, on Ellicott's Hill.

At a white stucco house, Luke and Baldridge made their way up the winding front steps and onto the columned porch. They were met at the doorway by Mrs. Murdoch and shown to an upstairs room, where Tenny Mays was being attended by a Negro maid.

"He's just not doing any better," Mrs. Murdoch said in a whisper. "The doctor says it won't be much longer." She forced back tears. "It seems so unreal. I remember Tenny when he was just a boy. He'd come and visit with his mother . . . that's my mother's sister. He was always such a strong boy. It just makes me sick to see him that way."

The two men stepped up to the side of the bed; the attendant left the room. Mrs. Murdoch stayed back near the window. Kneeling down beside the bed, Luke touched Tenny lightly on the arm.

"Tenny? Tenny, it's Luke Williamson."

There was no response, and while Luke thought he noticed a change in the man's breathing, Tenny's eyes remained closed.

"He's in and out," Mrs. Murdoch said. "Sometimes he talks, but mostly he just lies there."

"Tenny, can you hear me?" Luke asked. Masey Baldridge stood beside him looking about the room. Luke turned to Mrs. Murdoch. "Has he said anything about the accident?"

"Very little," she said. "Or if he did, I couldn't understand it. He just babbles sometimes. One day he was lifting his arms, as if he were struggling. I guess he was remembering being in the water. I can't say for sure."

The sound of Tenny's voice, weak from the fever and infection, grabbed Luke's attention.

"Luke."

"Yes, Tenny. It's Luke."

"Luke . . ."

Even Mrs. Murdoch seemed surprised to hear him respond; she moved closer to the bed. Tenny's lower lip quivered as he tried to speak, and Luke saw him attempt to lift his hand; but it fell uselessly against the sheet.

"Tenny, listen to me," Luke began. "I need to know . . . if you were at the wheel." Tenny didn't respond. "Were you at the wheel when she went down?" The movement was almost imperceptible, yet Luke noticed it and pointed at Tenny. "He's shaking his head no," he told Baldridge.

"Don't look to me like he's sayin' a damned thing."

"You weren't at the wheel? Is that right, Tenny?" Mays made a sound, but Luke couldn't make it out. "Was it Ed? Was it Captain Smythe?"

"C-c-captain."

"What did you hit? Tenny, what made her go down?"

The question seemed to disturb Mays, and his body began stirring, only slightly at first, then more and more. Mays was almost shaking now, and suddenly his eyes opened. He looked up at the ceiling, his gaze fixed as if viewing some strange scene playing out before him.

"To port," he groaned. "Take her to port, Captain. To port!" Tenny was now reaching up in the air as if trying to turn the pilot's wheel. Luke took his hand and Tenny squeezed hard. "Can't . . . can't get away. Can't get away!"

"What is it, Tenny? What can't you get away from?"

"C-c-can't get away!"

"Is it a sandbar?"

Tenny shook his head. "Can't . . . can't get away. Go to port, Captain. To port!"

"Get away from what, Tenny? A sandbar? A snag?" Luke asked.

Tenny began to settle down; his hands dropped to his side and his breathing became deep and regular. Luke looked at Baldridge and then at Mrs. Murdoch. "Has he said this before?"

"Once or twice," she said softly.

"What does he mean by 'Can't get away'?" Luke said, more to himself than to the others.

"Captain Williamson, I can't rightly say." Mrs. Murdoch shook her head. "I tell you, it's downright awful what he's going through." She looked at them and frowned. "I know this sounds terrible, but sometimes I think it would just be more merciful if the Lord went on and took him. I really do."

Tenny had left them again, his mind off in some realm where they could not follow. Luke stood up and took Mrs. Murdoch's hand.

"Thank you for letting us see him."

She nodded, still holding back her tears. "I don't know if what he said can help you, Mr. Williamson. Lord, I don't even know if he really knew who you were."

Luke grasped her hand with both of his. "Tenny's a good man. He was a good pilot, Mrs. Murdoch. He may pull through yet."

"Maybe so."

Luke offered her some money to take care of Mays, but Mrs. Murdoch refused. She said Tenny was family and she would keep him at Cherokee as long as it took. The three of them were nearing the doorway when they heard a groan from the bed. As Luke, Masey Baldridge, and Mrs. Murdoch turned in unison, Tenny Mays suddenly sat upright in the bed, his right arm extended and his index finger pointing straight ahead. His arm was trembling and his lower lip quivered; a stream of saliva crept down the left side of his chin. With his eyes wide in terror, as if viewing some apparition, Mays cried out.

"Tor . . . Tor!" His hand shook harder and his voice grew louder and more desperate. "T-t-tor." Then, just as suddenly as he'd sprung up from his repose, he sank back on to the mattress, his eyes rolling back in his head and his mouth gaping open. Mrs. Murdoch reached him first, and the others were close behind.

"Tenny?" she said, taking his wrist. "Tenny?" His breathing was shallow and labored; she touched his head. "The fever is worse," she said quietly, looking at the two men. "I think you'd better go now. He needs to rest." Luke agreed, but he'd clearly heard a death rattle from Tenny's throat; the pilot wouldn't last much longer.

While Mrs. Murdoch remained in the room, Luke and Baldridge moved down the stairs and through the sitting room; but as Luke opened the front door, Baldridge sidled over to a small table near the window. Luke paused with the door open and watched him lift a glass decanter, remove the lid, and pour himself a glass of brandy. A chilly breeze squeezed through the crack in the door and rushed up the edge of Luke's sleeve. Sending a cripple to investigate a wreck was bad enough, but a drunk, too? Luke studied Baldridge. He was a dark-complexioned man; if Luke had spotted him coming aboard he might have taken him for a farmer—not some planter with a fifteen-dollar beaver hat and a better-than-thou look, but a workingman, a tenant farmer like the dozens who rode among the deck passengers and jealously guarded their half-dozen bales of cotton and their piddly few sacks of wheat. Baldridge gripped his glass with large, rough hands, not with the thin, graceful fingers of the landed gentry, and he reminded Luke of the hundreds of Reb prisoners he'd hauled up to Cairo at the beginning of the war—simple men who always seemed to look lost, men he was sure had no notion of what they were fighting for.

Luke chuckled to himself and shook his head. *Wonder if he has any idea what he's doing!* As he inverted the glass and finished his brandy, Baldridge cut his eyes to the side and noticed Luke staring at him. He carefully replaced the glass in exactly the spot he had taken it, upside down among the three others on the elegant little table, and he looked over at Luke.

"What do you figure he meant by that?" Baldridge asked, joining Luke in the doorway.

Luke stepped out on the porch. The other man followed, closing the door behind him. "Meant by what?" Luke said.

"That word. 'Tor,' or whatever it was?"

"Who knows?" Luke offered. "Probably just the fever."

They hurried back toward the landing, since Luke needed to leave Natchez in less than an hour; but he was getting frustrated at having to walk slowly so Baldridge could keep up. They were talking about the accident as they reached the Pollock House, a four-story, brick-faced hotel farther down on Franklin Street. Baldridge stopped, and a few steps later Luke realized he wasn't beside him anymore.

"We haven't got time for another drink," Luke said sharply, beckoning Baldridge to continue. "I'm pulling out for New Orleans at five-fifteen, and I don't hold my boat for anybody."

Baldridge cupped his hand by his face and looked in the window of the Pollock House. Luke checked the time, then looked at Baldridge impatiently.

"I've got to get back to the landing. I've got to pull out before dark."

Baldridge continued looking in the window as he spoke. "Well, you have yourself a safe trip, Captain Williamson. And if I was you," he added, turning to look at Luke, "I wouldn't stop Under the Hill on my way back. I imagine some of those boys are still pretty upset.

"You're not going to New Orleans?"

Baldridge shook his head. "No, I don't think so."

"But I thought you wanted to talk to the others . . . the ones who got off the boat."

"You talk to 'em. There's still some things I want to do here in Natchez."

This guy was starting to make Luke mad. If he was supposed to be investigating the wreck, then why didn't he go to New Orleans? The wharfmaster said that was where most of the survivors went. Maybe Baldridge had no idea what he was doing. Maybe he just wanted to stay here and get drunk. Whatever. At least he would not be underfoot the rest of the trip down. He wasn't much help anyway. He didn't know shit about the river—he admitted that. And what could he possibly find out with his face in a glass of whiskey all the time? No, it was better if he stayed in Natchez. Luke would find out for himself what happened, and then pick this sodbuster up on the way back to St. Louis.

"I'll look you up when we come back through in a few days," Luke said.

Baldridge nodded. "I'll be staying right here."

It occurred to Luke that he ought to thank Baldridge for helping him out of that scrape, but the longer he looked at the man, the less he wanted to admit he might owe him anything. Thinking back on it, he would have probably taken those guys without Baldridge. Besides, he just didn't trust this ex-Johnny. He wouldn't be the first southerner to have it in for a northern businessman. He and his Mid-South Insurance Company were liable to renege on the *Mary Justice* anytime. No point in being friendly. It would just get in the way of doing what he had to do.

"I'll be back in about three days," Luke called as he started down Franklin Street. But he wasn't really sure he would find Baldridge around when he returned.

$\triangledown$

7

Sunday morning, October 27

BALDRIDGE'S BACK ACHED from the awkward way he had slept, and when he tried to sit up, the feather mattress sank in the middle, forcing him to grasp the iron headrail and pull himself to the side of the bed. His right eye was crusted over, and his left one opened only slightly, then quickly closed as a shaft of morning sunlight warmed his face. Lifting his hand to block the sun, he felt his head throb as he leaned forward and picked up his watch. Too much whiskey, too fast, too late at night had left him fighting the urge to lie back down. He should get up. He should have been up two hours ago, for that matter.

When he stood up he was shaky, and his bad leg felt stiff as a piece of sawmill lumber. He shuffled over to the washstand and poured some water in the bowl. Leaning forward he splashed his face and ran his hand across his whiskered cheek. His left eye cautiously opened now, and stared vaguely into the scarred metal mirror. With the edge of a rag he wiped out his right eye, then wet his hands and ran them through his hair, pulling it back on his head.

A saloon on Canal Street had waylaid him last night, and when he wanted to leave, it wouldn't let him. He tossed the rag over the water pitcher. Who was he kidding? He knew the minute he stopped there that the night's work was over. He knew damned well he wouldn't leave until . . . how had he left? Scratching his head, Baldridge managed only a shadowy image of entering the Pollock House.

He glanced around the room, noticing his jacket wadded up and nestled next to the runner of a rocking chair. When he leaned back and looked down at his feet, he realized he still had his shoes on. This had to stop, he told himself. He was acting like a drunk. He surveyed his features again in the mirror. That wasn't a drunk looking back. It was a man who used his whiskey medicinally. He rotated his leg at the hip and lifted it, bending his knee as far as it would go. Just three days. Three goddamned days, and he would be walking like a normal man. All God had needed to do was keep him safe three more days, and there would be no pain. That Yankee sharpshooter might have been posted in a different spot, or showed up a few minutes later. Or his aim could have been off—not much—just a couple of inches. The ache was coming back again. Must be rain on the way.

Baldridge bent over, his head splitting from last night's foray. Lifting his jacket from the floor, he checked the inside pocket and let out a relieved sigh when his fingers caressed his money roll. He removed the clip and counted it. He was doing all right, and with the way his leg was feeling this morning, he decided to splurge and get a horse from the livery stable down the street. His entertainment last night had put him hours behind, and he rationalized that having a mount would help him catch up.

At the livery, Baldridge haggled with the owner and eventually rented a slack-bellied gelding. The saddle leather was split on one side, but he settled for it considering it would save him a dollar. For the next two hours, he checked out a lead he had gotten—one of the few things he did remember from the night before—that Asa Turner was working in a restaurant there in Natchez. Turner had been a cabin steward on the *Mary Justice,* and Luke Williamson had described him as a pretty reliable and trustworthy hand. Baldridge figured he was bound to offer a better account than the one Luke had gotten out of Russell Flint.

At the fourth place he tried, a restaurant called the Boontoon, he found Asa Turner. A Negro attendant working the front door showed Baldridge back into the kitchen, where Turner was rotating some soup pots over the fire in a large, brick hearth. His right arm was in a sling.

"Are you Asa Turner?" Baldridge asked. The skinny man turned suddenly toward him, looking frightened. "I'm Masey Baldridge. I'm looking into the steamboat wreck that took place down here about a week ago. I understand you were employed on the *Mary Justice* the day she sank."

"Yes, sir, I was," Turner said, continuing to shift the pots awkwardly with his one free arm.

"Can I give you a hand with that?"

Turner looked at him hard. "I do my job by myself, sir."

"Okay." Turner seemed nervous, watching Baldridge out of the corner of his eye. "I was just wondering if you could tell me what happened that day. You know, a little about where you were and what you saw."

Using a large wooden spoon, Turner trapped a chicken neck against the side of one of the pots and carefully dipped it out and dropped it into a second pot of boiling water.

"I didn't see much of nothing, Mr. Baldridge." He looked at him as if to see how he was being received. "It was dark and all, and I was working the tables. I was cleaning them off after folks got through eating."

"Well, do you recall if the boat hit something?"

"Can't rightly say."

"Mr. Turner, you were clearing tables, you said?"

"Yes, sir, that's right."

"And you were probably hauling dishes back and forth to the kitchen, weren't you?"

"Yes, sir, that's what I do."

"But you say you don't remember if the boat hit anything. Now if you had your hands full of dishes, and a steamboat going as fast as the *Mary Justice* was to hit a sandbar or a snag or something, you sayin' you wouldn't know it?" Turner didn't answer. "It just seems to me that a collision would make you lose your balance at the least, maybe even drop a dish or two."

Turner peered into his chicken broth. "Yes, sir."

"So are you saying you didn't feel any impact before she went down?" Turner kept stirring the broth without looking up. "Mr. Turner?"

"No sir, I didn't say that."

"Well either you did or you didn't, Mr. Turner."

Turner glared at Masey. "Why you asking me all this? Are you the law?"

"No, I'm not the law. I work for the company that insured the *Mary Justice*." When Turner offered no response, Masey continued: "How is it you got off the boat?"

"Reckon the good Lord was just lookin' out for me."

"Well, how exactly did he do that? The Lord, that is? How did he get you off before she sunk?"

Turner walked across the kitchen and took a butcher knife from a rack on the wall, then got another chicken from a large painted-china bowl. Leaning his slung arm on the chicken wing, Turner began to cut up the rest of the bird. "I can't really remember. Everything happened too fast. I run out of the cabin and I seen the fire . . . and . . . I looked for the lifeboat. But I didn't see one, so I jumped in and swam for shore."

"Did you feel or hear an explosion before you left the deck?"

"Wouldn't know nothin' about that," Turner said sharply, forcing the knife through the joints of the chicken.

"Didn't you notice anything?"

"I didn't hear nothin' and I didn't see nothin'."

"Mr. Turner, Captain Williamson told me you were a smart fella. He said you were straight-down-the-middle. Now how is it that you survived an awful river accident and you didn't see or notice anything?"

"I done told you, Mr. Baldridge," Turner said, pointing the butcher knife to emphasize each word, "*I didn't see nothing*. Now, if you don't mind, I've got work to do."

Baldridge stood quietly in the doorway. "How'd you hurt your arm, Mr. Turner?" Turner began trying to skin a piece of the chicken. "Did you hurt it in the wreck?"

"I guess I did."

"You guess?" Turner didn't reply. "How come you didn't try to get on with the *Paragon* when it docked?"

"Maybe I'll catch it on the way back north."

"Maybe so. Well, I tell you what, Asa. Should you suddenly have an attack of memory, I'll be staying at the Pollock House for the next couple of days." Turner didn't appear to acknowledge him. "That's the Pollock House. You take care of that arm, now, Asa."

Since no one was talking about the wreck, or making much sense when they did, Baldridge decided he would ride the six or seven land miles north to the spot where the *Mary Justice* went down. It wasn't until he reached the intersection of Main Street and Union and saw St. Mary's Cathedral that he realized it was Sunday morning. The bells in the cathedral tower began to signal the end of morning mass as he turned north on Union and started out of town. He was glad to get past the church before the parishioners began filing out. Something about being seen outside of services on Sunday mornings made him feel self-conscious, and for the past eight years, he'd been feeling self-conscious just about every Sunday. But he enjoyed the rich, full music of the bells as he continued out Pine Ridge Road, until the sound melted away in the distance. The knowledge that no matter how far he strayed, the bells would still be ringing, gave him a sense of peace.

It had started to sprinkle when Baldridge reached the bluff near Bisland Bayou. The river appeared as a rusty ribbon that tumbled from his right and passed below him, then swung to the west in a broad crescent before weaving back east in its reach toward Natchez. The first thing that impressed him about the view was the difference in the two banks of the river. The bluff where he sat on his horse rose some three hundred feet above the water, in a steep grade covered with heavy undergrowth. The opposite side—the west side—was a low tidal plain across which the Mississippi had, over the centuries, meandered until she was comfortable and then settled in to create a channel. The channel might last a year, maybe a hundred years; but the many washouts across the neck of flat land, and the tiny lakes that stood out like pox scars, served as testament to the River Lady's fickle nature. The bluff afforded him a view as far north as the next bend, and south almost two miles. On a clear day, he suspected, he could have seen even farther.

On the far bank Masey saw two men in a small johnboat. They appeared to be using a seine and working their way along with the current. Just upriver from their boat, he spied the residue from one or two bales of waterlogged cotton, and what appeared to be some lumber and driftwood hooked around a sawyer along the bank. It was amazing that he could find no other traces of the wreck. As large a boat as the *Mary Justice* was, it certainly had been subject to a tidy demise. Luke Williamson said the water beneath the bluff was deep—how deep, he never did say, only that it could have swallowed up a boat. At other wrecks, in more shallow water where part of the boat remained topside, the salvagers and scavengers would work the hull for weeks, hauling off anything of value. But looking down toward Giles Point, Baldridge realized that except for the reports and the word of the survivors, the river had left little trace of her handiwork. Why couldn't this have been simple? Why couldn't he have gotten a case where he could just take a johnboat out to the wreck and stroll around the top deck for a while? Then he could see the pieces from the busted boiler, or note the hole in the hull, or talk to the crew and know what happened. He would be on the next boat back to Memphis and everybody would be satisfied. But this wouldn't be that easy. What he needed to see and touch was now home to catfish, and as sick as it made him to think about such on a Sunday morning, the people he needed to talk to were food for the alligator gars. From somewhere behind him, the lever action on a repeating rifle cracked through the dullness of the rainy morning. He sat motionless, listening carefully and trying to pinpoint the direction. The wet ground insulated the feet he was sure were moving behind him, so he gently turned his head to the right and peered out of the corner of his eye.

"Hold it right there, mister," a voice ordered from the woods. Baldridge kept the reins in his left hand as he lifted his arms slowly from his sides. "What you doin' on my land?"

He took a deep breath and let it out slowly, then pivoted in the saddle and leaned back on his right arm. "Mornin'," he said, forcing a smile.

The man who had challenged him held the butt of a Spencer rifle tucked under his right arm; the barrel pointed at Baldridge's head. A farmer's hat shadowed his face, which seemed weathered and worn, with hard features and dark eyebrows.

"You're trespassin'," the man declared.

Baldridge laughed slightly. "Well, I hate that. I really do. Didn't mean to do that."

"I'm gettin' tired of havin' to run you people off," the man continued. "It's got to where I can't get no work done for having to come up here. I've a mind to shoot you just to let 'em know I mean business." He looked Baldridge over carefully. "I could shoot you. I'd be within my right, you know."

"Mister, I'm not carrying a gun. I mean you no harm. I'm just sitting here looking at the river." He noticed that the man seemed to be checking the line of trees on the other side of the trail. "I'm by myself," he added.

"You ain't got no wagon up here, have you?"

"A wagon?"

"Yeah."

Baldridge continued to smile. "No, no wagon. Just me and this old nag."

"Well, the others had a wagon. And I done told 'em that if they come up here with it again, it'd be *my* wagon. You got no right comin' on my land without asking me."

"I'm sorry, Mr. . . . uh . . ."

"Jackson." The old man seemed to have a twitch in his left cheek.

"Mr. Jackson. But I'm just visiting down here from Memphis. I didn't see your house or I'd have stopped in."

"No, and you won't see it neither. I got it set back a ways." He was almost bragging. "I got it hid real good."

Baldridge played along. "I see. A man does need his privacy, doesn't he?"

"Damned straight, he does."

The thin old man studied him carefully, his dark eyebrows almost dancing as he spoke.

"So what's your business up here?"

"Mr. Jackson, do you think you might lower that Spencer a tad? I mean you no harm."

"You got a name?"

"Masey Baldridge."

Jackson eased the Spencer down to his side and rested the stock on his boot. "Well, I'll have to say you don't look like them others. So, what are you doin' up here?"

"Well, Mr. Jackson," he began, pointing out toward the river, "a steamboat went down out there about ten days ago—"

"And?"

"And I'm down here tryin' to find out how it happened." As he eased his jacket open with his left hand, he saw Jackson tighten his grip on his Spencer, so he held his other hand aloft as he showed him the inside pocket. "Thought I'd have a little warmer-upper." He reached in slowly and pulled out his flask, then held it out toward Jackson. The rain was coming down harder than before and slapping his bare hand. "Can I offer you a sip?"

For the first time he saw something other than suspicion in Jackson's face. The old man moved closer and took the flask from his hand, but he kept his eyes on Baldridge as he took a swig. He glanced quickly at the container and sneered, then returned the flask and pulled his hat down against the back of his neck to keep the rain out.

"You wouldn't have seen the *Mary Justice* go down, would you, Mr. Jackson?"

"Was that the name of the boat?"

"Yes, sir. The *Mary Justice*, out of St. Louis."

"No, didn't see no wreck. But I heard the whistle that night."

"Did you happen to come down to the river?"

"Not that night. 'Tweren't my business. I keep to myself. That's the way I like it. Had plenty to do the next day, though."

"How's that?"

"Well, between the bodies that came washing up, and having to run the horse thieves off from my land, I worked to way after dark."

"You found bodies from the wreck?"

"I had bodies all right. Eight or ten of 'em."

"What did you do with them?"

"Why, I give 'em a good Christian burial, that's what I done," Jackson said defensively. "I done what any man would've done."

Baldridge felt a shiver run down his back as he considered the possibility that Ed Smythe might have been among the men Jackson buried. He pressed the old man for details on what the bodies looked like and how they were dressed, and asked if he'd found any personal effects on them. Jackson described them as well as he could, but Baldridge could hear nothing that suggested Ed was among them, and the old man said he found nothing on the bodies to identify them. He explained how he'd put them on his pack mule and hauled them from the bank down below, up the steep slope, and back along the trail Baldridge had taken to this overlook. He had buried them some forty or fifty yards off the road in a stand of cedar, in what he said was an old Spanish cemetery. But when Baldridge questioned him about why he hadn't notified the authorities, Jackson became defensive again.

"Me and the law down in Natchez had a fallin'-out about five years ago," Jackson explained. "Got no use for no lawmen." He gestured with the barrel of his rifle. "That's what I figured you might be at first. But ain't no lawman crazy enough to come up here by himself. 'Cause I done told 'em that if I ever find one of 'em up here on my land again I'll send him straight to hell."

Baldridge wasn't sure what Jackson's idea of a falling-out was, but the old fellow was obviously not a man to be trifled with. Then he asked Jackson about the condition of the bodies he buried.

"Living along the river all these years, I've seen some strange things. Seen a few drowned men and I've seen some flatboats turned into kindling by the river currents. But it's the first time I ever seen bodies from a shipwreck wash up with bullets in their heads."

"You sayin' the men you buried were shot?"

"Not all of 'em. But four of the eight were shot deader'n Gerber's goat." Jackson saw the confusion on Baldridge's face. "I know what you're thinkin'. I was thinkin' it, too. It don't make no sense. That's when it hit me."

"What's that?"

"Them fellas didn't drown. At least not all of 'em. I figure four of 'em drowned—the woman, two of the men, and a young boy. Couldn't have been over twelve. It was a sad thing."

"And the others?"

"Every one of the four that was shot was laying along the side of the trail leadin' up from the water. They had to have come off the boat, though. Wouldn't be no reason for people to be down there with no horse, no supplies, no weapon."

Baldridge worked his left foot tighter into the stirrup. Pressing himself up with the saddle horn, he swung his right leg over and simultaneously slipped his left foot from the stirrup, making a controlled drop to his feet alongside his mount. He could see Jackson staring.

"What happened to your leg?" Jackson asked.

"The war." Baldridge took the reins in his hand and worked them in and out between his fingers. "So, let me get this straight. You're telling me that you found four people off the *Mary Justice* shot to death right down here on the riverbank?"

"Sure did."

Baldridge looked at him in disbelief. "And you didn't tell anybody?"

"What's the use? They dead anyway."

"But they have families. People who wonder about them."

"Ain't my affair," Jackson snapped. "I done told you, I ain't havin' no lawmen up here. If I go down to Natchez and say I got people up here that's been shot, I'll have half the town traipsin' around here and stickin' their nose in my business." Jackson spat into a rain puddle near his feet. "Besides, if I get the law up here, the ones that done it is liable to come back up here lookin' for me."

"And who do you figure that was?"

"Oh, I got me a pretty good idea."

"Who? I mean why would anybody shoot people that just survived a wreck?"

"Now I can't tell you why, but like I said, I got a pretty good idea who. The sorry rascals stole two of my best horses," Jackson said, "and if I get my hands on 'em . . ."

"Who?"

"Don't know their names."

"I thought you said you knew who did it."

"I seen 'em all right," Jackson explained. "It was the next morning before I got down to the river, before I come upon the bodies. They was out about a quarter of a mile from here," he said, pointing again in the direction of where he had buried the bodies, "almost to the road when I come upon 'em. It was five men on horseback and two drivin' a wagon."

"Is that why you asked me if I had a wagon?"

Jackson nodded. "At first I thought you was one of that bunch."

"Why do you think they were the ones that shot those people?"

"Well, they lied to me, first off. I asked them if they'd been on my land. And the tall one, a broad-shouldered dude of a fella as I recall—wore a real nice hat and talked real educated-like—he said they were lost. Said they were looking for Pine Ridge Road. Now, I didn't much believe 'em, mind you. I had my doubts right then. But there was seven of 'em, and since they wasn't actually on my land at the moment, I figured I'd best not cross 'em. When I come down the trail toward the river, sure enough I saw them."

"Saw what?"

"The tracks. Deep wagon tracks. I followed them all the way across my land and down this here trail"—he ran his hand along by his feet—"and right on down the draw to the water's edge. That's when I come upon the bodies, you know, as I was going down to the river."

"So do you think the men with the wagon shot these people the morning after the *Mary Justice* sank?"

Jackson shook his head. "Nope. Night of the accident."

"But you said they—"

"They was here," Jackson interrupted, "—or at least, somebody was down here—that night. There was three sets of wagon tracks the next morning, and only one set was fresh enough to have been made since daylight. The other set had to have been laid down the night before."

"What was in the wagon, Mr. Jackson?"

"Can't say. They had something covering it up, but I can tell you this. Whatever it was, it was heavy. Them tracks must've run four inches deep in places, and when I surprised them out by the road, their wagon team looked wore out."

"Mr. Jackson, do you think you could show me where you found those bodies?"

"I don't know . . ."

"I won't bring any law up here. It's just me and you. I've got a job to do, Mr. Jackson, and the sooner I do it, the sooner I can go home and the sooner I'm off your land. So, if you could just show me down to the river where you found the bodies, I'd be much obliged."

"Well, I don't reckon it would hurt," he said. "But you're

gonna leave after that. You gonna go back to Natchez and stay off my property. I'm not going to find you out here again, am I?"

"Nobody wants to leave here sooner than I do."

Jackson led Baldridge down a winding trail to the area where he had found the bodies and walked him to each spot. In spite of the rain, which had let up only slightly, Masey worked his way through the tanglefoot alongside the trail, parting the vines with his boot as he looked for anything that might have fallen from the pockets of the victims. Finding nothing where the bodies had been, Baldridge strolled to a slight ridge not more than fifty feet from where the trial led to the shoreline. He looked out across the water.

"Do you suppose those men you ran into could have been salvagers?"

"Didn't look like salvage men to me. Besides, chances are anything a man would salvage from a wreck out there would wash downstream and end up on the other side." Jackson pointed across the water. "There's been people on the west bank that's been haulin' things out of here since the day after the boat went down. But you ain't gonna find 'em over here, because the bank's too steep and the current in this bend sweeps by here too fast for much to get caught. Now down a little farther on this side, where the bank flattens out, I'm sure there's people salvaging. But not up here. Not below these bluffs."

Baldridge stared out over the river trying to piece together what he'd heard from Jackson, but it didn't seem to make sense. What were those men doing here the night of the wreck? What were they hauling away the next day when Jackson encountered them? And if they did shoot the survivors, why? How could four half-drowned men possibly threaten someone enough to get shot? As he turned to head back up the trail, he saw Jackson staring at the base of some briars.

"What you make of this?" Jackson asked, pointing to what looked like a piece of board sticking up from the mud. The old man picked it up and brushed the mud away. At the center of one end of the eight-inch-by-six-inch piece of sanded wood was a tiny brass knob. "What in the world is this thing?" he said, handing it to Baldridge. Baldridge turned it over in his hands and examined both sides; at first he could find no mark, no etching, nor any writing on it. But as he held it up before him, shielding it from the rain with is left hand, a bead of water settled on the tiny brass knob and magnified the fine, raised lettering: BPE.

"Look at this," Baldridge said.

After studying the object for several seconds, Jackson reached toward the metal. "I believe the center of this thing comes out. Look right there along the edges. Isn't that a metal runner? Don't you reckon you pull this here knob and the center of the thing slides out?"

It wasn't until Jackson had grasped the knob and begun to pull on it that Baldridge realized what he was holding.

"Stop!" he shouted, reaching across with his left hand and grasping Jackson's wrist. The old man started back slightly and glowered at him.

"What the hell—"

"Don't pull it any farther. I think I know what we've got here." When Jackson had released the knob, Baldridge gently pushed back the center section of the wooden box. The old man had managed to open it half an inch.

"Well, what is it?"

"I'm not exactly sure what you call it," Baldridge said, still shielding the case from the rain, "but I saw one about three or four years ago at a fair in Memphis. I hired this fellow to take a picture of my sister at one of those photographer tents. As I recall, I saw him pull something like this out of the back of his camera before he disappeared into another tent. When he came back a few minutes later, he gave me a tintype. I've still got the tintype."

"You saying that's a picture?" Jackson scratched his head. "I don't see no picture. All I see is a piece of wood."

"I'm not saying this is a picture, Mr. Jackson." He held the wooden casing in front of the old man's face. "But I'll bet you it was at one time. Who knows? Maybe it still is."

"So where's the picture?"

"I don't know much about this kind of thing, but my guess is that the picture is inside this frame." Baldridge took hold of the brass knob gently. "From what I understand about these things, this knob you started to pull is what makes the picture. The whole case goes in the camera, then the fella pulls this center section out, like you started to do; then he slides it back in. The image is captured in the box."

Jackson looked at him doubtfully. "You sayin' there's a picture in that box?"

"I don't know if there is or not, but if you'd pulled that center out, I'm pretty sure what was in there would have been gone."

"A picture of what? Where you reckon this come from?"

"Maybe it washed ashore from the wreck."

Jackson shook his head. "Uh-uh. Way too far up on the bank. It's been months since the water was high enough to wash something up that far. And with no more wear than it shows, I'd say this thing ain't been here more than a week or two."

Baldridge decided to look up a photographer when he got back to Natchez. It would be worth paying him a visit, before Luke returned with the *Paragon*. As they made their way back up the bluff and out toward Pine Ridge Road, Baldridge thought how Jackson reminded him of his uncle back in Tennessee. Uncle Taylor had wanted, more than anything else in the world, to be left alone. Like Jackson, he kept a cabin stuck back in the bottoms along the Wolf River, and dared anybody but family to come near him. But he suspected that Jackson, like his uncle, spent an inordinate amount of time keeping people at a distance; and that once you got to know him, he was probably a decent man—a man who would be there for you if you ever needed him. And while he knew he should report the shootings to the sheriff in Natchez, Baldridge reasoned that would be a poor way to repay the old man for his courtesy. Besides, he might yet require Jackson's help, and there was no reason to close the door till he was all the way out of the house.

It was after dark when Baldridge got back to town. Following directions from the desk clerk at the Pollock House, he made a swing past Gurney's Corner, at Main and Commerce streets. The photography shop was closed, so he decided to get a hot meal and a good night's sleep and return the next morning. By the time he dropped his mount off at the livery and walked the two blocks back to the Pollock House, it was almost seven o'clock. Chilly and damp from his day on horseback, Baldridge leaned out from beneath the second-floor balcony and shook the water off his oilcloth poncho. His nose caught the smell of onions on the damp night air, and turning his head toward the front door of the hotel, he inhaled the pleasing aroma of someone cooking meat. The desk clerk told him the evening meal was served in the dining room at seven; with no breakfast and no lunch that day, Baldridge felt he could probably clear the table by himself given the chance.

After a dinner of roast beef, potatoes, and beans, he excused himself and started upstairs for his room. Halfway up, he stopped and glanced down at the registration desk. A sign behind the clerk read:

Hot Bath: $1.00 in the Jones Room

He ran his hand down his left leg and began to gently massage the back and side of his knee. After a meal like that, one of those hot baths would feel pretty good. He could soak his leg and lie back and get the chill out of his bones. Then he would go to bed and sleep like a baby. There wasn't anything he could do about the investigation until morning anyway. He owed himself a quiet night. Baldridge limped back down the stairs and arranged with the desk clerk to have a bath drawn in twenty minutes.

The room was already steamy when Baldridge arrived.

Slipping out of his clothes, he handed them to the attendant, who hung them on a rack near the door. The bath attendant, a young man in his early twenties, showed him to the tub and, noticing his limp, stood by to help him in.

"I can get it," Baldridge said, waving him off. He tested the water with one foot. "Oh, boy," he sighed, "that's just right."

"Not too hot for you, sir?"

"No, no. It's just right. I like it hot as you can get it."

"Well, I can keep it hot for you, sir," the attendant assured him. "Here's your soap and some clean towels." He pointed to a small table beside the tub. "I'll be right over yonder by the stove. And unless you call for me earlier, I'll be coming back with some more hot water in just a few minutes."

"Sounds good." Baldridge lowered himself into the bath. "Uhmmmmmmm. Say, how long does my dollar get me?"

"You mean, how long is the bath?"

"Yeah."

"Oh, usually about half an hour. But since I don't have anyone else signed up until nine, it's all right with me if you want to stay a little longer. I'll keep the hot water comin'," he said with a grin.

Baldridge had closed his eyes and was neck deep in the steaming water. "You do that, son. You do that." Much of the ache in his leg, which had plagued him all day, began to disappear as the heat did its job. "Sleep," he mumbled, "sleep that knits up the ravelled hand of care." He had learned that as a boy, but he couldn't remember who said it.

He was thinking about nothing in particular when the attendant returned several minutes later with another pot of hot water. The renewed water momentarily sent a shiver through him, but he leaned back and settled in again. He began thinking over the last two days and trying to put things together. Luke Williamson would be back tomorrow, and he had hoped to have some answers by then. Instead, he had a lot more questions, and he didn't feel any closer to knowing what happened to the *Mary Justice*.

The *Mary Justice* did sink where Luke thought she had.

She did catch fire. She was completely submerged. Some of the passengers got off. But as Baldridge sat there pondering the situation, he realized that there was little else anyone agreed upon. The wharfmaster said she hit something; if the witnesses' reports were right, she must have. Russell Flint, at least according to Luke, also said the boat had struck something, but he didn't say what. From what Luke told him, it was clear that Flint had not wanted to talk about it. Maybe he was lying, but Baldridge doubted it. Something about facing a loaded gun tends to bring the truth out in a man. Both the wharfmaster and Flint confirmed that there was an explosion. But they didn't say if it came when the *Mary Justice* struck the snag—or whatever it was—or if the explosion came later. And Old Man Jackson mentioned nothing about an explosion. He said he heard the long whistle that night. And then there was Asa Tuner. Where Flint didn't want to talk, Turner was afraid to. But why? A man as sharp as Luke said Turner was doesn't got through a major river disaster and not see or hear anything. He needed to see Turner again. And what were those men doing on the riverbank the night of the accident? Baldridge adjusted his position in the tub and tried to put it all in perspective. A large steamboat with an experienced pilot and crew sink in the middle of a normal stretch of river during decent weather, leaving no trace of what happened. Despite hitting a sandbar, or a snag, or something, the pilot does not make for the nearest bank to discharge the passengers. Either the boiler blows up, disabling the engines, or something else happens to keep the burning riverboat in midstream, where it conveniently disappears in over a hundred feet of water. The few people who survive either don't remember what happened or are too scared to say. Some of the passengers who managed to swim ashore wind up strung along the bank with bullets in their heads. And these strange visitors on Jackson's land leave the next day with a loaded wagon and lie to him about what they were doing there. And all Baldridge had to show for his work was a small wood-frame tintype that might or might not have been left by the men Jackson saw, and might or might not have a picture in it. He only hoped Luke Williamson would come up with something in New Orleans.

The room was thick with steam from both the bath and the water the attendant was heating on the stove. It was impossible to see more than a couple of feet, but Baldridge was enjoying breathing the warm humid air and he felt that it was clearing his lungs. When he opened his eyes, he could make out a figure standing near the foot of the bathtub.

"You got me a warm-up?" Baldridge said, his eyes barely slits. The water had relaxed him completely. The attendant didn't answer. "I said you got me a warm-up?" he repeated. Still the man didn't answer. Baldridge strained to see him through the mist. "I told you, you can't get it too hot for me."

Suddenly he felt what seemed like a dozen needles thrust into his scalp, and his head slammed back against the porcelain tub. Before he could reach up, he felt someone grasp his right hand, and as the man moved closer he could smell the sweat and leather. Baldridge sloshed about in the water, struggling against what now appeared to be three men, all trying to keep him in the tub. As he struggled, someone moved toward him with a large pot of boiling water; when the steam cloud separated, he realized that the young attendant who had helped him get in had been replaced by an older man, dressed in riding clothes rather than the white uniform of the hotel staff.

"So I can't get it hot enough for you, can I?"

"What are you doing?"

"Just warming up your bath, Mr. Baldridge. That is your name, isn't it?"

The other men were struggling to keep his wet arms from slipping out of their grasp. "Who are you?" Baldridge said, wrestling frantically.

"We're soldiers."

"Soldiers?"

"That's right. Like you used to be. Only we ain't forgot

the cause like you have. Maybe a little hot water might just help you remember."

Though he tried to lift himself from the bathwater, his right foot could get no traction and his left leg was too stiff to bend enough to help. The man with the water stood beside him now and began pouring it into the bath. Baldridge battled to pull his feet under him as the man gradually moved the stream of boiling water closer.

"Let's fry his balls," the man said. "Down here stickin' his nose in business that ain't his." He moved the hot steam closer and Baldridge vainly tried to retreat. "We're doin' what ought to have been done seven years ago, and you're just gettin' in the way." Baldridge's head was stinging as the man who had hold of his hair twisted it to get a better grip.

"Turncoat, that's what you are. We'll boil you like a shrimp, boy."

Unable to make himself any smaller in the tub, Baldridge could feel the scalding water splashing up on the ankle of his bad leg. In only seconds the entire stream would be cascading over his skin, blistering it and moving up his body.

"You and that Yankee captain just had to keep on, didn't you?"

Baldridge screamed as the water began pouring on his calf, and just when he thought he could stand it no more, he heard a voice from across the room.

"Daniel, you got another customer that wants a bath at— Daniel?"

From beside him a shot rang out as one of the men let go of him and fired into the haze.

"Goddamn it, Jenkins! What'd you go and fire for?" the man with the hot water shouted. From the anger and fear in his eyes, Baldridge knew instantly what he was about to do. Taking advantage of his free hand, he pulled himself hard to the left, throwing his weight into the side of the tub. The suddenness of his movement, coupled with the sloshing water, tipped the tub over on its side, dumping Baldridge and the bathwater in a wild flow toward the wall. In the instant the tub rocked over, the man had tossed his pot full of boiling water directly at Baldridge's face. Some of it dashed against his forehead and his right ear, but most was caught by the outside edge of the tub and fell on the feet of the man who had fired.

"You scalded my leg, Curry!" the gunman squalled as Baldridge scrambled for cover. In the steam and the heat and the confusion, the three men wasted no time looking for him, but escaped out a window and onto the balcony. They fired two shots into the cloudy room as they left, but neither round came near Baldridge.

In a few seconds the hotel employees began to gather in the room; only after a few chaotic moments did they realize that Baldridge was naked and hand him a towel to cover himself. The desk clerk apologized profusely while Baldridge got dressed; when the manager arrived, he too, began to offer an apology. A quick check of the area in and around the hotel revealed that the assailants had made good their escape. The bath attendant was unconscious in a closet at the end of the hall. Except for a rather sizable knot on his head, and a second-degree burn on his ankle, Baldridge was all right.

For almost half an hour he tried to explain to the manager how the men simply appeared and disappeared in a cloud of steam. He would just as soon have been done with the matter, but the hotel manager kept gushing about how sorry he was and how things like that just did not happen at the Pollock House. Baldridge begged to differ with him on that last point, but he finally took leave of the man and went up to his room.

He checked the room carefully and looked in the closet before settling in, then bolted the door from the inside. Once in the bed he realized just how tender his blistered left foot and ankle were, and he kept his leg outside the sheet as he covered up.

Baldridge looked over at his bowie knife, which hung in a scabbard on his belt. Although an excellent shot with pistol and rifle, he had not carried a gun since the war. He'd had his fill of seeing people shooting other people and of seeing his friends torn apart. Now he preferred the bowie knife to a revolver. As a close-range weapon, it forced him to look his opponent in the eye when he used it, and that kept him from taking the killing of a man lightly. Shooting someone just seemed too easy, too likely to be done in the heat of the moment. But the close call he had experienced tonight had him reconsidering the matter. If he had been armed he could have returned fire. If he were a whole man, with full use of both legs, maybe they couldn't have held him down in that tub. Perhaps he could have stopped them.

It was a silly notion and he dismissed it as quickly. Who would have thought a man had to take a gun with him to his bath? But he would be more careful from now on. He reached over and slipped his knife and scabbard from his belt, unsnapped the retaining strap, and placed the weapon under his pillow. He practiced pulling it twice before he was satisfied with the way it lay. The light from the coal-oil lantern beside his bed sent shadows dancing across the flowery wallpaper around the room. With his hands behind his head, he tried to recall the faces of the men who attacked him; but they were all blurry, every bit as cloudy as the room had been—all except for the sight of that water streaming from the pot and edging closer to him.

He rotated his ankle and peered down at the reddened area. That would feel good in a boot tomorrow. They were crazy. That was all there was to it. They had to be crazy to try and scald a man to death. But they had to be scared, too—scared, and maybe a little desperate, which told Baldridge he was getting close to finding something that mattered in this case. The more he thought about that bathtub the angrier he became. It was personal now. Now he would find out who those men were if it killed him. And it was beginning to look as if it might. Baldridge reached over and put out the light. He should have gone drinking. It would have been safer.

$\triangledown$

8

CARRIAGE TRAFFIC WAS heavy Monday morning when Baldridge tied his rented horse near Gurney's Corner. He glanced across the intersection of Main and Commerce streets, where a well-dressed lady stood giving instructions to an eager young Negro boy. Nearby, the proprietor swept the wooden walkway in front of a mercantile store and used his broom to shoo two determined cats from an empty milk pail beside the door. Baldridge took the wooden photographic casing from his saddlebag as two young boys ran down the street, yelling and shooting finger guns at one another. His horse stirred slightly as one of them ducked under the tying rail and dashed just beneath the animal's neck.

"Boy, watch what you're doing," Baldridge called, stroking the horse to calm it; but the youngster, without looking back, disappeared around the corner of the photography shop in hot pursuit of his playmate. As he secured the strap on his saddle bag, Baldridge gazed over the back of his horse and noticed two men standing across the street just down from the mercantile. Perhaps he was just getting jittery, but he thought they were watching him. They seemed somehow out of place: Both wore riding boots, and one had on a long overcoat that, with the sun as warm as it was, seemed a little much even for this brisk autumn morning. He pulled the case snugly under his arm and went inside the photographer's shop.

Inside the poorly lighted room, Baldridge got a whiff of

what smelled like rotten eggs. The front windows had dark
green blinds pulled three quarter's of the way down. The
papered walls were lined with all manner of photographs.

"Anybody here?" he said. "Hello?"

"Just a minute," someone called from behind a dark
curtain hanging in the doorway to an adjacent room.

He studied some of the photographs near the door, until
a man emerged from behind the curtain.

"What can I do for you?"

"Good morning. I'm Masey Baldridge." He offered the
man his hand.

"Henry C. Norman," the man said. "I run the shop for
Mr. Gurney."

"I've got something here I hope you can help me with."
Baldridge unlaced the string and unwrapped the wooden
case. "Is this what I think it is?" He handed the case to
Norman, who turned it over and over, peering closely at the
tiny brass knob on the end. "I figure it's got something to
do with a camera," Baldridge added. "I saw something like
this when a fella took my picture back in Memphis."

With his thumb and index finger, Norman tugged gently
on the knob, then quickly pushed it back. "Yes, sir, this is a
photographic plate all right. But it looks as if it's been
mistreated."

"Well, Mr. Norman, it has. It was left out in the mud for
a least a week, and I'm wondering if it could still have a
picture in it."

"Well, why on earth would somebody leave—"

"I don't know."

The photographer continued to inspect the casing. "Well,
the slide still works," he said, glancing up. "It could have
rusted shut, you know, but everything seems to be working.
Of course, there may not be an exposure. It could just be a
blank plate somebody lost."

"I see."

"You know, even if there is an exposure, and assuming
the elements haven't gotten to it, you're not going to get a

very high quality image out of one of these Melainotypes."

"A what?"

"A Melainotype," Norman said. "That's what this is, you know. Most people call it a tintype."

"Yeah, I know what a tintype is."

"Yes sir." Norman frowned, and spoke apologetically. "You see, this is a very cheap way to make a picture. You're not going to get the quality out of this that you would with one of my shots."

"Is that right?"

"Oh, yes." He held the case up to catch the light along the edge, and rubbed his finger over the end of the brass knob. "You mostly find these operations at fairs, carnivals . . . they're usually done by some traveling outfit."

"Got any idea who might have done this one?"

"Hard to say." He held the edge close to his face. "It has an imprint here on the handle. Looks like 'BPE.' Can't say I've ever seen that one. Of course, I don't deal in these tintypes, you understand."

"I understand." Baldridge pointed at the case. "But you think there could still be something in there?"

"Oh, I suppose it could."

"And could you develop it?"

"I don't handle Melainotypes, Mr. Baldridge."

"I understand you don't normally—"

"Look right over here," Norman said, walking over behind a desk. "See right here? See how sharp my images are? A tintype like this just can't give you that kind of finish."

"Mr. Norman, I'm sure your process is much better. I don't doubt that. But I really need to know if there's a picture in that case. Do you think you can make it come out?"

Norman studied the case again. "I don't know, Mr. Baldridge. The chemicals I use are different from those it takes to develop a tintype."

"But could you try? I'd be willing to pay you well."

"I couldn't guarantee anything," Norman said. He looked back toward his darkroom as he thought about Baldridge's request. "I'd have to mix up some silver chloride," he said, more to himself than to Baldridge, "and if I combine that with my collodium . . . and smear it on the plate . . . that should react the silver." He turned back to Baldridge. "I could wash off the unreacted silver and it might—mind you, I said *might*—give us an exposure. Assuming there is one here, and assuming the weather or the light hasn't gotten to it."

"That sounds fine, Mr. Norman. Whatever you think."

"I'd have to charge you extra, though, what with making up a special solution and all."

"That's fine. I'm willing to pay to have it done right."

"Well, if it can be done—and I'm not promising that it can—Henry C. Norman is your man." He smiled.

"Great, Mr. Norman. How long will it take you?"

"Oh, I need most of the day anyway. I've got some other orders to finish first. But I suppose I could have it for you first thing in the morning. That is, providing—"

"I know, I know. If there's anything there."

Norman smiled again. "Yes, sir."

When Baldridge emerged from the building, the two men he had seen earlier were gone, and he decided he must have been making something out of nothing. There was no use in getting spooked; it would just make the job harder, and with information in this case as scarce as virtue in a whorehouse, he was beginning to wonder just what kind of report he was going to provide the insurance company.

Mr. Ferguson's questions were simple: How did the accident happen and was the pilot negligent? Those should have been easy enough to answer, but the more questions he asked, the more he created, and with the survivors scattering, there were damned few people left to ask. Between all the conflicting accounts of the incident, and what Jackson told him, it was clear that he was dealing with more than a shipwreck. There was something ominous, something sinister, lurking in the shadows of this investigation, and Baldridge was edgy, expecting any moment that that something would jump out and grab him.

The image of that boiling water inching closer and closer to his crotch made him cringe, and he kept recalling how those men used the phrase "Yankee captain." They had even called themselves "soldiers." Baldridge had heard stories of men who wouldn't give up the fight after the war, but these were usually isolated cases of mountain men, holed up in their cabins way back in the middle of nowhere. Feelings ran deep, there was no doubting that. Not a day passed that his leg didn't remind him of the price he'd paid. But while the notion that something could have happened to Ed Smythe simply because he was a Yankee seemed remote, something Ferguson had said that day at Mid-South Insurance kept bothering Baldridge:

"I swear, I think someone has declared war on steamboats."

On Saturday the wharfmaster had commented that the *Mary Justice* was the strangest wreck he had heard of since the *T. H. Thorndike*, a small packet based in Cairo, Illinois. Baldridge hadn't paid much attention to it at the time, but on a hunch, he stopped by the telegraph office and sent a message to Ferguson in Memphis. It was probably a silly notion, and perhaps a waste of money; but since he would be wasting Ferguson's money and not his own, Baldridge decided to check it out.

OCTOBER 28, 1872

ROBERT FERGUSON
PRESIDENT MID-SOUTH INSURANCE COMPANY
MEMPHIS TENNESSEE

PLEASE CHECK COMPANY RECORDS FOR WARTIME OCCUPATION OF EDWARD SMYTHE AS WELL AS THAT OF LATE CAPTAIN OF STEAMBOAT MERCURY STOP ALSO FOR CAPTAIN OF T H THORNDIKE WRECKED OFF COLES POINT FEBRUARY THIS YEAR STOP DO NOT KNOW THORNDIKES INSURER STOP IMMEDIATE REPLY REQUESTED STOP

MASEY BALDRIDGE
POLLOCK HOUSE
NATCHEZ MISSISSIPPI

Not only was he concerned about having to report to Ferguson, but he had also hoped to have something solid to tell Luke Williamson when he returned tonight. Williamson seemed a little quick-tempered, but there was something about him Baldridge liked.

He wanted to board the *Paragon* tonight and tell Luke that Captain Ed Smythe, through no fault of his own, lost his boat to natural causes and an unforgiving river. He wanted to be able to say that the terrible loss of life was a freak accident of nature and would likely not be repeated in a hundred years. But he knew that was not going to happen; and while he wasn't exactly sure what he *would* tell Williamson, he was sadly resigned to knowing what he would *not* say.

Yet the prospect of remaining in Natchez for a few more days, at least until he got to the bottom of this mess, was not all bad. This was a steady job, and Ferguson's money was still holding out. Baldridge could eat at a decent restaurant, sleep in a feather bed, and have himself a drink whenever he wanted to. It was the best he'd had it in several years, and he reasoned there was no use in rushing things. Even if he could come up with some reasonable explanation for the wreck, it would be stupid to finish up too soon. Ferguson had given him the money to cover expenses, and with the off-and-on nature of the work at the insurance company, who was to say when he would live this well again? So Baldridge decided that whatever he turned up in the next few days, this investigation was bound to take another week, unless the money ran out sooner.

Over a glass of whiskey that afternoon, he borrowed a pen and some writing paper from the bartender and drew a sketch map of the river from St. Louis to New Orleans. He placed a circle for all of the major cities in between; recalling what he'd learned investigating the wreck of the *Mercury,* and the newspaper accounts he had read, and what he had heard from pilots, he began to place X's along the river at spots where major wrecks had occurred. Back in March an excursion boat had gone down in the Graveyard, as rivermen called a dangerous stretch of river a few miles below St. Louis. He also recalled reading something about a packet that in May ran aground and burned on a sandbar near Columbus, Kentucky. Neither accident was remarkable and the loss of life was minimal, but he marked them anyway. He X'ed in two boats that had burned on the lower stretch of river between Memphis and Vicksburg. The *Commercial Appeal* had reported that in one case the spark arrester was damaged by high winds, allowing a hot ember from the smokestack to ignite some cotton bales the crew had stupidly loaded on the hurricane deck. The pilot wisely ran her aground, and most of the passengers got off safely. The other boat, he recalled, burned and sank to the second deck in low water. As he moved down his sketch map, Masey placed an X for the *T. H. Thorndike* at approximately where he thought Coles Point might be, and another for the *Mercury* at his best guess for St. Joseph's Landing. For the *Mary Justice,* he next marked where Giles Bend would be, and finally he placed another X down well below Natchez for a showboat that back in the summer accidentally rammed a packet during an early-morning fog. According to the papers, the showboat limped to shore, but the packet sank to her smokestacks in mid-channel.

The bartender refilled Baldridge's glass and he lifted it to his lips, sipping bourbon and rolling it around in his mouth until it began to tingle, then swallowing it down. He studied the map for some connection—something to tie any two of the wrecks together, anything that might indicate a pattern. But they were all in different locations, and from what he recalled reading, they all happened at different times of day or night. No two boats belonged to the same shipping line. He took another drink of whiskey, placed his elbow on the table, and rested his head in his left hand. He picked at a tiny bump near his hairline as he scanned the page. Then he picked up his pen and circled three of the X's: the *T. H. Thorndike*, the *Mercury*, and the *Mary Justice*. The accidents that resisted explanation had all occurred in the stretch of river between Grand Gulf and Natchez. Masey realized that of all those he had listed, only these three boats had sunk in water deep enough to swallow the entire craft. The river was high when the *T. H. Thorndike* sank, so her disappearance was easy enough to explain. But the other two boats had gone down during low water, and from what he had gathered from talking to pilots, there just weren't that many spots deep enough this time of year to swallow an entire steamboat.

While investigating the *Mercury*, he had turned up survivors who reported an explosion before the boat went down. Like the *Mary Justice*, the *Mercury* had dropped in mid-channel, in water so deep as to leave no trace. And the witnesses said the boat was completely submerged in less than two minutes. Baldridge remembered what Jacob Lusk had told him that night on the rear deck of the *Paragon*: A good pilot would have grounded a disabled steamboat to let his passengers get ashore. Ed Smythe should have grounded the *Mary Justice*, but he didn't, and that still bothered him. With his pen he sketched both sides of the river bank near Giles Bend and between the lines drew an oval to represent the *Mary Justice*. Smythe could not have been more than a quarter mile from the east bank. Closing his eyes, Masey pictured the spot where he and Jackson had stood on Sunday. Even a crippled boat should have made it to shore in a couple of minutes. He sat his glass on the table and stared out the window. What manner of snag or sandbar could a boat hit that would damage it badly enough to sink it in less than a minute?

As he scanned the drawings, it seemed odd that three disastrous accidents would occur so near each other, and in such a questionable manner. He took another drink and rotated the glass around on its base. But it wasn't impossible. It could be just a run of bad luck. Maybe the Grand Gulf-to-Natchez stretch was just dangerous water. Maybe none of it meant anything. Luke Williamson would know about the river, and rather than dismiss these accidents out of hand, Baldridge decided to wait for an answer to his telegram to Ferguson, and for a look at the photo he'd left with Norman.

The wind was whipping the sawgrass alongside Silver Street as Baldridge rode down the bluff about nine-thirty P.M. to meet the *Paragon*. The huge riverboat kissed the edge of the dock as she bobbed on the rough water, and the blaze from a dozen torches cast an uneven light on the roustabouts hustling new cargo aboard. Smoke from her stacks played hide-and-seek with the crescent moon that hung like a crooked grin on the western horizon. Tying his horse near a caretaker's shack, Baldridge limped past the busy crewmen and weaved in between cotton bales to reach the landing stage. His leg was stiff again. He had been on it too much today. Pausing for a quick sip from his flask, he saw the big black first mate watching him from the lower deck, his arms folded and his eyebrows hinting of displeasure. As he continued on to the ship, Baldridge waved the container at him. "Care to cut the chill?"

"No, sir," Jacob Lusk said, unsmiling. "The cap'n don't allow no drinkin' on duty."

"Suit yourself," Baldridge said as he passed. Lusk was an intense man who seemed never to relax. A good shot of bourbon would fix whatever ailed him.

He found Luke Williamson on the hurricane deck, dressing down one of the stewards for failing to clean up a passenger's cabin. The two of them returned to Luke's cabin, where they talked for almost an hour.

"What difference does it make?" Luke shouted, as Baldridge pressed him for information about the *T. H. Thorndike*. "It's like I told you. Three different people down in New Orleans said Creed Haskins's boat, the *Apollo*, was racing the *Mary Justice* when they left Vicksburg. What more do you want?"

The investigator shook his head. "I want a connection."

"A connection? Hell, man, Creed Haskins has hated me ever since he refused to run the Reb batteries at Island Number Ten. I volunteered for the mission, took his boat and showed him to be the coward he is and he ain't never forgot it." Luke was furious over what he had heard down in New Orleans from some survivors of the *Mary Justice*. Even after Baldridge produced his drawing and suggested a connection between what had happened to the *Mercury*, the *T. H. Thorndike*, and the *Mary Justice*, Luke wasn't impressed. It was as if he didn't want to hear anything about the investigation, unless it pointed to Hudson VanGeer.

"That's a bad stretch of water," Luke said. "It's claimed a lot of boats. The fact that they went down near each other doesn't mean anything."

"Don't you think it's a little strange that all three of these boats sank in water deep enough to hide 'em?"

"It's a deep river . . . in places."

Even when Baldridge told him of his encounter with Jackson and the incident in the hotel, Luke dismissed it.

"Probably just some rivermen from Under-the-Hill trying to settle the score for Saturday."

"What about all that talk about 'the cause' and Yankees getting what they deserve?"

"Well, you tell me," Luke snapped. "You're the Johnny!"

Baldridge was angry; that remark was uncalled-for.

"Look, Captain, maybe Haskins is involved, maybe not. But it sure doesn't fit what I'm seeing. Haskins is a Federal man. It ain't likely he'd be mixed up with the kind of men I came up against."

"What's somebody got to do? Hit you in the head with a board?" Luke tapped the used tobacco from his pipe into an ashtray. "Haskins works for Hudson VanGeer. Me and Ed have been giving VanGeer hell on this St.-Louis-to-New-Orleans run. We undercut his prices and offer the passengers better service. There's no tellin' how much business he's lost to us."

"But did anybody see Haskins or his crew do anything to the *Mary Justice*? You said Haskins came along after she went down."

"Look, I don't know how they did it. Maybe they hired somebody. I don't know. But it's clear enough to me. VanGeer and his houseboy Haskins are the only ones with anything to gain by sinking the *Mary Justice*."

"What about another company? Another packet service?"

"Nobody else is low enough to pull something like this. It's like I told you, we go back a long ways. When we get back to St. Louis, we'll confront VanGeer. You'll see."

"I'm not going back to St. Louis just yet."

"What?"

"I'm staying on in Natchez a few more days."

"Staying in Natchez? What the hell for?"

Baldridge looked up at the lights that winked from the mansion windows along the bluff. "The answer to the wreck is right here."

"Have you heard a word I said? I just laid it out for you. It's VanGeer. Sure, maybe he hired some men to help him, and maybe you pissed 'em off, and maybe they don't like Union men."

"Oh, I pissed 'em off all right."

"Don't get me wrong. Ed Smythe was the best friend I had in the world. I'd personally shoot any man that had a hand in what happened. But I know who ordered it. I know who's behind it, and it's Hudson VanGeer."

"You may be right. Hell, you probably are. But right now you got no proof. You can't go cruising into St. Louis accusing a man like Hudson VanGeer of murder. Give me a few more days. Let me see what I can come up with."

"You'll have a few more days, all right. The *Paragon*'s the last boat you'll see until the water rises. And God knows when that'll be. The longer you're down here, the longer VanGeer's going to think he's getting away with it." Luke tapped his fingers on the desk. "And the longer it's going to be before I see a settlement from your company."

"I'll settle the claim when I've got facts."

"You know, I trusted you. I believed you when you said you weren't looking for a way to back out of my rightful claim—when you said you were really interested in finding out what happened to Ed."

"There's questions to be answered."

Luke leaned closer to Baldridge and sniffed his breath. "Well, you're not going to find the answers in the bottom of a whiskey bottle."

Baldridge's eyes cut hard into Luke's. "I'll take care of my business, Captain. You take care of yours."

"Well, you have at it," Luke said, leaning out of the cabin and motioning to Jacob on the lower deck. "I'm going to St. Louis, and I'll thank you to get your ass off my boat."

Standing on the dock, Baldridge watched the *Paragon* back out into the channel and head west in the direction of Merengo Bend. He had not told Luke Williamson about the people Jackson had found shot along the bank; since he couldn't be sure Smythe was not one of them, it seemed needlessly cruel to raise the matter at all. Whatever he said, Luke was determined that VanGeer was behind the loss of the *Mary Justice,* and if there was anything the captain didn't need, it was another reason to go after VanGeer. If VanGeer was behind the wreck, Baldridge figured the trail had to begin in Natchez; at first light tomorrow, he would start tracking.

About nine o'clock Tuesday morning Baldridge entered the photographer's shop and immediately noticed that the blinds were pulled completely down.

"Mr. Norman?" he called as he shut the door behind him. Only a sliver of light reached across the floor from where the front door did not fit snugly to the frame. "Mr. Norman, it's Masey Baldridge. I'm here about the tintype."

That rotten-egg smell was stronger than ever—a result, no doubt, of whatever potions Norman had conjured. Although he called to him twice more, Baldridge got no answer, so he moved slowly through the dark room toward the curtain that led into the back. Reaching up to pull the curtain, he hesitated. What if he exposed something? He shouted for Norman again but got no answer. The building was silent, and only the clip-clop and rumble of a horse and wagon bled through from the street outside.

Slowly Baldridge pulled the curtain to one side and eased his head past it.

"Mr. Norman?" The back room was completely dark and that foul smell almost took his breath away as he felt along the wall past a shelf that held some glass bottles, bumping one and almost tipping it over before he could catch it. Something was wrong. Norman had seemed like a precise man. He had said first thing in the morning. He should be here. Baldridge slid first one foot, then the other, into the dark room, still feeling his way along the wall and giving his eyes time to adjust to the dark. As he moved his right foot forward, it struck something, and he heard a groan.

"Who's there?" Baldridge said, recoiling slightly from the sound.

A weak voice moaned from the darkness. Baldridge leaned over and felt around in the blackness. He found a foot, then moved his hand up the pants leg to the shin.

"Norman? Mr. Norman?"

"Help me," Norman groaned. "Help me."

Baldridge reached over and pulled the curtain completely aside, but there was still too little light. "I can't see shit," he said, stumbling to his feet.

"In . . . in the corner." Norman groaned again. "Near the . . . the bottles." As he felt for a lamp, Baldridge could hear the man stirring on the floor.

"Just lie still, Mr. Norman. I've got the lamp." Baldridge found some matches and quickly managed to strike a struggling flame. In the erratic light, he could see Norman lying on his side, clutching his left temple. He placed the lamp on a nearby table and carefully moved Norman to a chair in the other room. Returning to the darkroom, he dipped his hand into a dish of water and sniffed it. Satisfied that it was pure, he pulled a rag from the shelf over the table, wet it, and returned to Norman. He folded the rag and placed it over an abrasion oozing blood from just in front of Norman's ear.

"What the hell happened to you?" Baldridge asked as he walked toward the windows at the front of the shop.

"Somebody . . . somebody jumped me." Norman pressed the cloth against the wound and leaned back in the chair. Baldridge lifted one of the blinds, but the photographer protested mildly, so he lowered it halfway. "Must've come through the back while I was working," Norman said.

"Have you been there all night?"

"Yeah, I guess so."

"You want me to take you to a doctor?"

Norman shook his head very slowly. "I don't think so. I don't know. Not right this minute. I think I just want to sit here awhile. But there is one thing," he said, adjusting the damp rag and shading his eyes from the window glare. "There is one thing you can do."

"What's that?"

"You can tell me"—Norman groaned as he shifted on the chair—"where you got that picture." He leaned toward Baldridge. "And why in the world . . . why somebody would knock me upside the head to get it."

Pulling up a chair, Baldridge sat down across from him. "Someone took the picture?"

"Damnedest thing I ever saw," Norman said, still groggy from the blow. "I can't quite understand why a fella . . . a fella with that kind of talent would still be using a Melaino-type process."

"What was in the picture, Mr. Norman?"

"Can't say I've ever seen anybody take a picture like that." Norman's eyes seemed to brighten somewhat as he dabbed the rag against his temple. "Being nighttime and all, I just don't—"

"The picture, Mr. Norman. What was the picture?"

"Oh, uh . . . it was what looked like a riverboat."

"A riverboat?"

"Yes, except it was on fire. Damnedest shot I ever saw. A riverboat on fire out over the water."

"What was—"

"At night! That's the strangest part," Norman continued, seeming to find renewed strength from the subject itself. "Now I've heard tell about people taking shots in the dark. There's supposed to be a newfangled gadget that lights up the subject—"

"Mr. Norman—"

"—but that would be a close-up subject. I don't know how in the world this fella shot this—"

"The name of the boat, Mr. Norman!" Baldridge shouted. "Hell, man, what was the name of the boat?"

"Please don't shout, Mr. Baldridge," Norman said softly, a hurt look coming over him. "I don't like it when people shout at me. Besides, I've got a pretty bad headache at the moment." He paused, but soon spoke up again. "And I couldn't make out the name of the boat. There was a strip on the plate that didn't come out. Probably a light leak, or maybe the weather got to it."

"You couldn't read the name?"

"No, sir, I couldn't."

"And the ones who hit you run off with my picture?"

Norman nodded. "They said it wasn't your picture. Said it belonged to them. I wasn't going to give it to them, you understand, but, uh"—Norman rubbed his head—"I guess you could say they persuaded me. Now, don't get me wrong." Norman glanced at the rag and returned it to his head. "That's good photography, even with the bad streak in it. But why would somebody try to hurt me over it?"

"I don't know," Baldridge said, "but I figure it's the same crowd that tried to boil me alive the other night."

"Boil you alive?"

"It's a long story." Baldridge stood up and walked to the

front door, where he lifted another shade up and stared out into the street. He watched the traffic for several moments, then added, "If I knew who those men were, I'd probably have the answers to a lot of things."

"Well, I can't give you a name, but I've seen one of them before," Norman said matter-of-factly.

Baldridge's head snapped around. "You know the men who hit you?"

"No, not exactly," Norman began, trying to get to his feet.

Baldridge hurried over to him. "Let me help you."

Once on his feet, Norman crept over to the display of photographs Baldridge had noticed the day before.

"I see a lot of faces, Mr. Baldridge. That's how I make my living." He leaned closer to the images and ran his finger along them. "And I don't forget many."

"But it was dark back there."

Norman was still studying the pictures. "I finished with your tintype about eight-thirty, and I was examining it when I heard a rustling in my storeroom. When I turned the corner, there they were. Two of'em."

Baldridge glanced out the window in the direction of the mercantile. "Was one a tall fella with a long overcoat?"

"Sure was," Norman said. "Say, they came after you, too, did they?"

"Maybe."

"Anyway, they said they come for the tintype, and I told them they couldn't have it, and—"

"This man you say you recognized," Baldridge said, "did he know you?"

"Oh, I doubt it. See, I take lots of people's pictures. About all they see of me is a wave of the hand from behind the camera. Me, I see them real well."

"Where did you see this man before?"

"That's what I can't figure. Maybe it's this whop on the head, but I just can't bring it to mind. But I took his picture, I do know that. And it's been in the last two years."

"How do you know that?"

" 'Cause I've only been in Natchez two years. I came down in 'seventy to take over the shop for Mr. Gurney." Norman eased down into the chair near his desk. "I think I better sit a spell. I'm feeling a little dizzy."

"Are you sure you don't need to see the doctor?"

"I doubt it, Mr. Baldridge."

"I could stay with you awhile," Baldridge offered, "but I don't expect they'll be back. They got what they wanted."

"Yes, sir, I guess they did. But you still haven't told me why they wanted it."

Over the next half-hour Baldridge related to Norman the story of the *Mary Justice* and what he had encountered trying to settle the claim. When he prepared to leave, an intrigued Henry Norman stood up on shaky legs.

"That's quite a story, Mr. Baldridge. Quite a story indeed." Norman steadied himself on the arm of a chair. "I tell you what I'll do," he added as Baldridge started for the door. "I'll check through some of my old pictures. I might come across our friend in my file. You see, sometimes I take more than one shot. I generally keep a record."

"You do that, Mr. Norman," Baldridge said. "You can find me at the Pollock House if you come up with anything."

"I thought you were going back to St. Louis."

"Not now," Baldridge said with a grin. "Not when I'm just starting to make people nervous."

After lunch Baldridge went to the telegraph office and found that Ferguson had wired him shortly before noon. The boy was halfway out the door to deliver the telegram to the Pollock House when the operator called him back inside. Baldridge tossed him a nickel and opened the envelope.

OCTOBER 29 1872

ST. LOUIS MISSOURI
MASEY BALDRIDGE
POLLOCK HOUSE
NATCHEZ MISSISSIPPI

REGARDING INQUIRY OF YESTERDAY STOP CAPTAIN
EDWARD SMYTHE WAS CIVILIAN PILOT USS JOHN RAINE
STOP JOHN D BALLARD, CAPTAIN STEAMBOAT MER-
CURY SERVED AS PILOT OF STEAMER BALTIC STOP

VERNON MARLEY WAS CAPTAIN OF THORNDIKE
STOP SINCE WE DID NOT INSURE CANNOT SAY WITH
CERTAINTY STOP RELIABLE RIVERMAN WHO CLAIMED
TO KNOW HIM SAYS MARLEY WAS PILOT OF USS
FAIRCHILD STOP RECORDS SHOW FAIRCHILD WAS COM-
MISSARY BOAT IN MISSISSIPPI MARINE BRIGADE STOP
BALTIC AND RAINE ALSO MARINE BRIGADE COM-
MANDED BRIGADIER GENERAL ALFRED W ELLET STOP

WILLIAMSON'S BANK PRESSING FOR SETTLEMENT
STOP WIRE AS SOON AS YOU HAVE FACTS REGARDING
WRECK STOP

ROBERT FERGUSON
MID-SOUTH INSURANCE COMPANY
MEMPHIS TENNESSEE

Baldridge smiled as he folded the telegram. He had been
right. There *was* a connection between the wrecks—the
Mississippi Marine Brigade. The names of Alfred W. Ellet
and his Mississippi Marine Brigade were sure to draw some
harsh words from southerners along the river. Ellet had
commanded a U.S. Army outfit, subject to orders from the
navy, whose mission was to ride transports up and down the
Mississippi River, engaging Confederate guerrilla units that
emerged to check the river traffic. Baldridge recalled a brief
encounter with them a few miles south of Dyersburg,
Tennessee, in the fall of 1863. It hadn't amounted to much,
only himself and six or seven other scouts, taking potshots
at the passing boats to determine how many men they
carried. By the time Ellet's shallow-draft boats had landed
and dispatched their cavalry, Baldridge and his fellow scouts
had disappeared into the woods. But a number of people
along the river, particularly civilians, had claimed to suffer

at the hands of Ellet's men, frequently complaining to the Federal authorities about the so-called depredations the brigade committed in the name of war.

The pilots' service in the Marine Brigade was the only link between the wrecks. Baldridge knew that Williamson and Smythe had served together, and if he were a betting man, he'd bet Williamson had been a pilot in the Marine Brigade too. He thought about wiring the captain, but it would be two more days before the *Paragon* arrived in St. Louis, and Baldridge's information was sketchy at best. Even if he could contact him, he didn't know what to tell him to look out for, and from their last conversation, he doubted Luke would believe him anyway. But if his guess was right, and someone was sinking riverboats belonging to ex-pilots from the Marine Brigade, Luke Williamson might figure as the next target. At least Baldridge took comfort in knowing that once the *Paragon* reached St. Louis, she'd be idle until the river came up, affording him time to check out his theory.

▽

9

Thursday afternoon, October 31

W HEN LUKE WILLIAMSON arrived at St. Louis, he wasted no time turning the boat over to Steven Tibedeau and going ashore. Hailing a carriage along Front Street, he climbed inside.

"Baker Street. VanGeer Shipping Line," Luke said, and the driver moved out. If that crippled drunk didn't have enough gumption to come to St. Louis and confront Hudson Van-Geer, then he would do it himself. He had heard all he needed to hear in New Orleans to know that VanGeer was behind what happened to the *Mary Justice*, and he wasn't going to let him get away with it.

He had explained to Baldridge how four different people, all located at different places on the *Mary Justice*, told the same basic story. He'd outlined in detail how they said there was an explosion. To blow a boat apart the way they said the *Mary Justice* went, Luke figured the explosion had to be that of a boiler. It was plain as a Quaker's hat. Somebody did something to one of the boilers. That was the only explanation. That had to be it. That whiskey-breathed ex-Reb just wouldn't listen to reason.

All that ridiculous business about Asa Turner running scared, and some old codger up on Bisland Bayou, and that unbelievable tale of somebody trying to scald him in a bathtub—Baldridge was probably drunk the whole time. He'd most likely dreamed up the whole thing. Even if somebody had come after him, the man should have sense enough to see that VanGeer was behind it. VanGeer had more than enough money to hire a few thugs to rough up a cripple. Looking out the window of the carriage at the storefronts, Luke grumbled to himself.

Let him stay at Natchez. To hell with him. To hell with his insurance company, too.

The carriage halted before a Baker Street storefront, and tossing the driver a half-dollar Luke rushed through the front room and burst into Hudson VanGeer's office. The door swung back and slapped the wall, bringing VanGeer's head up from the papers on his desk. Beside him stood his chief pilot, Creed Haskins.

"What the—"

"Oh, this is perfect," Luke said as he continued toward the two men. "You got your errand boy with you."

"What do you want here, Williamson?"

"I know damned well you did it. And I know this asshole was involved."

Haskins started to come around the desk, but VanGeer held him back. He tossed his pen onto the desktop. "What are you talking about?"

"I'm talking about murder." Luke edged closer, placed his hands on the edge of the desk, and leaned forward. "I'm talking about how you sank the *Mary Justice* and murdered my partner and over a hundred passengers and crew."

"Ol'Crazy Luke," Haskins said. "They're right about you. You're crazy as hell."

"Shut up, Haskins."

But Creed Haskins kept talking: "I'm not used to seein' you up this close, Williamson. You and that tub of yours are usually disappearing in my backwash."

"You're a fool, Haskins. The day hasn't dawned when I couldn't outrun you."

"Sheeeyut," Haskins said, glancing at two of VanGeer's men who had stepped into the doorway behind Luke.

"Now see here, Williamson," VanGeer said. "I didn't have

anything to do with what happened to your boat. It's a
tragedy. We all hate to see lives lost. It's bad for business all
around." He pushed away from his desk and leaned back in
his chair. "But the truth is, you were through long before the
Mary Justice went down. It was just a matter of time. You
and Smythe couldn't hope to keep up with me."

"We were doing a pretty good job of it."

"The fact is, you're through," VanGeer said. "Finished.
You just don't know it yet. Why don't you face it? You're up
to your neck in debt. You're down to one boat. The public's
downright afraid of you. And I hear your insurance company
is about to cancel you."

"Well, you hear wrong."

"Do I?"

"Yeah."

"Facts are facts."

"That's right, VanGeer. And the fact is you killed my
partner and destroyed our boat." As VanGeer stared coolly
into his face, apparently unbothered by anything he said,
Luke got angrier. He turned to Haskins.

"You were racing the *Mary Justice* that night."

"So what? I race a lot of boats. Beat 'em, too. Including
yours."

"You left Vicksburg over an hour before the *Mary Justice.*
A couple of crewmen I found in New Orleans told me so.
What were you? Five, six miles ahead?"

"What difference does it make?"

"So how was it that Ed passed you? How is it you got
behind?"

Haskins glared at Luke. "I had engine trouble."

"The hell you did!" Luke turned to VanGeer. "You told
him to do it, didn't you? You told him to hold back and let
Ed Smythe pass. You wanted the *Mary Justice* to reach Giles
Point first, didn't you?

"Now why would I do something like that?" VanGeer grew
frustrated. "How could I know what was happening three or
four hundred miles away?"

"I don't know how you did it. At least, not yet. But I know you were behind it, and when I find out how you did it, I'm coming after you."

As Luke spoke, another man entered the room and stood near the door. There were now three of them watching him, listening, waiting for VanGeer's command to remove him from the room.

VanGeer got up from his chair and stood beside Creed Haskins. "You've got no right to come into my building accusing me and my staff of—"

"You sayin' you didn't want Ed and me out of the way? You sayin' your business isn't better now that the *Mary Justice* is gone?"

"Listen, Williamson," VanGeer said, "it's true I wanted you two out of my hair. Your puny two-packet service has cost me some business."

"*Some* business?"

VanGeer lifted his hands in front of him. "Okay. A lot of business. But I don't have to sink a riverboat to get rid of you. I can just outhaul you. I've got more boats, better boats." VanGeer glanced at Haskins. "And better pilots."

"Like hell you have!"

VanGeer laughed. "Customers are afraid of you, Williamson. Word is, you take chances with people's lives. Word is, you're more interested in building a reputation than in taking care of your passengers. Haskins here is right," VanGeer said, with a tilt of his head. "People are calling you 'Crazy Luke.' Been calling you that for more than a year now."

"My cabins are all full," Luke said.

"Only because it's late in the season." He looked at Creed Haskins, grinned, and turned back to Luke. "And I've got a feeling that come spring, I'll have more business than I can handle. By the time I'm through, I'll see to it you can't get a contract to haul pig iron."

Luke stared first at VanGeer, then at Haskins. "You two are not going to get away with this."

"I'm getting tired of this shit," Haskins said, jabbing his finger toward Luke. "I already told you, I had nothing to do with what happened to Smythe. Hell, I even stopped my boat to help. I hauled five or six of your cold, wet passengers to Natchez. And they were *very* grateful to me and to Mr. VanGeer's Shipping Line for keeping our riverboats *on top of the water.*"

"You bastard!" Luke shoved a chair out of the way and started around the desk. Grabbing Haskins by the lapel, he shoved him against the wall and, holding him with his left hand, delivered first a backhand, then a forehand, across his face. VanGeer signaled, and in seconds his men had pulled Luke off Haskins.

"See?" Haskins said, using his wrist to wipe blood from his cracked lower lip. "See what I mean? You *are* crazy! People are starting to figure that out now, but I've known it a long time." He removed a handkerchief from his coat pocket and pressed it against his mouth, looking at VanGeer and the men holding Luke as he spoke. "He was crazy back during the war, you know. But nobody would listen." Luke struggled to free himself as Haskins continued. "They called me a coward. Said I was afraid to run those guns at Island Number Ten. Then he up and volunteers. You were lucky you made it through. Just lucky, that's all. I wasn't afraid. I could have made that run the same as you. I just had better sense."

Luke pulled free of the men holding him. One of them quickly stepped between him and Haskins. Luke peered around the man. "You didn't have the guts to do it then, and you haven't got the guts to admit what you've done now." Luke looked at VanGeer. "You'll never run me off this river. Not now. Not after what you did to Ed Smythe."

"For the last time, Williamson," VanGeer said, "I had nothing to do with the wreck of the *Mary Justice.*"

Luke started backing toward the office door. "It may take me the rest of my life, VanGeer, but I'll make you pay for this. Both of you."

At the Mercantile Bank the next morning, Luke could not believe what he was hearing. Jeremiah Palmer and Jack Aubrey had tracked down the money Ed Smythe borrowed before he died: He used it as a down payment on a boat from an Ohio River packet service that had fallen on hard times. Luke was disheartened, and he sat there for several moments just staring into the fireplace across the lobby of the bank.

"Captain Williamson," Aubrey said, "from what we can tell, it seems to have been a reasonably sound investment. Mr. Smy—that is, *Captain* Smythe—appears to have obtained a very fair price."

That wasn't the point, Luke thought as he watched the flames dancing in the hearth. Ed had kept something from him. He had intentionally closed a deal without telling him. Ed had always consulted him on investments. And Luke had specifically told him he thought it was too soon to buy into another boat. He balled his fist and pounded the arm of the chair. What could Ed have been thinking?"

"So we have the matter of the eight-thousand-dollar loan," Aubrey droned, "but of course the boat Captain Smythe purchased can act as collateral on that."

Palmer jumped in. "But we do need to get a settlement out of your insurance company as soon as possible. I trust you've made arrangements to reimburse the customers for the cargo they lost?"

Luke kept looking at the fire. "Steven's handling all that. He's got the records. As soon as we get a settlement he'll take care of it."

Palmer laced his fingers together and leaned over the desk. "And when, Captain, do you think that might be?"

Luke snapped his head toward Palmer. "How the hell do I know?" Some nearby customers turned and stared at Luke, and he lowered his voice. "They've got some half . . . some investigator down in Natchez asking questions." Luke looked at Palmer and Aubrey. The concern in their eyes told him he should watch what he said. Telling them it wasn't an accident, and that the insurance company might take months to pay him off, would only prompt more questions—questions Luke couldn't answer. He turned his gaze back to the fireplace. "Probably won't be too long." Luke wished that were so. But with Baldridge down in Natchez when he should be in St. Louis, his investigation might take forever.

"So, Captain," Aubrey said, "what do you expect to do with this new boat?"

"Do with it? I don't even know where the hell it is. Louisville or someplace, isn't that what you said?" The men nodded. "What am I supposed to 'do with it?' " The two bankers stirred uncomfortably. "Look, I guess I'll go up there in a couple of weeks and if the water's high enough, I'll bring her down here and see what we've got."

Palmer shuffled some papers until he came up with a sheet with some figures on it. "Captain, with the season ending, we still show a balance of twenty-eight hundred dollars due the bank for unsettled expenses during the period August through October."

"I'll make it up next season."

The bankers looked at each other grimly. "Captain Williamson, the bank is concerned that you might not be able to do that."

"What do you mean?"

"With the loss of the *Mary Justice*, people—the customers, that is—are getting worried. There seems to be some doubt among many that your packet service will be able to continue."

"And what's that supposed to mean?"

"It's just that with only the one boat left," Palmer said, "and with a sense that you are, well"—he glanced at Aubrey—"perhaps a little incautious—"

"Spit it out," Luke snapped. "If you've got something to say, just say it, for God's sake. I'm sick and tired of you dollar-counters talking out your ass."

Palmer and Aubrey sat quietly for a moment, until Aubrey finally spoke. "It's our job to know what people think—to manage the bank's money as efficiently as possible." Aubrey smiled. "Anyway, we think your customers are losing confidence in the packet service. And frankly, Captain, if you don't do something soon, many of them just won't come back next spring. They'll take their business elsewhere. Then you'll be out of business and we'll be out the money we loaned you."

"You want me to restore your confidence?"

"Yes, that would be fair to say."

"And just how am I supposed to do that? How am I supposed to do that if I can't run the river till spring?"

The two bankers looked at each other again; then Aubrey handed Luke a sheet of paper. "There may be a way."

Luke looked at the paper, dated two days earlier: Carlton Distillery, Roman's Grain Cooperative, and the St. Louis Cotton Exchange were looking for two boats to make a late-season haul to New Orleans. It was to be a combination cargo run and promotional campaign to drum up business for the coming spring. And the companies specified that they wanted two different packet lines to furnish a boat. Aubrey said he had talked to the merchants as late as yesterday morning, and while they had succeeded in signing up one carrier about a week ago, they were disappointed that half their cargo would remain in St. Louis for lack of a ship to haul it.

"When do they want to make this run?"

"Sunday," Aubrey said.

"Sunday?" Luke shook his head. "Out of the question. That's just two days. Why I couldn't even refit in two days." He tossed the paper back at Aubrey. "Nobody's going to run the river this late. I bet I didn't meet a dozen packets coming back from New Orleans, and most of those were local carriers, running maybe fifty or sixty miles at the most." Luke pointed to the east. "I just came off this river and I'm telling you the water's too low. I don't know who they got to agree to this, but no serious pilot would make a run now."

"But if somebody did," Aubrey said, "and did it successfully, think what that could do."

"It could get somebody killed, that's what it could do."

"Captain, if people are losing confidence in your line," Aubrey said, "and I've already said they are, then think what making this run could do for you. It could restore that confidence. Why, any man who could complete a run in this weather, with water this low, could take his pick of business come spring."

"It's too risky. Besides, you just got through saying I was reckless."

Palmer jumped in. "Now, that's not exactly what we said, Captain. We said some people *think* you're a bit . . ."

"Incautious," Aubrey said.

Palmer smiled. "Yes, that's the word."

"And if I take this run they'll *know* I am," Luke replied. "Besides, I thought you were worried about getting your money. What happens if I take the *Paragon* out in this low water and snag her? Then we're both out our investments."

"We're trying to take the long view, Captain Williamson. Sure, there is some risk in making another run this season," Aubrey said. "But we believe it's manageable."

"Manageable," Luke repeated.

"Yes, Captain. Whereas, if you wait until spring . . ."

"We think the public will see this as a sign of pluck," Palmer added. "It certainly would get you some attention. And I'm talking about the good kind of attention—perhaps put the business about the *Mary Justice* behind you."

"I don't want it behind me."

"You know what I mean, Captain."

Luke shook his head. There was still the VanGeer business to clean up, and the settlement from the insurance company.

"I've got things to take care of right here in St. Louis."

Palmer looked over his glasses at Luke. "Captain, we strongly recommend you look into this offer."

For a second, Luke didn't get it. Then he saw: They were not really "recommending" at all. They were telling him to do it—do it or they would pull his financing out from under him. All they gave a damn about was their money. They didn't care about Ed Smythe, or the *Mary Justice*, or the *Paragon*, or what might happen to the crew. They just wanted to protect their precious investment. Luke looked at the two men for almost a minute without saying a word, then began to nod slowly.

"Who do I see?"

When Luke first heard the terms from the man at the Cotton Exchange, he had to admit they sounded good. The money was more than reasonable, and with the promise of a full contract the following spring, Luke decided the run would be worth a shot. His half of the cargo would fill the *Paragon* to no more than 75 percent of capacity, meaning she would draw slightly over five feet of water. Yes, the river was low—lower than it had been in almost a decade—and despite a one-day rain, it was still dropping. But since most of the pilots based in St. Louis had quit running over a week ago, Luke figured they didn't know what he knew. His view of the river conditions was fresh; he recalled only about three or four soundings that were under eight feet, and should they get another rain, even those would be no problem. The bankers were right. A chance to get solid business commitments for next spring was too much to pass up. With guaranteed contracts, and the insurance money for the *Mary Justice*, he could use the off season to fix up the boat Ed bought in Louisville. Aubrey and Palmer at the bank would back him because they would smell the money to be made. He could hire another crew and be ready by early March. It seemed to be the answer.

But what Aubrey and Palmer had not known, or at least had not told Luke, was that just hauling goods to New Orleans didn't guarantee the spring contract. The merchants had something a little bigger, a bit more flashy in mind. A delighted and relieved Mr. Garrett, representing the combined merchants, immediately hired Luke to haul the second half of the cargo; but Garrett would not say which shipping line had agreed to run the other half. The spring contract, Luke discovered, would go to the shipper who reached New Orleans first.

Racing under these water conditions seemed risky even to Luke, but when he considered the alterative, and recalled the tone of Aubrey and Palmer, he knew he had little choice. He left the Cotton Exchange determined to win the contract and save his business.

While Luke rushed to regather his crew and begin a hasty refitting for the run, Garrett immediately contacted the newspapers with the details of the race. Both boats would leave the St. Louis wharf on Sunday. There would be only two required stops: Memphis and Vicksburg. Any other stops would be at the discretion of the captain. The boat that first secured a lead line at Station Number Twelve along the Canal Street Dock in New Orleans would receive the contract for the following spring. The losing boat would be paid only for costs involved in the race.

Later in the afternoon, when he picked up a copy of the St. Louis *Democrat*, Luke found a more important reason to be first to New Orleans.

STEAMBOAT RACE TO THE FINISH

Two respected riverboats will depart at one P.M. on Sunday, November 3, for what promises to be one of the most thrilling maritime competitions our fair city has observed since the *Natchez* dueled the *Robert E. Lee*. The firing of the ceremonial cannon at Visitor's Point Wharf will signal the start of the race between the Hudson VanGeer Line's *Apollo*, under the command of the dependable and experienced Captain Creed Haskins, and the swift and luxurious *Paragon* of the Smythe-Williamson Packet Service, whose daring captain, Luke Williamson, is known to all. Both boats boast clean, luxurious cabins and cuisine to rival any found on this side of the Atlantic Ocean. As of press time, both the *Apollo* and the *Paragon* had space available for those wishing to make the exciting journey. We wish Godspeed to both vessels and anticipate an exciting contest. —A. Paige

It was not enough to have destroyed the *Mary Justice* and killed Ed. Now VanGeer was seeking a monopoly on the business next spring. Whatever it took, Luke decided he would not be beaten to New Orleans. He might never prove VanGeer was behind the wreck—he might never see a penny from the Mid-South Insurance Company—but he would show everyone who had the best boat and who was the best riverman. He figured he owed Ed Smythe that much.

▽

10

MASEY BALDRIDGE WAS looking for 337 Clifton Street, the address of former acting master Zedekiah McDaniel, late of the Confederate States Navy. The trail to McDaniel had come courtesy of the diligent, but still smarting, Henry C. Norman, who showed up at the Pollock House at nine-thirty A.M. Baldridge felt rotten. While Norman, still hurting from the blow on his head, and sporting a rather prominent pump knot, had spent most of Thursday searching through his stock of photographs to identify his assailant, Baldridge had spent the day drunk. He'd had every good intention of rising early Thursday morning and getting to work on the case; but the dull ache in his knee screamed for a drink from Smiley's Saloon, and then he found himself in a card game, and someone bought another bottle of whiskey, and the last thing he remembered was being escorted into the street as a result of something he said to the owner's lady. If he had made it back to the hotel, he would have found Norman at his door Thursday afternoon, excited about the photo he had located. But instead of waking up in the feather bed he so enjoyed, Baldridge came to at dusk Thursday evening in an alley behind Madison Street, staring at the shiny silver spurs of Dan Powell, the town sheriff. Despite his protests, Powell escorted Baldridge to jail for the night and wouldn't let him out until eight o'clock Friday morning. Angry with himself for having wasted an entire day, Baldridge returned to his room and had just finished cleaning up when Henry C. Norman again knocked at his door.

Producing a photograph of seven men posing on a bluff with the river behind them, Norman pointed out the man who had hit him and taken the tintype. Six of the men were standing around what appeared to be some packing crates, barrels, grain sacks, and a couple of large glass demijohns. One knelt in front. The man on the left, the one Norman recognized, wore a full beard, and with his right hand he held a sword across his chest. The second from the right was a dignified-looking gentleman, as was the third, who was not looking directly into the camera. The fourth man held a pistol in a pose reminiscent of wartime daguerreotypes Baldridge had seen; and the last two men standing were rather sloppily dressed, rugged-looking types, as was the seventh man, who was kneeling in front of the others. Norman could remember only that he'd taken the picture a couple of years ago, on what was a chance encounter. He had been doing a series of shots near the wharf, getting used to some new equipment, when one of the men approached him about making a photo of their group. Norman had no idea why they were gathered there, and they offered no explanation. But they paid him cash and had him mail the finished photo, though Norman said he no longer retained the address. He recalled making three exposures, all very much alike, and choosing the best one to send them. The picture he had brought Masey was a file copy; he had destroyed the other because he wasn't satisfied with the quality.

Fortunately, Norman could match a name to the third gentleman from the right, the best-dressed of the group. His gaze was slightly askew of the camera and he seemed rather uncomfortable in his pose. Norman identified him as Zedekiah McDaniel, an ex-Confederate naval officer who lived in Natchez. He had been introduced to McDaniel less than a year ago at a gentlemen's club in the city, and seeing the old photograph, he was sure it was the same man. After checking at the club for McDaniel's current address, Baldridge rode over to ask him about the others in the photograph.

A modest two-story frame house, in want of a decent whitewash, turned out to be the target of his search, and he knocked on the front. The door stuck as it was being opened, and after a second tug, it swung clear to reveal a soft-featured woman in her mid-thirties, her blond hair pulled back tightly against her head. Baldridge introduced himself and discovered he was talking to the daughter of the man he sought. She seemed rather suspicious of him, and asked him several times to repeat who he was and what he wanted. Then she disappeared into the house, returning in about two minutes to say that her father would see him.

The house carried the smell of herbs, and the furnishings in the hall and parlor were modest; in fact, some of the chairs had fallen into disrepair and were covered with a blanket or cloth. The woman took Baldridge to a rocking chair near a window on the east side of the house, where a rather frail old gentleman sat looking through a book. As his eyes lifted to meet Baldridge's, the investigator noticed how they seemed cloudy and distant.

"Father, this is Mr. Masey Baldridge. He's with an insurance company from Memphis. He wants to talk to you. Mr. Baldridge, this my father. Mr. Zedekiah McDaniel."

Baldridge acknowledged the gentleman and shook his hand.

"Won't you have a seat, Mr. Baldridge?" McDaniel said, the left side of his mouth drooping and appearing rather sluggish. "What does an insurance man want with me? I'm already poor, and I've never seen a dime come of any I ever bought."

"I'm not here to sell you anything, Mr. McDaniel. I was hoping you could help me identify someone."

The old man looked a little surprised. "Well, if I can. I don't get out much anymore."

Baldridge reached into his jacket and produced the photograph Norman had given him. "I've got a picture right here, and if you could just take a look at it . . ."

McDaniel turned closer to the window and held the photograph at an angle. His daughter leaned over his shoulder to view it as well. He studied it for several moments without speaking, then looked up at Baldridge as if anticipating a question.

"I believe that's you right there," Baldridge said, pointing. "Isn't it, Mr. McDaniel?"

McDaniel eyed the photograph. "Sure looks like me." He adjusted the angle of the photograph. "Yes, yes, I believe that is me."

"Do you recall having that picture made, sir?"

McDaniel again glanced at Baldridge then at the picture.

"Well, yes, I believe I do." He glanced out the window. "Seems like that was about two years ago—back before I had my stroke."

"My father has been in poor health for some time now, Mr. Baldridge. He doesn't often receive visitors. He's rather weak, you see."

Waving his hand at his daughter, the old man chuckled. "My daughter babies me too much. I'm a little slower, I guess, but you can't keep a navy man down. Are you a naval man, Mr. Baldridge?"

"No, I'm afraid not."

"But I bet you were a soldier."

"Yes, sir, I was."

"I knew it," McDaniel said, mildly pleased with himself. "I can usually tell. Your accent there, Mr. Baldridge." He paused to study him a moment. "I'd say that would be western Kentucky, or maybe Tennessee."

"You're pretty sharp, Mr. McDaniel. I'm from around Memphis."

"Oh, that wasn't fair," he complained, looking up at his daughter. "You said he was from Memphis, didn't you? You shouldn't have given me a hint."

"My father prides himself on recognizing people's accents. He's quite an observer."

"I see."

"Why are you carrying around a picture of me?" McDaniel asked.

"Well sir, the man I'm trying to identify is in this photograph, and since someone pointed you out to me, I thought you might be able to help." Baldridge pointed to the first subject on the left in the photograph.

Again McDaniel looked at the picture. "That'd be a man named Curry."

"Curry?"

"Yes, that's right."

"Would that be his first name or his last?"

"Last," McDaniel said, handing the picture back. "Afraid I wouldn't know his first name." McDaniel turned and started looking out the window. Baldridge glanced quickly at the daughter, noting a rather impatient look about her, then turned again to McDaniel.

"If it's not too much trouble, sir, would you have any idea where I might find this man Curry?"

McDaniel spoke without looking at him. "Afraid I wouldn't know that. Why're you looking for him, anyway?"

"It may be possible that he has some information regarding the recent wreck of the riverboat *Mary Justice*."

"Riverboat wreck, huh?" McDaniel looked up from the corner of his eye. "Well, that might be and it might not."

"Could you tell me where you knew Curry from, or what this is a picture of?" Baldridge asked.

"Just some old war veterans, that's all. Some of us got together a couple of years back."

"A reunion?"

"I guess you could call it that." McDaniel quickly added, "It was just for one day. Never saw none of them after that."

"These other men," Baldridge asked, "are they all veterans?"

"More or less."

"What do you mean?"

"I mean what I said," McDaniel said curtly. "More or less."

"Mr. Baldridge, my father grows weary rather quickly, so if you would be so kind—"

He didn't even look at the woman. "What kind of reunion was this, sir?"

McDaniel explained that about two years ago he had received an unsigned invitation to join some of his old comrades for a day of reminiscing and honoring their wartime experiences. Since gatherings of Confederate veterans were still outlawed, they had simply called the affair a meeting of the River Wartime History Club. After debating whether to go, he finally decided it might be pleasant to renew old acquaintances, so he traveled to the north end of the Natchez wharf, where he found a small group of ex-Confederate soldiers, sailors, and civilians, only three or four of whom he recognized.

Baldridge could sense that the old man was growing increasingly uncomfortable as he described this meeting, and at first he thought McDaniel feared he might be working for the federal government. The old man had almost asked as much once, then seemed to withdraw the question. Baldridge assured him that he had served the Confederacy under General Nathan Bedford Forrest. Those words, particularly the mention of Forrest, seemed to calm the old man.

"Like I said," McDaniel continued, "I'll admit I was intrigued to see how some of the boys were faring after the war, so I went. We spent the afternoon down at the river eating a picnic lunch of fried chicken and potato cakes some ladies had prepared for us." He paused a moment as if in deep thought. "To this day they were some of the best potato cakes I ever ate. Anyway, things was going along all right for a while, with the boys talking about the *Cairo* and all."

"The *Cairo*?"

"Yankee gunboat we sunk back in 1862. Fact is, this meeting was on the anniversary of that day—December twelfth. Two or three of these boys were present at the sinking, and we talked about it a long time, but the others I'd never met before. Never seen them since, either."

"You said things were going all right for a while. Did something happen?"

"Well, one of the men got to talking, and the more he said, the crazier it sounded, until me and Thomas Courtenay got a little nervous."

"What kind of talk?"

"Crazy talk," McDaniel repeated. "They were fighting the war all over again. You know, saying some pretty bad things."

"Like what?"

"Things like sailing up the Mississippi and shelling northern towns in the middle of the night, and putting together a fleet of gunboats and raiding ports along the Gulf, and well, just all kind of crazy things." McDaniel looked directly at Baldridge, his watery eyes checking their drift as he made his point. "But me and Thomas, we told them to forget it."

"Why would this particular group of veterans want to do something like that?" Baldridge asked. "A lot of people are bitter about the war. Hell, I'm one of 'em, but I ain't in no hurry to get back in it."

"I really can't say." McDaniel returned his gaze to the window.

"You were a master in the navy, is that right, sir?"

McDaniel nodded.

"Were these men on your boat during the war? Is that why they asked you to join them at the river?"

McDaniel hesitated. "We, uh . . . we served together, some of us."

"You were together when you sank the *Cairo*? You were in command of the boat?" Still looking out the window, McDaniel declined to answer. "Mr. McDaniel, I asked you a question."

"My father is old and his health is failing, Mr. Baldridge," his daughter interrupted, "and I think he's growing tired of your questions now."

"The ship, Mr. McDaniel?" Baldridge ignored an exasperated sigh from his daughter.

"That was a long time ago, sir. I see no need to go back over—"

"Mr. McDaniel, you say you're a navy man. A navy man should care about boats and seamen above everything else." McDaniel still did not look his way. "I'm investigating the wreck of a riverboat that claimed the lives of over a hundred decent, God-fearin' people." He held the picture in front of the old man and tapped it with his finger. "I'm sure this Curry was involved in the wreck. Now I don't see why you can't help me with a little information."

McDaniel began rocking gently in his chair. "I took an oath, Mr. Baldridge. You're asking me questions I can't rightly agree to answer."

"All I'm asking you is who these men are and what boat they were on." Baldridge was getting frustrated. "I don't see how that could betray anyone's trust."

"They weren't on a ship."

"All right, then. What outfit were they with?"

McDaniel took a deep breath. "I took an oath to the Confederate States of America, Mr. Baldridge, and men's lives depended upon—"

"Mr. McDaniel," Baldridge said, trying to preserve his patience, "there is no Confederate States of America. We lost the war. Any oath you took to the government of the South don't amount to a hill of beans now."

"An oath's an oath," McDaniel said softly, continuing to rock and stare out the window. "You know, I get the best view of the morning sun through this window."

Baldridge reached over and pulled down the blind. McDaniel sat back with a start. For a moment, Baldridge thought the daughter might come after him; she stepped close beside her father, as though to shield him. He stepped between McDaniel and the window, so the old man could not help but face him.

"Listen, Mr. McDaniel, I'm sure you were a fine sailor. No man could ever say you didn't do your very best for the cause. The gentlemen down at the club where I got your address spoke very highly of you. But this is not a game I'm playing here. People's lives are at stake. I have reason to believe that at least one of the men in the picture, maybe some of the others, had something to do with sinking the *Mary Justice.* A man who would take an oath—a man of integrity— wouldn't let this crime go unpunished." He held the picture up in front of him. "Now please, sir, tell me the names of the other men in this picture, and tell me as much about them as you can."

There was a momentary silence, but Baldridge remained adamant, unmoving, refusing to lift his gaze from McDaniel's face. Just when he was beginning to think he had reached a dead end, McDaniel slowly lifted his head and looked him in the eye.

"I was sworn to secrecy," he said.

"Oh, Father, tell someone! Perhaps Mr. Baldridge can help," the daughter blurted.

"Help what?"

The old man took a deep breath and let it out slowly. "During the war I worked with several of the men in this picture. As I said, two of them I've never seen before, but the others I know."

"Please go on," Baldridge said, stepping back and taking his chair.

"In October of eighteen and sixty-two, General Gabriel Rains in Richmond formed a special branch of the engineers called the Torpedo Bureau. He sent a Lieutenant Kennon to New Orleans to instruct me, Master Francis Ewing, and then-lieutenant Isaac N. Brown on how to emplace and operate submarine torpedoes. It was one of Kennon's torpe- does, a big ol' glass demijohn filed with a hundred pounds of powder and detonated with an electrical wire, that sank the *Cairo* in December of that year. Then we got the Federal gunboat *Baron DeKalb* in the Yazoo River in July of eighteen and sixty-three."

Baldridge confessed to being ignorant of torpedoes, so McDaniel explained how the devices worked. The old sailor told him of the various stages he, Kennon, and Ewing went through to perfect a design for underwater ordnance that would either destroy a ship upon impact or electrically detonate from the shore. McDaniel explained some of the failed designs, then told him in some detail how the bureau eventually came to use torpedoes on the *Cairo* and the *Baron DeKalb*. They loaded a hundred pounds of high-quality gunpowder into a glass demijohn three feet tall, twenty inches wide at its center. Using gutta-percha for a watertight seal, McDaniel explained, they either attached friction primers to the outside, or ran two pieces of thin platinum wire back to a shore battery. As soon as a Federal ship came over the torpedoes, they were detonated, tearing a hole in the belly of the vessel and usually sinking her in less than a minute. As he listened to the old man, Baldridge realized that what he knew of the wrecks of the *Mary Justice*, the *Mercury*, and the *T. H. Thorndike* was certainly consistent with the effects McDaniel described.

"And the men in this picture worked for you?"

"No. Just Curry. He was with us from the very beginning. But the others"—he pointed to the fourth and fifth men— "Bether and John Peyton, didn't come along until later. Bether and Peyton weren't in the navy."

"Then how did they come to work for you?"

Again McDaniel hesitated. He looked over at Baldridge. "If you are a Federal man, what I'm telling you could get me and a lot of good men hung."

"Mr. McDaniel, I'm not a Federal man. I told you who I am. All I want to do is find out what's happening on the river."

"The man I told you about earlier, Thomas Courtenay, was authorized in eighteen and sixty-four to set up a secret-service corps for torpedo warfare along the Mississippi." He spoke as if apologizing. "You have to understand, Mr. Baldridge, the war was going bad for the South. Well, you know, you were there. People were looking for any way to stem the tide."

"These were navy men?"

"No. And that's what's so dangerous. Later on in the war, these civilians came along, and Courtenay, he tried to control them, but he didn't have much luck. Curry and some of the others fell right in with them."

McDaniel stood up.

"Let me help you, Father," his daughter said.

"No, no. The cat's out of the bag now." With the aid of his cane, he moved to a roll-top desk and from the false bottom in a side drawer carefully removed a yellowed envelope. Settling back to his rocking chair, he handed it to Baldridge.

"This is a copy of a letter from Thomas Courtenay." He pointed his cane at Baldridge. "Now, mind you, Courtenay was a good man. He did his job during the war and he did it well. But like me, he was glad to see it end. The day of this picture, Courtenay would have no part in all that craziness they was talking. But that's what worries me."

"Why is that?" Baldridge asked, carefully lifting the letter from its envelope.

"Mr. Baldridge, me and Courtenay and most of the men I served with during the war did what we did because we were sailors. It was a war and we had a duty."

Baldridge unfolded the letter and glanced at it. "I understand that."

"But these civilians who came into this secret torpedo corps toward the end of the war, some of these men acted downright crazy—crazy enough to be involved in something . . . something awful. And without Courtenay there to keep them straight, well, I'm not sure what some of them might do."

"What did civilians have to gain by sinking Federal ships during the war?"

"Well, some might say they acted out of patriotism, but I know better. They did it for the bounty. The government in Richmond was paying them half the value of the ships they sank and the property they destroyed."

"But there's no bounty now," Baldridge said, looking up

from the paper. "Can you imagine why anyone would be involved in sinking commercial vessels now?"

"No. No, I can't. Unless, of course, somebody was still paying them."

While Baldridge read the letter the old man sat quietly and watched his expression.

Richmond, Virginia, January 19, 1864

My Dear Sir:

I met with much delay and annoyance since you left. The castings have all been completed some time, and the coal is so perfect that the most critical eye could not detect it. The President thinks them perfect, but Mr. Seddon will do nothing without Congressional action, so I have been engaged for the last two weeks in getting up a bill that will cover my case; at last it met with approval and will today go to the Senate, thence to the House in secret session. It provides the Secretary of War shall have the power to organize a secret-service corps, commission, enlist, and detail parties, who shall retain former rank and pay; also give such compensation as he may deem fit, not exceeding 50 per cent, for property partially and totally destroyed; also to advance, when necessary, out of the secret-service fund, money to parties engaging to injure the enemy. As soon as this bill becomes a law I have no doubt but I shall get a suitable commission and means to progress with, and that all the appointments you or I have made will be confirmed. I hope to be in funds very soon, for if the Government does not advance me, I have a most respectable gambler ready at any time to buy an interest and put up the money. It will be necessity that will cause me to make such an association, but how true is the old adage, "Any port in a storm." Keep me informed of your field operations and I shall contact you via special messenger when I have all matters arranged here.

Your friend,

T. E. Courtenay

"What's all this about coal and castings?"

"Just before I was reassigned from the torpedo service, the engineers in Richmond developed a 'coal torpedo.' They cast a hollowed-out block of cast iron to look just like a piece of coal. Inside they loaded about ten pounds of powder, then coated the outside with tar and coal dust. I saw one of them myself. You couldn't have told it from the real thing."

"To load it on board and burn in the boiler, right?"

"That's right. They made one from wood, too. As I recall, they stuck a sawed-off rifle barrel full of powder inside a hollowed-out piece of cordwood. Then they plugged the end and put the thing in the middle of a stack. Before you know it, some fireman's pitching a hot-loaded stick of wood into the boiler. The rest is easy to figure out."

"My God, Mr. McDaniel. If someone is using these contraptions, there's no telling how many people could get killed."

"That wasn't ever the purpose. None of these things were made to use against civilians."

"Mr. McDaniel, when you were in the navy did you ever encounter the Mississippi Marine Brigade under the command of a man named Ellet?"

"I ran up against them a couple of times. Why?"

"Can you think of any reason someone might be trying to get back at the men in that unit?"

"There's lots of reasons, Mr. Baldridge," McDaniel said. "A lot of people suffered at the hands of the Marine Brigade. But I can't imagine anyone still harboring enough of a grudge to be dangerous this long after the war. Besides, how on earth would anyone know who was in the Marine Brigade and who wasn't?"

"I'm not sure."

"Most of us are trying to put the war behind us and go on." McDaniel lifted the photograph and examined it again. "But I suppose it's possible that some men don't want to do that." He looked up. "Do you really believe all this is connected to the riverboats that have sunk?"

"Yes, I do." Baldridge took the picture back. "If the men from the torpedo corps wanted to sink a boat, would they still be able to build one of these torpedo things? I mean, would they have the knowledge and equipment?"

McDaniel shook his head. "Oh, yes. It wouldn't be hard. These men, particularly Curry, were good at their jobs."

"But I thought the Federals collected all the weapons and ammunition after the war."

"Well, they may have gotten the regular ordnance," McDaniel said, "but I doubt they knew a lot of this was around. And even if they did, they weren't likely to have gotten it all."

"Could a man like Curry put together a troup of ex–torpedo service men?"

"Not Curry. He was good with his hands, but Curry wouldn't be smart enough to carry off something like you're talking about."

Baldridge studied the letter. "But if not Curry, then who? Courtenay?" he asked, noticing how the old man's daughter began gently stroking her father's hair.

"Thomas Courtenay would have nothing to do with such a project," McDaniel declared. "I knew the man for twenty years, and—"

"Knew him?"

"Yes. Thomas died a little over six months ago—a hunting accident."

"Hunting accident, my foot!" his daughter said. Her eyes flashed. "He was murdered. I know it."

"Now dear, we don't know—"

"I know all I need to know," she said, taking her hand from his head. "Listen, Mr. Baldridge, it didn't exactly come as a surprise to my father that you showed up here today."

"You were expecting me?"

"No, not you in particular, but we knew someone would be coming. Actually, I'm quite relieved it's you—if you're who you claim to be. My father wanted no part of this lunatic scheme," she said, speaking rapidly. "He told them to go to hell. He told them to leave him be—"

"Now dear—"

"What scheme?" Baldridge asked.

"Mr. Courtenay was a friend of our family for a long time. I'd known him since I was a child. Then, about six weeks before his so-called accident, he wrote my father a letter. He

explained how he had been approached by some of the men
in his old unit—how they wanted him to help them—"

"Dear, you mustn't—"

"Oh, yes, Father. I certainly must!" she said, kneading her
fingers into his shoulders. "They wanted Mr. Courtenay to
help them in some devious scheme, but he would have none
of it. He told them the same thing my father did, and look
what they did to him! My father's next. I'm sure of it, Mr.
Baldridge. I'm sure of it. I tell you, not a day passes that I
don't expect someone to show up at our door—"

"I'm an old man, Mr. Baldridge," McDaniel interrupted,
"and my daughter fears too much for my well-being."

"Father, it's true! There's no point in hiding it anymore.
If Mr. Baldridge meant to do you harm he would already have
done it." She turned back to Baldridge. "The only reason I
can think of that they haven't come for him is his health.
Perhaps they believe he can't hurt them now. Perhaps they're
just waiting for him to die." The daughter became increasingly agitated; her voice broke as she described the fear they
had lived in over the past several months. The old man sat
quietly while she talked, occasionally adjusting the blanket
on his lap.

"Father still clings to his misplaced code of silence," she
said. "Why, you're the first person he's ever told. Father was
afraid to go to the authorities. With the Federal government
just looking for illegal veterans' groups, a lot of good people
could have gotten hurt. Decent men doing nothing wrong,
and with no ax to grind against the Yankees, would have
been rounded up and—and—God knows what would have
happened to them."

Finally, Baldridge knelt on his good knee, the photograph
in one hand and the letter in the other, and spoke to
McDaniel in a careful, measured tone. "Mr. McDaniel, I
understand why you, as a sailor in the Confederate States
Navy, would want to keep your word to another sailor. And
I respect you for that. But judging by the story you've told
me, and by what your daughter is saying, I think you know

as well as I do that the people involved in sinking the *Mary Justice* aren't sailors. They're not operating under the rules of war. They're renegades, sir. They're murderers taking the lives of innocent people either for money or out of some crazy notion of continuing the war."

The old man continued to rock gently, staring into space.

"Who, Mr. McDaniel? Who do you believe could finance and control such an operation?"

McDaniel rocked.

"It's not like it was when you sank the *Cairo*. That was war. People were supposed to get killed." Baldridge pointed in the direction of the window. "When one of these boats sinks, innocent people die, sir," he said softly. "Young women like your daughter, young children."

A tear crept down the old man's right cheek.

"Father, for God's sake, if you know anything, tell him!"

Baldridge held the photograph before him. "Is it one of the men in this photograph?"

McDaniel lowered his gaze and shook his head.

"Who then, sir?" Baldridge glanced at the letter again, studying the second page attached. "There must be forty names on this list of agents, from all up and down the river. Mr. McDaniel, it would take two years to track all these people down. We don't have that kind of time."

"Father, please!"

"The gambler," he whispered, almost in spite of himself.

"What gambler?"

"In the letter. The one mentioned in the letter."

Masey scanned down the page and read aloud. " 'For if the Government does not advance me, I have a most respectable gambler ready at any time to buy an interest and put up the money.' " He looked up at McDaniel. "This man? This is the one organizing it?"

"I'm not sure."

"But you think it could be?"

McDaniel nodded.

"Who is he and where can I find him?"

Speaking slowly and deliberately, McDaniel now made eye contact with Baldridge. "I didn't know who the man was myself until six months ago. He wasn't at the river when we made the picture. In his letter just before he died, Thomas Courtenay said he believed the man behind the scheme was Victor Burl."

"Victor Burl?" Baldridge repeated. "I met Burl. He was on the *Paragon* with me." He looked back at McDaniel. "Why Burl?"

"Mr. Baldridge, I don't know. I never met this Burl fella. Thomas dealt with him for money to finance the operation, but that was toward the end of the war, when I wasn't much involved anymore. I wouldn't know the man if I saw him."

"Can I keep this letter?"

"Please, Mr. Baldridge," he said, reaching to take it back. "There's good men on that list. Men who never did anything wrong. Men with families and children trying to rebuild their lives. If this falls into Federal hands, I'll be responsible for the result." McDaniel's hand was quivering as he grasped the page, with Baldridge still holding the other end. "Find this Burl man. Find Curry and stop him. Stop all of them. But please," he said, tugging on the page, "please don't destroy the lives of decent people."

Reluctantly Baldridge released the letter. When he looked up at McDaniel's daughter, she was crying.

"Help us, Mr. Baldridge. Stop these men before they come after my father."

"I'll try, ma'am." He slipped the photograph into his inside pocket and spoke to McDaniel. "Thank you, sir." As he turned to leave, McDaniel grasped his wrist with a grip that hinted at the tremendous strength the old man must have possessed in his youth.

"We did what we had to do, Mr. Baldridge," he said, his watery eyes beseeching. "We did what we had to do."

"I know, Mr. McDaniel," Baldridge said with a smile. "And you did the same thing today."

As he left McDaniel's home, Baldridge put it all together.

He recalled that night on the *Paragon,* when Burl had made such a scene over the singing. He seemed bitter, all right, but certainly not bitter enough to do something like this. And where was the money in it? If he had learned anything about Burl that night on the boat, it was that the gambler jealously guarded his money. Why would he bankroll something like this? What could he hope to gain? And if he was right, why target only the Marine Brigade?

He figured if Burl was involved, there was a good chance he might still be in Natchez; perhaps Curry could be the key to finding him. Baldridge would stop at the Pollock House for some supper, then start hitting the hottest gambling spots at Natchez-Under-the-Hill. As he rode toward the hotel, he removed his flask and took two quick sips. That would have to hold him for tonight. There was too much to do; besides, returning to the hellhole along the river required a clear head if he planned to get out alive. He resolved not to even buy the first drink.

▽

11

STANDING IN THE center of the five-piece brass band, the tuba player wiggled his fingers in between notes to keep his knuckles from stiffening in the chilly November air. His music left the stage of the gazebo and floated along the dock at Visitor's Point Wharf, delighting a growing crowd of onlookers who had braved a whipping wind to view the start of the race. In the last two days, the contest had been the talk of St. Louis, and news of the pending race had appeared in the Louisville *Courier-Journal*, the Cincinnati *Gazette*, and even the New Orleans *Picayune*. Excitement and anticipation swelled as the clock in the gazebo neared one. By agreement with the Merchants Association, Luke stood near the gazebo, waiting for Mr. Garrett.

"I can't believe you're making this run," one citizen said. "Can't say anybody's ever raced under these river conditions."

"What's the river stage?" another asked. "Four feet? Couldn't be much more."

"That Haskins has a mighty fast boat," one man had warned Luke. As if he needed to be reminded.

"Step over here, Captain Williamson," a skinny little man begged him. "This fella wants to shoot your picture." Luke really didn't have time for a picture, but he was supposed to make the most of the publicity for the event, so he agreed. While the man was making the photograph, Luke saw Creed Haskins arrive amid a throng of locals congratulating him on what they fully expected to be a runaway victory. The *Paragon* was a nice boat, they reasoned, but the reputation of the VanGeer Shipping Line was enough to convince most people that the *Paragon* would simply be outclassed.

"I'm not racing the whole line," Luke reminded one vocal gentleman, "just one boat."

Once the photographer had finished with Luke's photo, he stepped out from under the black cloth cover, and seeing Haskins nearby, called to him.

"Captain Haskins! Captain Haskins! Do you suppose we could get a picture of the two of you?" As Haskins approached, Luke started to walk away, but he ran into Garrett.

"Good day, Captain Williamson."

"Mr. Garrett."

"Uh, Captain? Captain Williamson!" the photographer called. "Could we get a group picture? The two captains and you, Mr. Garrett."

Luke shook his head, but Garrett grabbed his arm.

"It's good advertising, Luke. We can all use some of that."

Luke reluctantly stood on one side of Garrett while Haskins stood on the other; the photographer took their picture, while the crowed pressed closer to the base of the gazebo.

"Great!" the photographer said. "Now can we get one of the two captains shaking hands?"

"This is bullshit," Luke said, turning to walk away.

"Captain," Garrett said, "please . . ."

Luke chewed on his lower lip and stared at Haskins, who returned his glare.

"Captain?" Garrett said again, beseeching Luke with his eyes.

Reluctantly, Luke stepped in front of Garrett and took Haskins's outstretched hand. He would have liked to do the nasty deed and pull away, but the photographer needed time.

"Hold it. Hold it steady there," the man shouted from beneath his cloth head cover.

Luke felt Haskins squeezing his hand harder and harder.

He responded by tightening his grip in return. Neither man spoke; they eyed each other, unsmiling. By the time the photographer was satisfied, Luke could feel the knuckle at the base of Haskins's little finger giving way under the pressure.

"Okay, got it!" the photographer said.

Luke pulled his hand away and stepped back.

"Gentlemen," Garrett said, in a grand elocutionary style directed more to the crowd than to the captains, "on behalf of the St. Louis Merchants Association, Carlton Distillery, Roman's Grain Cooperative, and the St. Louis Cotton Exchange . . ." He paused to ensure that the advertisement had time to sink in. " . . . I want to wish you both the best of luck in the race to New Orleans." Garrett turned to the band and cued it. "And may the best boat win!"

As the crowd cheered, the band struck up "The Year of Jubilee," and Luke immediately began weaving his way through the crowd to the landing stage of the *Paragon*. Ladies called out their best wishes, gentlemen slapped him on the back, and children tried to reach out and shake his hand. As he reached the landing stage, he cast a knowing glance at Jacob Lusk, who stood in the middle of the walkway, arms folded, looking stern. Jacob shook his head as if he were already weary of it all, and stepped aside to allow Luke to pass.

"Sho' is lots of foolishness, ain't it, Cap'n?"

"Sure is, Jacob," he said in passing. Luke stopped at the boat end of the landing stage when he heard seven or eight of his roustabouts begin to sing along with the band.

Their voices were strong and full, and they immediately drew the attention of the crowd along the dock. And as they sang, many of the onlookers joined in for what was fast turning out to be an endorsement of the *Paragon*'s plucky challenge to the mighty VanGeer Shipping Line. Luke turned to the shore, watched and listened to the voices for several moments, then lifted his hat to the crowd, bringing forth a roar of applause. He glanced over at Jacob.

"You put this together, didn't you?"

Jacob smiled.

Luke nodded and waved again to the cheering crowd. "Where'd you find these singers?"

"I editioned from the crew," Jacob said with a broad, toothy grin.

"You what?"

"Editioned them myself, Cap'n. I figured we ought to start this here race off right."

Luke glanced around him at the rest of the roustabouts, who were lined up on the second deck, waving, singing, dancing, and calling out to the line of well-wishers along the dock.

"Huh," Luke mused. "I don't think I've ever seen deckhands that happy before. They seem really excited to be in the race."

Jacob paused a moment, then looked away from Luke and waved at the crowd himself. "I 'spect they're more excited about the double wages they're gettin' for this trip."

The smile vanished from Luke's face as he looked over at Jacob.

"Now, don't even say nothin', Cap'n. We was lucky to even find hands who would make a run like this."

"Well," Luke said thoughtfully, as he watched the enthusiastic workers, "I guess we can afford that." He put his hat back on and started down the deck. "At least the cabin crew won't be getting double pay."

"No sir," Jacob called out after him, lowering his voice a little. "They be gettin' a tad more." Jacob turned and quickly shouted to one of the roustabouts near the bow. "Bring in the stage. We headin' for New Orleans."

For the past two days Steven Tibedeau had been working until late in the night to accommodate the many last-minute travelers who wanted to be a part of the race. Jacob Lusk had been driving the deck crew fifteen hours a day to store the cargo for the journey. After preparing to shut them down for the season, Ham had suddenly been asked to clean and refit the engines for one more passage south. And instead of cleaning the stoves and storing the nonperishables until spring, Anabel had quickly prepared new menus, bought supplies on two days' notice, and begun preparing to feed the passengers in the grand style that the Paragon's name demanded. As he ascended the stairs to the pilothouse, Luke realized what he had put his crew through, and he knew Jacob was right about the pay. Winning this race would depend more on them than it would on him, and he resolved that if he won—when he won—he would find an appropriate way to make it up to them. Luke smelled the rosin-rich mixture Ham had force-fed the boilers to create the characteristic twin black, billow clouds of a departing steamboat. The black smoke was all for looks; once they hit the channel, Ham would have those boilers white-hot and burning clean with cordwood. Martin in the pilothouse was now laying on the steam whistle in a battle of blasts with the Apollo that whipped the crowd into near frenzy. And with each step up toward the texas, Luke bathed in the music from the shore, and the voices of the singers, and the lonesome squall of the whistle. From the deck he felt the rumble and shutter of the twin engines far beneath him—awaiting only his signal and Ham's sweep of a lever to engage the huge paddle wheel at the rear.

His heart began to pound, and a warm sensation traveled through his body. Every breath felt fresh. He'd never felt more alive. When he reached the door of the pilothouse, he turned and looked out at the crowd. The clock on the gazebo said two minutes to one; he could see the gunners readying the cannon. On the deck below him, Jacob stared up at the pilothouse, awaiting his order to release the lines. Martin peered from inside the window of the pilothouse, his hand on the speaker tube, ready to instantly relay the command to Ham in the engine room. The *Paragon* trembled beneath Luke as if she were a chained beast ready to break free and dash into the wilderness. In that moment he knew, more than ever before in his life, why a river man was all he would ever be.

At the cannon's blast, the *Paragon*'s huge wheel churned the brown water into a froth as she backed away from the dock amid the cheers of the crowd. Luke watched quietly as Martin, occasionally glancing at him for approval, shouted orders through the speaking tube. Luke would keep his mouth shut, at least for a little while. It was a long way to New Orleans, and Martin needed to know Luke believed in him. For several minutes he just stood and watched out the window of the pilothouse, knowing that Martin was struggling to make all the right moves. Luke also knew what Ham was going through in the engine room. It was a hot, squalid, nasty job, with a dozen things to do at once and no one to note how well you did them; you were noticed only if something went wrong. Luke could picture him down there, sweating through his shirt, checking the gauges, shouting instructions to the boiler crew, and in all likelihood, cussing the captain. Fortunately for Luke, the big end of the voice tube was in the pilothouse, saving him from Ham's blistering blue phrases. But after all the noise, and all the complaints, and maybe a threat or two, Ham would come through. He always did. He was the best, and he handled those engines as if they were a beautiful woman.

"You got to warm 'em up if you want 'em to put out, Captain," Ham liked to say. "And when she's had all she can stand, you've got to let her blow off some steam or she'll damned near kill you."

The *Paragon* and the *Apollo* were side by side as they raced south, with first one boat, then the other, inching ahead. No more than fifty yards separated the speeding steamers, and the passengers had lined their decks and were screaming challenges back and forth across the water. Satisfied that Martin was taking the best angle on the channel, and forgetting his vow to remain quiet, he offered some instructions on how to handle the jetty up ahead, then left the pilothouse and went down to cabin level.

"We're gonna get 'em, Captain!" one of the passengers yelled.

"The *Paragon*'s bound to win, you know." another offered. "We're counting on you, Captain Williamson."

Luke nodded and smiled and thanked them for their confidence. He walked the deck, searching the crowd for a familiar face. With all the publicity, he fully expected to see some of the regulars. A reporter from the St. Louis *Democrat* was scribbling something on a pad, and there were a number of wealthy-looking couples already sipping mint juleps and placing bets on what time they would get to New Orleans. Seeing Luke, one man left the others momentarily and tried to quietly pump him for some inside information. Luke dodged his questioning as gracefully as possible and continued along the deck. The notion of gambling brought to mind Victor Burl; Luke was glad the gambler had not booked a return from Natchez. That troublemaker was one headache he did not need on this trip. Too bad for Burl, though; with all the money waiting to be taken among these passengers, the man could have made a killing.

One face, or body, he did recognize was that of Salina Tyner, who was talking to Steven Tibedeau near the gentlemen's cabins.

"Making another trip so soon, Miss Tyner?" Luke said as he stepped up beside Steven.

"Good afternoon, Captain," she said with a wide smile. "This is an unexpected pleasure. I thought you would have your fingers dug into the wheel and sweating to pull us ahead of that nasty ol' *Apollo*."

"That's what I pay my pilot good money to do."

"I understand. Good money will get you all kinds of things." She eyed him discreetly. "All kinds of wonderful things."

"Well, I'm glad you chose to ride with us," Tibedeau said.

"Oh, I don't care for the *Apollo*. Creed Haskins doesn't treat me as nice as your captain does." She looked at Luke again. "And I find this boat so much more entertaining."

Jacob Lusk approached the group from the front of the boat. "Afternoon, Miss Tyner."

"Good afternoon, Jacob."

"You wanted to see me, Captain?"

"Yes, yes I did. You and Steven join me in my cabin for a few minutes." Luke tipped his hat to Salina. "If you'll excuse us, Miss Tyner . . ."

"Of course, Captain."

Once in the cabin, he sat both men down and explained his suspicion about VanGeer's role in the wreck of the *Mary Justice*. They listened intently as he shared what he had learned of the wreck, what Masey Baldridge had told him, and finally, what he feared most about this trip.

"I think they'll try something. I don't know when or how, but I'm sure they won't risk us winning this race."

"I don't see how they could do that short of rammin' us, Cap'n," Jacob said. "And then they'd be liable to bust up their own boat, too."

"VanGeer's smart. He wouldn't try something that obvious. He's got somebody on this boat. You can bet on it. There's somebody he's planted either in our crew or among the passengers . . . somebody to sabotage our run."

Steven pulled a passenger manifest from his leather case. "Captain, we've got more than a hundred and twenty passengers on board." He glanced down the list. "There's no way to know if any of them are mixed up with VanGeer."

"The deckhands I hired come from all over, Cap'n. Like I told you, I was lucky just to find enough men to run with. Ain't no way to know who might be up to somethin'."

Luke sat down on the edge of his bunk. "I know it's not easy. I know there are a lot of people on board. But we've got to keep our eyes open. We've got to be looking for anybody doing anything strange—anything out of the ordinary. People hanging around the engine room, or straying around the paddle wheel, or showing up near the pilothouse."

"Like your insurance man did on the last run?" Jacob said.

Luke laughed. "Yeah, Jacob. Like that."

"He was right about the brandy, though," Jacob added.

"The what?"

"Oh, just somethin' he said."

"Well, he's wrong about what happened to the *Mary Justice,* and he ought to be up here with us. But he's not, and that's neither here nor there. It's VanGeer we have to be concerned with. He's not going to settle for losing this race. This is his chance to get rid of us. He's not going to miss it."

"We'll be watching, Captain," Steven said.

"See to it that you do. And I want to know about anything you see that makes you suspicious. Anything. Got that?"

"Yes, sir," Jacob said.

"Yes, sir," Steven echoed.

"Leave me that passenger list. I want to take a look at it for myself."

"Yes, sir," Steven said, placing the list on Luke's desk.

Luke looked first at Steven, then at Jacob. "This is it, men. There won't be a second chance for the *Paragon* if we don't get to New Orleans first. We've been running this river together too long to give it up. We've been through too much. You're just like me. You need this river like you need your next breath." Luke swallowed hard. "And I don't want any of us to quit breathing anytime soon."

$\triangledown$

12

WITH A FIERCE backhanded blow, Jacob Lusk sent a mulatto roustabout tumbling over a whiskey barrel and crashing into the cabin wall. Out of the darkness where he'd landed, the broad, muscular man came diving at Jacob, wrapping his arms around him and forcing him to the deck. Several of the other deckhands stepped back to avoid the two as they rolled in the narrow space between the cotton bales. Trying to hold Jacob down and punch him in the face, the roustabout, several years Jacob's junior, took a sweeping blow to the right side of the head and bounced against a cotton bale. Struggling to his knees, Jacob grabbed the man by the hair and pulled his head down, slamming his face into the deck. Dazed, but still unwilling to quit, the roustabout lifted himself from the floor and flailed wildly, his fists falling short as the first mate held him just out of reach. In desperation, the man rolled over, screaming in pain and leaving Jacob holding only a handful of his hair. Again he rushed, but this time Jacob rose to his feet and stepped aside, giving the deckhand a healthy shove as he passed. He fell into a crowd of other deckhands who were whistling and shouting and encouraging the fracas. With the noise getting louder, and the deckhand getting more and more desperate, Jacob knew he had to end it soon. As the man pulled himself free of the crowd, Jacob drove his boot into the back of his leg, sending him to his knees. Then, wrapping his massive bicep around the man's throat, he asked him a question.

"I'm gonna ask you one more time, boy. Do you want to work on this boat and follow the rules, or do you want to breathe your last right here and now?" Every second the man struggled against him, Jacob flexed his arm more tightly around his throat, until the roustabout, seeing the futility of the struggle, managed to choke out a few words.

"Yes . . . sir," he grunted. Yes . . . sir . . . I do what you says."

Jacob maintained his grip. "Are you gonna touch my whiskey barrels again?"

"No, no," he choked out. "No . . . sir."

And tighter Jacob flexed.

"Am I gonna have any more trouble out of yo' black ass?"

The man was nearly unconscious by now, his hands hanging limp at his sides, as the crowd of deckhands watched in silence. Jacob leaned over and looked into the man's face. Seeing his eyes roll back in his head, he said, loudly enough for the others to hear. "Well, I take that to mean no." When he released him, the deckhand slumped to the floor, his hand moving slowly to his throat as he struggled to breathe.

Jacob eyed the deckhands around him, most of whom were men he had hired in the two days prior to the run. The last thing he wanted to do was make a trip as dangerous as this one with a crew thrown together at the last minute. Without a chance to screen the men he'd hired, Jacob wasn't exactly surprised to find some thugs in the crowd. But now, before the river got bad and he didn't have time to be looking over his shoulder, he had to show them who was boss, and he could leave no doubt as to what would happen should they step out of line. He waved his arm in front of them, pointing toward the half-lit faces that peered back at him from under the deck.

"Any of you other men got ideas about stealing whiskey?" The men stood quietly. The music from the dining room above filtered down on the night air and merged with the slosh of the paddle wheel as Jacob waited for his answer.

" 'Cause if you do," he said, pausing for their attention, "then I got somethin' for you." After several moments with no reply, Jacob glanced down at the man still lying at his feet. "A couple of you men take care of him. And in case he should forget, be sure you tell this nigger how close he come to seein' Jesus tonight." As he walked off in the darkness, Jacob realized it was going to be that kind of a voyage.

"I'm too damned old to be settlin' things like this," he grumbled, rotating his shoulder to ease the pain from the dumping he'd taken on the deck. But that was the price he paid for having to throw together a crew. If he'd known—but who would have dreamed they'd be going out again? By the time he found out the captain had agreed to this race, he'd already cut most of the men loose for the season and they had scattered to the winds. That Captain Luke would even consider making such a run surprised him—and yet it didn't. That was the captain.

"That man don't cull nothin'," he mumbled as he walked toward the stairwell near the bow. One thing was for sure. There was no other man Jacob would have dared to run with under these conditions. Not only would most boats not be on the river, they sure wouldn't be moving at night in such low water. That was what made him so mad about this disturbance—it took time away from what he should have been doing: watching the river from the bow and managing the sounding crew. There was no telling what they would run up on. He only hoped he'd gotten the message through to the others.

That Captain Williamson expected a difficult run was clear. Jacob had already seen more of him in the first day of travel than he usually saw the whole trip. If he wasn't down below asking Ham about the engines, he was wandering among the deckhands and inspecting the cargo. Jacob had never seen Luke behave like this. Although the captain was always interested in the work on deck, this time he was getting on Jacob's nerves. Maybe some of the hired men weren't the best available, but Jacob had the situation under control and he'd just as soon the captain not stick his nose in his business.

Late Monday afternoon Jacob found Luke standing near the bow, shadowing the men on the lead line and watching the *Apollo* churn water not more than a quarter mile ahead. When he raced, Luke always liked to lay back and let the other boat break water. Often the opponent would find the sandbars the hard way, and when he slowed to find a bypass, Luke would order the boilers double-fired and slingshot past the competition on some near-invisible channel he had committed to memory on the previous trip. But as Jacob leaned against a support beam under the overhang of the second deck, he couldn't recall ever seeing the captain so nervous.

"Three fathoms," one of the sounders sang out toward the pilothouse.

Jacob moved up behind Luke.

"She's stayin' up real good, Cap'n."

Luke nodded, but his face reflected concern. They were a little more than two hours out of Memphis, and Jacob knew Luke was thinking about Council Bend up ahead. On the last trip they had cleared this sandbar with no more than three feet to spare. With any more silt buildup, and with the water still dropping, it was bound to be a tight squeeze.

"Are the spars all set?" Luke asked, referring to the long poles mounted upright near the nose of the boat.

"Yes, sir. I checked 'em myself."

Luke eyed the crewmen nearby. "Do they know what to do?"

Jacob tried to reassure Luke, all the while wondering himself how the men would handle the challenge up ahead. He hated grasshoppering, the long, arduous technique for working across a shoal or a sandbar too shallow for the draft of the riverboat. Using the spars like giant legs, the men drove them into the sandy bottom on each side of the boat once the craft went aground. Then, as the engines drove the paddlewheel in a burst of power, the bow would actually lift up out of the water, sending the craft lurching forward on its two wooden "legs," settling back into the water several feet ahead. The process was repeated as often as necessary to clear the shallow stretch and regain the channel. The passengers frequently enjoyed the whole effort—provided, of course, it wasn't conducted during mealtime—but for Jacob it was pure drudgery. After talking with Luke for a while, Jacob heard the man on the lead line calling "mark twain," a twelve-foot depth of water. He stepped up to monitor his soundings as Luke shouted up for Neely, the night pilot, to bring her over to the far right of the channel.

"Quarter less twain," sang the sounder moments later.

"Quarter less twain," Jacob echoed up to Neely in his rich, bass voice. Ten and a half feet: They were fast approaching the sandbar. Anticipating Luke's next order, Neely slowed the *Paragon* to half speed. Jacob sent four deckhands to bring the yawl forward, and ordered two others to prepare the candles and bobbing boards. It was fully dark now, with only a tad more than a half-moon floating on the horizon; and straining to monitor the water ahead, Jacob figured the next couple of hours would be tough. While the *Paragon* made for the right side of the channel, the *Apollo* had moved left; and Jacob knew that a wide sandbar, more than a thousand feet across, lay hidden only a few feet beneath the steady current at Council Bend. During high water, the bottom was subject to arbitrary shifts with the current; with the river low, the bar would remain constant—it would just be closer than ever to the surface. Jacob wasn't surprised when Creed Haskins veered left; that approach offered a deeper, though less direct, passage back into the regular channel. And he knew Luke would take the riskier route to the right, which, if negotiated successfully, would allow him to overtake Haskins. So after calling instructions to the hands, Jacob made a quick survey of the deck. So far, the chill of the night air was keeping most of the passengers inside and out of the way, but that was likely to change as soon as they realized what was happening. The last thing Jacob needed was some half-tipsy planter tumbling into the river right in the middle of the passage. There would be no room to turn the boat around, and that meant stopping the engines and backing up to get him. Such a fool would be lucky if Captain Luke didn't kill him. Between listening to the sounders and studying the water ahead, he occasionally stole a glance to his left to see if the *Apollo* was slowing. Some eight hundred yards on the far side of the river and slightly farther south, Jacob could see the lights on Haskins's boat twinkling across the dark water. Judging from his location, Haskins would be hitting the most shallow part of the river any minute now. *Maybe he'll get stuck,* Jacob thought.

"One fathom!" a lanky black man sang out as he retrieved the measuring rope and held it up for Jacob, noting where the water had met the first knot.

"We got six feet, Cap'n," Jacob shouted to Luke, who by now had positioned himself on a cotton bale where he could observe the action. Neely heard the call up in the pilothouse and instantly slowed the boat. When the men arrived with the rowboat, Jacob ordered them to lower it. Motioning for the men with the candles and bobbing boards to climb over the side and into the craft, he started to follow them, then paused a few feet from Luke. "Sho' wish there was another way, Cap'n."

Luke glanced over Jacob's head in the direction of the *Apollo.* "They're going to have to do it, too." He looked down at Jacob. "We'll just do it faster, won't we?"

"Ain't nothin' to it, Cap'n."

The *Paragon* had now come to a full stop and was drifting slowly forward with the current as Jacob climbed into the rowboat and ordered the hands to row out ahead of the riverboat. Twenty or thirty feet in front of the paddle wheeler, one of the hands began checking the depth with a long pole, while another lit a candle, placed it in a treated paper bag, and attached it to a board tied with a six-foot rope and anchor. Every five to ten feet, all the way across the sandbar, Jacob would locate a minimum depth of five and a half feet and mark the channel with the floating lights, while the *Paragon*, under Neely's careful hand and the practiced eye of Luke Williamson, would creep along the path of candle-light. Every ear on deck would be straining to hear the gravelly scrape of the river bottom clawing at the boat as she passed over. Although he'd gone through the drill dozens of times in the past fifteen years, Jacob couldn't help but feel nervous tonight. Captain Luke had made it plain: If they didn't get to New Orleans ahead of the *Apollo*, Jacob would be looking for a job. And nobody but Captain Luke was hiring colored first mates. The notion of going back to working the decks for another man almost made him sick to his stomach. Sitting at the lead end of the boat, Jacob spat tobacco juice into the watery darkness.

"Boy, you better get that light in the water and quit playin' around," he snapped at one of the men in the rowboat. "We gotta get finished and get on through here." Jacob peered into the darkness. "Why, you're Anabel's boy, ain't you?"

"Yes, sir."

"You ain't got no business out here. How come—"

"They—they just called for somebody," the boy protested, "somebody to bring the yawl forward, Mr. Jacob. I was there, so I come."

Glancing to the east, Jacob noted that the *Apollo* now appeared to have stopped as well. "You see that boat over yonder, boy?"

The young black man fumbled to light another candle, which revealed his wide-eyed, frightened stare.

"Yes, sir, I see it."

"You other men see that boat? You see them lights out front? You see them men doin' what we're doin'?" he asked.

They did.

"Well, just you be damned sure them little lights over there don't get far enough ahead of us that I can't see 'em without turnin' my head. You understand?" Jacob spat again over the side. " 'Cause if I got to turn my head, I'll have to lighten this here boat."

For almost an hour they worked in the darkness, lighting a serpentine course over the sandbar as the *Paragon* followed some forty feet behind. At last they reached a sounding of four feet—a shoal around which Jacob and his men could find no bypass—and the horrible notion that they might have to retrace their path burned in the back of the first mate's mind. What if he'd let Captain Luke down? What if he'd failed? The whole crew would suffer because of him. Frantically he ordered the oarsmen to move first right, then left, trying to find a deeper bypass; but for a stretch as wide as he dared to search, Jacob could find only a clearance of four feet, and sometimes as little as three, over the sandbar. Eventually he rowed farther ahead, and checking the depth again, he found the river bottom sloping back to a firm channel: five feet, five and a half, seven feet, then on to nine and ten. The channel was in reach. It was only fifty yards from the last safe sounding. He stood up in the rowboat, keeping his feet wide for balance.

"Hold this damned boat steady!" he shouted at the oarsman, looking first to the clear channel ahead in the darkness, then back at the stretch of water that lay unmarked between the rowboat and the last bobbing board that marked a good depth. The wind was flapping Jacob's collar and giving the oarsmen hell as they tried to hold the rowboat steady for the first mate to evaluate the situation. If they backed up they would lose two hours at least, retracing their route and beginning all over again to mark a new passage. On the other hand, they were facing a long stretch of sandbar at three, maybe four feet of water if they were lucky. In the distance Jacob could see Captain Luke standing on that cotton bale, pipe in hand, peering out in the darkness, waiting for his signal to move ahead. By now, many of the passengers, alerted by the slowing of the boat, had emerged on the hurricane deck to watch the action. He could hear the rumblings of their conversations across the water, and he could sense they were growing impatient. It was as if every passenger and crewman on the boat were looking at him.

Jacob lowered himself into his seat and spoke to the men.

"Mark the beginning of the clear channel with two buoy lights anchored a hundred feet apart at the seven-foot sounding."

The men quickly complied, and Jacob ordered them to return to the *Paragon*. As he climbed over the rail, Luke met him.

"What is it?"

"A shoal, Cap'n." He pointed toward the last of the regular marking lights. "See the last light? That's five feet. Past there she get down to four, maybe three in places."

"Damn."

"But on up ahead," Jacob added, "where I got the double lights, is the channel. It's smooth going from there on."

"How far?"

"Fifty yards, maybe sixty."

Luke studied the lights, looked toward the stern as if considering backing up, then, with a slight grin, turned back to Jacob. "Let's jump it."

"Ain't nothin' to it,' Cap'n." Jacob turned to the deckhands gathered nearby. "Lower those spars. On my order you'll make 'em fast to the bottom and stand by on those pulleys."

"What we gonna do, Captain?" a well-attired passenger called from the hurricane deck.

"Are we stuck?" another one yelled.

Luke looked up. "Not yet." He turned to Steven Tibedeau, who was standing near the stairs. "Get up there and get those passengers inside, and don't take no for an answer. I don't need them hanging from the rails while we do this. They can watch through the portholes."

"But, Captain, what'll I tell them?"

"I don't give a good goddamn what you tell 'em, Steven. Tell 'em they're throwing the boat out of balance, tell 'em they're catching wind out there, I don't care. Just get 'em inside."

"Yes, sir." Steven dashed off and Luke disappeared up to

the pilothouse to brief Neely. Meanwhile Jacob supervised the deckhands preparing the spars. Given that he'd never worked with some of them, their speed in setting up the rig surprised him. Maybe that extra pay was helping after all. Gradually they crept to the last of the safe-running buoys, and Jacob stood by awaiting the signal from Neely to plant the spars. As they attempted to move farther and the sounder sang out a depth of four feet, Jacob could feel the hull grinding against the bottom. He knew what was coming, so he ordered his men to brace for it. A quick scan of the upper decks revealed no gawkers standing by the rails, and he only hoped Steven had gotten all the passengers inside. With a cry from the steam whistle, the engines engaged the paddle wheels at full speed and attempted to drive the boat over the sandbar. She made a short distance before she was completely aground, only the paddle wheel and the aft section of the riverboat resting at full draft. They were committed now. There was no backing up. They would either clear the shoal or sit there until the water rose, which could be a week or more. Ham and Neely had already had their shot. Now it was Jacob's turn. When Luke's signal finally came, Jacob lowered the huge wooden poles into the water on each side of the bow, burying their ends firmly in the river bottom. Securing the other end of the poles to a wooden brace that stuck upward at an angle from the deck, Jacob double-checked to ensure his men were in position.

"We're ready, Cap'n."

"Give it hell, Mr. Neely!" Luke shouted up to the pilothouse.

The paddle wheel began thrashing water behind the *Paragon*, slowly at first, then with increasing ferocity, until the bow began to lift out of the water and onto its wooden supports. Once the first twenty feet of the boat had cleared the river, Jacob could feel her moving forward, supported against the river bottom by the wooden spars, which gradually sank deep into the mud as they took the full weight of the craft slipping forward. Once the spars were vertical, the bow began to descend again to the surface, angling the wooden poles to the nose. Again she was aground, but now closer to the double lights that marked the awaiting channel. Twice more they repeated the process; each time the paddle wheel pitched up more mud and silt as it dug into the sandbar. On the fourth and final lift, the *Paragon* again settled on the shoal, this time within ten yards of the channel markers. Sensing an end to their hard work, the deckhands began cheering and shouting and urging her on.

"Lift again, Cap'n?" Jacob yelled toward the pilothouse, sweat pouring from his face and darkening the front and back of his shirt.

"I think not, Jacob. Let's see what Ham can do now."

Building steam pressure for some five minutes, and driving the paddle wheel until the whole boat shuddered as if it would come apart at the center beam, the boys in the engine room managed to generate enough force to begin sliding the boat along the sandbar, slowly at first, then with increasing speed, until at last, accompanied by a hearty cheer from the crew, the *Paragon* bolted from the grip of the river bottom and into the channel.

Luke Williamson shouted his gratitude to Jacob and the men and moved off into the crowd of excited passengers now pouring from the dining hall and cabins to congratulate the captain on his passage. Busy with the grasshoppering, Jacob had lost his watch on the *Apollo*, but when he spotted the craft in the distance, he could see the tiny navigation lights still dancing on the water in front of her, and he knew Haskins and his crew would be a while in completing the passage. He took a deep breath and let it out slowly. Running against the *Apollo*, they would need all the lead they could get.

Later that night, just before midnight, Jacob was still on the deck, supervising the crew. He had been up since three that morning, and with water conditions this bad and a crew he wasn't sure of, he would likely be up all night tonight. Settling back on a barrel of flour, he leaned up against the wall and closed his eyes for a few moments, allowing himself

to court sleep while listening to the calls of the crewmen on
the bow. No more than two or three minutes had passed
when he heard a rustling nearby.

"What is it?" he mumbled, turning to the figure beside him.

"Didn't mean to wake you, Jacob," came Anabel's soft
voice, as she placed a covered dish on the barrel beside him.
"It's just that you didn't come by for supper tonight, and
from what I heard up in the kitchen, I 'spect you had your
hands full."

"Evenin', Anabel."

"Here's something to eat."

Jacob reached in the dark and picked up the plate, his
hand touching hers, and pausing ever so briefly against her
soft, warm skin.

"Thank you, Anabel. We've had a right smart of work
tonight."

She ran her hand through her hair and looked out toward
the bow. "Is everything all right now?"

"I think so," he said, biting into a chicken leg. "Me and
the cap'n figure the channel will hold for a while now."

"Well, all the passengers are fed and most of 'em have gone
to their cabins," she said, "and I 'spect I'd best turn in pretty
soon myself. I really should be going." She appeared to be in
a hurry. "You enjoy your supper now."

As she turned to leave, Jacob called out to her.

"Anabel!"

"Yes?"

"Do you have to go just yet?" She looked at him in
puzzlement. "I mean, I've got to sit up and keep an eye on
these fellas. . . ."

Anabel chuckled. "Like the eye you was keeping on 'em
when I walked up?"

"Oh, I wasn't asleep. I was just restin' my eyes."

She smiled. "If you say so."

"I was just thinkin' that if you didn't have to go to bed
just yet, you might keep me company for a while. Not long,"
he quickly added. "I know you got to get up early and all."

"Well, I suppose I could stay for a little," she said with a grin, taking a seat on the barrel. "Jacob, I want to thank you for hiring my boy on for this run." Jacob nodded and continued to chew. " 'Cause you didn't have to do it."

"He's a good boy. A hard worker," Jacob confirmed, "like his mama."

"Well, he sho' is taken with you," she said. "He come by about an hour ago and couldn't say enough about how you tackled that sandbar back a ways."

"Come by the kitchen?"

"Yes."

Jacob frowned. "He's supposed to be working with Ham down below. He ain't got no business up in the kitchen."

"He may be your deckhand, Jacob Lusk, but he's still my boy. And when his mama sends for him, then he'd better come."

"You sent for him?"

"I sure did."

"What for?"

"To make sure he got his supper."

"Anabel, you can't be pullin' that boy off his job to—"

"Now, you just hush, Jacob. I fed you didn't I?"

"Well . . ."

"Then I can see to it my boy's fed, too." Jacob said nothing. "We gonna win this race, Jacob?"

"We'll win. We got to."

"That's what I'm hearing." She stood up and straightened her skirt. "You know, I just can't imagine working for nobody but Captain Luke. If he was to lose the *Paragon*, I just don't know what I'd do. I'm too old to be starting over again with another shipping line."

Jacob looked at Anabel intently. "That why we can't let him lose. We got to pull together. He needs all of us." He took her hand gently. "And we need each other." Anabel allowed him to hold her hand for several moments before she pulled away. She seemed somewhat embarrassed, and Jacob feared he might have offended her. He had surprised himself by the gesture, but in the moments she'd sat with him, he realized, perhaps for the first time, just how much having Anabel around meant to him.

"I'd better get back in," she said nervously. "Now, don't you stay up all night, Jacob. You need your sleep same as the rest of us." She smiled. "We can't have the first mate falling asleep on us when we need him."

"All right, Anabel."

"Well . . . good night, Jacob."

"Good night. And I thank you for the supper . . . and the company."

"You're welcome," she said, as she turned and moved quickly along the deck.

Late Tuesday afternoon Jacob informed Martin that firewood was running low and they would have to put in at King's Woodyard for resupply. He had hoped to stretch their fuel to Natchez, but it was too risky. King's Woodyard lay on the east side of the river across from Rosedale Landing, some nine river miles north of where the *Mary Justice* had gone down. A wood stop frequented by most steamers on the downriver jaunt, Kings employed a yard boss named Ike, whom Jacob had known for five years. With the *Apollo* fast making up the distance between them, he figured Ike would see to it they made a quick load.

Woodyards along the river were big business during the busy season, and King's was one of the few that continued to operate even during poor water conditions. Like most woodyards, King's cut timber well inland, bringing the product to the yard through a series of chutes and slides. To speed up the loading, King's had a flatboat tied to the landing where they cross-stacked the wood in four-foot lengths, standing eight feet high and eighty-four feet long. While it was Jacob's responsibility to have the crew standing by to transfer the wood, it was Steven Tibedeau's job to check the cords for the correct size and to negotiate the price. Jacob had slipped on the white silk cap identifying him to all as the boat's first mate and had lined his crewmen along the lower port deck in anticipation of snugging up against the flatboat. Tibedeau came up beside him.

"Looks like they're ready for us," Steven said. He tapped the floor with the eight-foot measuring stick he used to check the cords. Jacob nodded as Tibedeau continued. "You don't think they'd try to be slick today, do you?"

"I sure hope not," Jacob said, adjusting his cap to get just the right tilt. Tibedeau was referring to the practice some woodyards had of short-stacking the cords and trying to get away with charging full price. One and a half dollars a cord was reasonable, but only for a full-size cord, relatively free of crooked pieces. King's had usually been straight with the *Paragon*, but then Steven always checked meticulously. Sometimes his diligence frustrated Jacob, who just wanted to get the wood aboard and get gone; but Steven wouldn't be satisfied until he'd measured and eyed every cord.

Looking past the paddle wheel, Jacob saw the *Apollo* rounding Coles Point and coming up even with Mesopotamia Plantation; then he glanced at Tibedeau out of the corner of his eye. The man reminded him of a bantam rooster, his eyes constantly blinking, his head darting here and there; Jacob sure hoped he'd be strutting and pecking fast today.

The *Paragon* made fast to the flatboat; Ike and another man Jacob didn't recognize were standing by the stacked wood. Steven jumped the two or three feet from the deck to the loaded flatboat, followed quickly by Jacob and his crew. At Jacob's order the men stationed themselves in a relay line from the first cord to the riverboat, awaiting his signal to begin loading. Jacob listened as Steven talked with Ike and the other man, but he noticed that Ike, who was usually friendly, wouldn't look directly at him.

"I must've heard you wrong," Steven said to the man beside Ike. "Did I hear him right?" he asked Ike. Ike stirred nervously and didn't answer.

"You heard me," the man said.

Steven's eyes were flashing. "Five dollars a cord? You're out of your mind!"

"That's the price if you want wood here."

"Wood's never been more'n a dollar and a half a cord—a dollar seventy-five at the most—here." The man pointed at a crude sign hung on one of the nearby stacks.

"It's gone up."

"Since when?"

"Since it went up," the man said with a grin.

"Ike, what's going on here?" Steven asked.

"That's what the man says, Mr. Tibedoo. I—I can't rightly say no different."

"I want to see Mr. King."

"Mr. King ain't here," the man said.

Steven surveyed the stranger. "Who the hell are you? I've never seen you around here before."

"I'm helping Mr. King out."

Jacob kept looking upriver as the *Apollo* was now pulling alongside another flatboat loaded with fuel. The *Paragon*'s lead was evaporating while Steven haggled with the stranger; but he couldn't really blame the mud clerk. Five dollars a cord was robbery, no doubt about it. It was just that losing all this time was making his stomach do flips. He leaned over to Steven.

"I'm gonna start loadin' while you get this straight," Jacob whispered; then he gave his men the signal to begin the human chain.

"But I haven't checked the cords," Steven said.

Jacob pointed to the *Apollo* pulling up alongside the second raft. "We ain't got time."

The deckhands hadn't tossed a dozen pieces of lumber along their chain when the stranger shouted toward them.

"Get away from there!" He looked at Steven. "You get your boys away from that wood until you've paid for it. Once you've paid for it, you can load it. My men over there will even help you."

Jacob noticed three men standing at the end of the row of

wood. He didn't recognize them as the usual hands that King employed, but he figured with traffic on the river so scarce, King might have had to settle for what he could get, just as Jacob had in St. Louis. They certainly didn't have the husky build of the hands King usually had working the woodyard. One looked vaguely familiar and another was sporting a bandage on the side of his head, as if he'd been in a fight with a bobcat. But it was the man talking to Tibedeau who bothered the first mate most. He had that arrogant, uppity tone Jacob frequently heard from what he called white trash, and he kept looking at Jacob's hat as if to say a colored man had no business being an officer on a riverboat. Steven looked back at the deckhands, who had paused momentarily in the loading and were awaiting Jacob's instructions. Jacob looked at Steven, then at Ike. Ike still wouldn't meet his eyes.

"Well, what's it gonna be?" the stranger asked.

Steven left the man and walked back onto the boat while Jacob stood awkwardly awaiting instructions. Ike looked nervous, constantly glancing back at the shack where King normally oversaw the operation. And all the while the whistle on the *Apollo* kept reminding Jacob that the race was getting tighter.

Steven Tibedeau finally returned.

"The captain says he'll pay it," he said reluctantly, producing some gold coins from his pouch. After watching Steven count out enough to cover twenty cords, Jacob signaled the men to continue loading.

"My boys will make sure everything goes right," the stranger said, pointing to the men Jacob had been watching earlier. "Pleasure doin' business with you," he said with a tip of his hat; signaling for Ike to follow him, he headed back to the shack. As he turned to leave, Ike cast a worried glance at Jacob. On another run the mate might have stopped to talk, but now he had more than enough to do just getting the fuel aboard.

Forty-five minutes later, the deckhands climbed aboard in sweat-soaked shirts having completed the loading; with a moan from her steam whistle, and with her paddle wheel slapping the muddy water, the *Paragon* eased away from the nearly empty flatboat and made for the channel. Jacob had climbed to the hurricane deck and was watching King's Woodyard shrink in the wake of the paddle wheel. Ike had acted strange. And those other characters kept sticking their noses in Jacob's business, ordering him around and telling him which cord to load next. It was none of their business in what order he loaded the wood. What the hell difference did it make? And that vaguely familiar face kept troubling him.

Music from a band on the *Apollo* reached across the water to remind him she would not be far behind; several passengers on the *Paragon* had lined the deck below, jeering and shouting challenges at people on the *Apollo*. As Jacob leaned over the rail and looked down at the passengers, he thought how it was all just a game to them—a source of entertainment, something on which to wager, something for people with more money than sense to do with their time. It was election day, and while the rest of the country was electing a new president, these people didn't even care. They'd rather be aboard for a steamboat race, and they wanted to win only so they could say they'd ridden on the fastest boat. If they could only know what the race meant to him, to Captain Luke, to Steven and Ham and Anabel and the others.

Jacob stared at the lengthening stretch of water between him and the *Apollo*. Too bad he couldn't be like Old Man River and not care one way or the other. Old Man River'd be the same tomorrow as today, and next week and next year. He could swallow a boat whole and just keep rushing toward the sea, unmindful of the lives that he'd snapped up or changed forever. Nobody could see past his muddy surface, or know his soul, or tell him what to do. And just when you thought you had him tamed, he'd up and surprise you.

$\triangledown$

13

ASA TURNER PEERED out the back window of a room above the dress store just across from the Pollock House.

"They're all right," he said, referring to the two horses saddled and tied behind the building.

Baldridge yawned. "Keep checking on 'em," he said, still looking out the front window. The two men he observed on Franklin Street below tried to look nonchalant as they stood in the early-morning light, watching the Pollock House from the corner of Market Street. They were the same men he had seen at the studio the day the tintype was stolen, and he was sure one of them was Curry. Turner, his arm still in a sling and his clothes smelling like every bit of their three days' wear, came near and looked over Baldridge's shoulder.

"The man who broke your arm," Baldridge said, pointing to the street corner below, "was he one of those two?"

Turner pointed out Curry, as Baldridge raised the window a few inches to get some fresh air. He was grateful to have Turner around, but he just wished the man would stand a little farther away. It wasn't Turner's fault that he smelled so bad; he had, after all, been on the run since last Friday. That was the day Curry and two others, apparently believing Turner had been talking to Baldridge about the wreck of the *Mary Justice,* returned to the restaurant where he worked and tried to finish him off. But seeing them come through the front door of the restaurant, Turner left hoecakes frying on the stove and disappeared out the back. Curry and the others chased him down the alley behind the restaurant, firing a shot that ricocheted off a brick wall and passed close enough for Turner to feel the breeze. Ducking between two buildings, he dropped into a storm cellar to hide, but soon heard his pursuers banging away at the trapdoor. So he hurried up a staircase, and to the horror of the store owner, emerged in a dress shop and dashed into the street. The move succeeded in losing Curry and his men, but Turner doubted they would give up until they found him, so he slipped away to the heavily forested area north of Natchez known as the Devil's Punchbowl, where he hid out for three days. Uncertain whom to turn to, he remembered Baldridge's visit, and at dark on Monday evening he slipped into town to find him. Once at the Pollock House, he used a delivery wagon to shield him from view, and moved unobserved through the back door of the hotel. Hiding in a broom closet until well after midnight, Turner made his way up the stairs to Baldridge's room.

"You better have another look at them horses," Baldridge said, more to keep the smell away than anything else. When Turner moved to the other window, Baldridge glanced at him, thinking what a pitiful-looking man he was—all skin and bones. Most of the kitchen folks he knew were fat, and he wondered how Turner had managed to stay so little. He smiled. The man was lucky to be alive, not only with Curry's men after him, but because of the way he came creeping around his room the night before.

Baldridge had spent three hours that Monday evening fruitlessly searching the bars and gambling houses Under-the-Hill for Curry, until he returned to the Pollock House and went to bed. Recalling all too vividly his near-lethal bath, he made sure to lock the door; he even balanced a chair gently against the handle. Sometime before two A.M., his light sleep was interrupted by the telltale sound of the chair sliding against the face of the door. Sitting up in bed, he pulled his Bowie knife from beneath the pillow, threw the sheet back, and stood up. A half moon cast soft shadows throughout the room. Back against the wall, easing toward

the door, Baldridge watched the knob slowly begin to turn
again. He tiptoed past the door and anchored himself against
the wall nearest the door knob. Gripping the knife with his
right hand, he used his left to silently slide the bolt back
from the door facing; then, taking the handle in a near
caress, he instantly jerked the door open. The sudden action
brought Asa Turner partially into the room before he could
release the handle, so Baldridge slammed him against the
door frame and slapped cold steel against his throat.

Turner tried to speak. "Mr. Baldridge! Mr. Bald—"

Baldridge had pressed the knife hard against the man's
windpipe and was leaning in for a last look before he
completed the stroke, when in the moonlight he noticed the
slung arm and made out the terrified face of Asa Turner.
Pulling Turner into the room, he kicked the door shut with
his good leg and tossed the man across the bed.

"What the hell are you doin' skulking outside my room,
Turner?"

Lifting his hands to show he was unarmed, Turner began
to talk fast—too fast to follow; only after Baldridge put the
Bowie knife away did Turner calm down enough to be
understood. He explained how Curry, upon hearing that
he'd survived the wreck, searched all over Natchez until he
found him. After breaking his arm, he threatened to kill him
if he talked to anyone about what he saw. Turner told how
the men returned for him and how he got away; but what
intrigued Baldridge most was Turner's story of the *Mary
Justice*—the story he had been too scared to tell the day
Baldridge visited him at the restaurant.

He had been on the second deck that night, taking a break
from his duties in the dining room, when he heard the
deckhands near the bow yelling something up at the pilothouse. Turner remembered how they seemed desperate to
get Captain Smythe's attention. He confirmed that Smythe
was in the pilothouse, and that the *Mary Justice* had pulled
almost a mile ahead of the boat they had been racing that
afternoon. He verified that there was an explosion, but he

made it clear that the blast came from beneath the boat—somewhere near the bow, on the port side, as he recalled. The force sent him crashing against the cabin wall, and the ship began to list heavily to port. By the time he regained his feet, he felt a second blast; this one spewed water into the air from near the lifeboat mounted amidships and sent him tumbling into the cold, dark river. He recalled struggling to the surface and gasping for air, and he described how the blazing *Mary Justice* had listed to port and was sinking fast. Knowing that his only hope was to swim for shore, Turner had made it some hundred yards when he heard shots ring out in the darkness on the bank. Eventually reaching water shallow enough to stand in, he was slogging through the sticky mud when he heard another shot. It was too dark to tell what was happening, but he could make out motion on the bank and he could hear voices, so he eased down into the water. Glancing back toward the river, he saw that the riverboat was nearly gone, with only the texas, spitting flames toward the sky, extending above the surface. Soon he heard the hiss of the red-hot smokestacks kissing the water in a maritime death rattle as the rest of the *Mary Justice* disappeared below the surface. And then there was darkness—darkness and silence. But the silence was interrupted by more shooting on the shore, and he heard angry voices shouting back and forth. Cold and stiff remaining in the water, yet afraid of the gunplay, Turner forced himself to swim ten or fifteen feet back into the channel, where he began drifting with the current. After a few moments he located some debris from the wreck, and clasping it, drifted a little more than half a mile southward, where he went ashore at Grafton Plantation.

As he recalled Turner's story, Baldridge sat watching Curry and his companion. It was no wonder they'd come after Turner. Baldridge's search of the area by the river, coupled with his visit to Henry C. Norman, must have convinced someone that the river man had talked; and to judge by what he'd learned from McDaniel, these weren't the kind of men who'd allow anyone to know too much. They had, after all, managed to keep their torpedoes a secret for most of the war.

The men watching the Pollock House would eventually have to leave. Someone would take their places, and Baldridge had decided to see where the departing men would lead him. About eight o'clock in the morning he got his break. Two riders approached Curry and his companion and spoke with them for several minutes. They appeared to be arguing, with Curry growing increasingly angry and impatient. Eventually, one of the men dismounted and Curry took his horse. Then, after another heated exchange, Curry and the new rider moved out along Franklin Street and passed just under the window where Baldridge sat watching them.

"Let's go," he called to Turner, not bothering to lower the window, and the two men hurried down the back stairs, Baldridge hobbling well behind the other man, until they reached their horses and mounted up. Setting off at a gallop to follow Curry, Baldridge traveled the back alley paralleling Franklin Street; it wasn't until he had covered almost a city block that he realized Turner was lagging behind. Maneuvering his horse so he could see down Franklin, yet still keep out of sight, he motioned for Turner to hurry up. But Turner was clearly struggling to manage the horse Baldridge had rented for him with ol' Ferguson's money, and it took several seconds for him to come up alongside.

"What the hell's wrong with you?" Baldridge said. "We're gonna lose 'em if you don't keep up."

"I ain't real good on a horse, Mr. Baldridge," Turner said sheepishly.

"What?" Baldridge shouted.

With one hand holding the saddle horn in a death grip, and his knuckles white from squeezing the reins in the other hand, Turner averted his eyes. "I'm a dining room steward, Mr. Baldridge. I ain't never really spent much time on horseback."

His eyes darted down Franklin Street to keep Curry and

his comrade in sight; then Baldridge looked back at Turner.
"Why didn't you tell me you couldn't ride?"

"I didn't say I couldn't ride," Turner offered, his voice
shaking almost as much as his hands. "I just said—"

"Well, I ain't got time to be givin' you no lessons,"
Baldridge barked. "So I'll put it to you like this. You can
either lay back here and let those men at the Pollock House
find you, or you can ride with me." Turner had the same
look Baldridge had seen that night in the doorway of his
room. "You do what the hell you want to, but I'm going after
Curry." With those words, Baldridge eased on to Franklin
Street, checking quickly to his left to make sure Curry's
replacement hadn't seen him; then he began to shadow the
two riders at a safe distance. He had gone maybe a quarter
of a mile when he heard someone closing in behind him.
Afraid he might have been seen, he glanced back, to see
Turner bouncing clumsily in the saddle as he pushed his
horse to catch up.

"I'll . . . stay . . . with you . . . Mr. . . . . Baldridge," Turner
said between bounces.

Baldridge turned around and locked his eyes on Curry up
ahead.

"You learn real fast, Turner. Real fast."

Curry and his companion were heading out Pine Ridge
Road, the same route Baldridge had taken the day he went
to Bisland Bayou. But slightly over a mile outside the city,
and just past a creek, the two men took a wooded trail
leading southeast. Baldridge and Turner entered the woods
and paralleled the trail a safe distance behind. Calling upon
his wartime experience as a cavalryman, Baldridge wove his
mount through the undergrowth and easily outdistanced
Turner, who found every low-hanging branch a challenge.
For nearly eight hundred yards, he rode through the black-
jack woods, occasionally moving out to the road to sight the
men he was following. Finally, when he saw Curry and his
companion dismount near an elaborate Creole-style mansion, he also dismounted, tied his horse to a tree, and moved

forward on foot. Although he tried to keep his eyes on the men, Baldridge's attention kept returning to the plantation house that lay before him. Well back from the main road and nestled in a clearing among huge oaks and beech trees, the house was weather-worn and in need of repair, yet its elegance showed through the hard times it had seen. The lower level was brick, with a tunnel directly in the middle, surrounded by a double staircase that led to the main door, located on the second floor. The circular drive in front was overgrown and barely visible. Baldridge wondered how such a grand house could have fallen into disuse.

The sound of Turner breaking every twig in the forest as he approached snapped Baldridge out of the spell the old house cast over him, and he began waving his arms to stop the man. Turner looked at him incredulously, so Baldridge quietly moved into the woods to confront him.

"Get off the horse," he whispered in a tone leaving no room for Turner to disagree. Turner's awkward dismount made even more noise. "You've got to be quiet!" Baldridge scolded.

Turner began to protest. "I'm not used to this kinda thing, Mr. Baldridge. I—I don't—"

"Just shut up, Turner, and stay close to me." He took the man back to the edge of the clearing. "Do you know anything about this place?" Turner viewed the mansion for a few moments, then confessed ignorance.

"All right. All right," Baldridge whispered. "You stay here. I'm going around the edge of this clearing to get behind the place. Keep the horses quiet."

"Mr. Baldridge, I don't know how to—"

"Fine. Just stay here and don't make noise."

The rear of the mansion revealed what must have once been a stately courtyard, and it wasn't hard to picture the gardens that would have lined the aging brick walkway leading up to the back of the house. Two horses were tied near the back door; off to the right, out of view of his initial position in front of the home, was a large barn. The pressed grass leading from the double doors in front betrayed recent traffic, so using the huge oaks to shield his movement, Baldridge decided to get a closer look. The barn had no windows, only front and back doors; he tried the back. Slipping his knife from its scabbard, he paused and listened for voices; hearing none, he started to force his way in. He had almost lifted the two-by-four that barred the rear door when he heard a voice around the corner of the barn.

"I don't care if you *are* hungry," a man was saying, "I told you to stay out here and watch the barn. Curry's back and he's talking to Mr. Burl. They're liable to be out here any minute. If they find nobody watching the barn they'll skin both of us alive."

Fearing the guard might come around the corner at any moment, Baldridge pulled the board off its support and pulled the door open. Once inside, he checked quickly to make sure he was alone, but the building was dark, with only an occasional crack in the sideboards allowing light inside. Squeezing his hand through the gap as he pulled the door closed, he tried to slip the two-by-four back in place, but the angle was no good, and the board slipped from his hand and fell to the ground. He felt his way underneath a wagon parked near the door and awaited the guard's approach. He was sure the man had heard the board drop. But several minutes passed and the guard never came, so Baldridge sat quietly allowing his eyes to adjust to the darkness.

So Burl was still in Natchez. But why? If he was behind the wreck of the *Mary Justice,* it would make sense to get out of town as soon as possible. Crawling from underneath the wagon, Baldridge stifled a cough and fanned the dust illuminated by slivers of light piercing the cracks in the wall. Drawing the canvas cover from the back of a wagon, he peered inside. Even in the poor light he recognized two large, chestnut-colored glass demijohns, with a long rope coiled nearby, and wires leading from the gutta-percha seal at the top. He returned the canvas to its original position and eased over to a second wagon, where he found two more of the contraptions. A third and fourth wagon near the front doors each held a large rowboat. Pulling a phosphorus match from his pocket, he struck it and held it aloft; by its modest light, he could see several barrels of gunpowder stacked against the far wall, and more empty demijohns lined up near a long worktable. Hearing voices and footsteps near the door, he shook out the match and crawled under the wagon nearest the front doors. The light hurt his eyes as the double doors swung open. Four men came inside. Baldridge immediately recognized the voice of Victor Burl.

"I want everything ready to move by midnight—all the wagons lined up out front, all the torpedoes wired and set—and I want a man watching Pine Ridge Road from now until we leave."

"Got it, Mr. Burl."

"You smell something?" Burl asked.

"No, sir."

The men were standing so close that Baldridge could hear Burl sniffing the air.

"I smell something." He turned to a third man. "Who's been in here?"

"Ain't nobody been in here, Mr. Burl. McGraw here's been watching the barn."

"That's right, Mr. Burl," McGraw added nervously. "Ain't been nobody in here since I came on this morning."

"You men check the place out," Burl said. "Smells like something's been burning in here."

As the men moved about the barn, Baldridge grasped the chassis above him; hooking the foot of his good leg on a cross-brace, he lifted himself off the ground and hugged the underbody of the wagon. Burl's men scurried around for what seemed an eternity. Baldridge's fingers were growing numb as they wrapped around the metal undercarriage, and his biceps were aching as he battled to hold himself off the ground. Eventually one of the men yelled that the back door had been opened.

"Round up the men," Burl ordered. "Find out if anyone

has come through the back. If they haven't, search the grounds. We can't afford to have visitors now." Baldridge's arms were quivering, and he knew he must soon let go. If he dropped they would find him for sure. Squeezing his jaw tightly, he tried not to think of the burning sensation in his arms and the ache that had now spread down his good leg to his ankle.

Any time now his hands would slip away. Just as he thought he could hold on no longer, he heard Burl order the wagons moved outside: "Get them outside. Now! Search this barn. Search it completely."

If he could just hold on a few more seconds, he would have a chance. His shoulders were cramping and he wanted to cry out as he felt the wagon begin to roll. Four men, one at each corner, pushed and pulled it out of the barn while a fifth controlled the tongue. Baldridge watched their feet as they rolled it out the front door and parked it near the trees in front of the barn. His right hand slipped from its hold and he rested it on the ground momentarily, praying the men wouldn't see it. Luckily, after tossing back the canvas and making a hasty inspection of the torpedoes, they hurried back to the barn to remove the other wagons. Lowering his hand again, he leaned down and, assured that their backs were turned, he dropped to the ground and rolled out from under the wagon on the side nearest the woods and away from the barn. He kept rolling until he felt the leaves crunch under him and the brush surround him. Then he began crawling until he was a safe distance into the cover of the trees. His arms hurt, his legs hurt, and all he wanted to do was get away. But then he thought of Turner. If they started searching the woods, they'd be sure to find him. After a cursory count of the men scurrying about the back of the house and working in the barn, Baldridge figured Burl had ten or twelve men with him. To stop the gambler he would need help, so he took a circuitous route around the opposite way he had come, crossed the trail leading up to the mansion, and slipped up on Turner, who was still sitting where he'd been left. Baldridge touched Turner's shoulder, startling him.

"Shhhhh!" Grabbing the little man by the sleeve, he pulled him from the edge of the clearing back to where the horses were tied.

"What's happenin' out there, Mr. Baldridge?" Turner asked. "There's men running all over the place."

"Now, listen to me," Baldridge began in a low voice, pointing in the direction of the house. "We've got to stop these men before they get out of here, 'cause once they're gone, we're liable not to find 'em again."

Turner nodded. "What are we gonna do?"

"Take your horse and ride back to Pine Ridge Road. Stay in the woods as long as you can, and be careful. They got men watching the main road."

"Do you want me to get the law?"

"Yeah, Turner, I want you to get the sheriff." But when Baldridge considered the possibility that Burl might get spooked and move out early, he corrected himself. "But not yet. First, I want you to ride north up Pine Ridge Road to Bisland Bayou. Find a man named Jackson. Tell him Masey Baldridge sent you and that if he wants to find the men that trespassed on his land and stole his horses, he should bring his rifle and come with you."

"Jackson? Is that right?"

"Right."

"What makes you think he'll come?"

"He'll come. Just tell him what I said."

"All right, Mr. Baldridge, I'll tell him."

"Send him to this spot, then you make for town and tell the sheriff that Victor Burl and a gang of men responsible for sinking the *Mary Justice* are holed up out here."

"Victor Burl?"

"That's right. And make sure Ol' Man Jackson brings a gun for me. And one for you."

"Mr. Baldridge, I don't—"

"Don't even say it," Baldridge snapped. "Just come back with Jackson and the weapons."

"Jackson," Turner repeated. "At Bisland Bayou."

"Right."

"And . . . Victor Burl's the one that sunk the *Mary Justice*?"

"Right, right. Now get out of here."

Baldridge watched Turner mount up and ride off, still struggling to maneuver his horse through the brush, and he got the sick sensation that he'd never see him again. He checked his watch. It was just past noon. He had a little less than twelve hours, which even with a man like Turner going for help, should be enough time. He found a spot where he could watch the front of the mansion, and settled back against the trunk of a shaggy bark hickory tree.

It was almost five o'clock and growing dark quickly. Baldridge turned at the sound of every windblown branch in hopes it was Turner and Jackson. They should have been here by now. Turner'd had more than enough time to get to Bisland Bayou. Maybe he'd gotten lost. Maybe he'd run into Burl's men. Maybe he'd turned tail and run. Baldridge had drained the last of his flask more than two hours ago, and with the coming darkness the breeze was picking up and beginning to chill him. His bad leg was stiff from sitting for so long, and once it got dark, he'd have to move closer to the house. The idea of facing Burl and his men alone made him shiver. Or was it the wind? He wasn't sure. Either way, the sight of Jackson or Turner and a posse from Natchez would go a long way to warm him up.

A half hour later, shadows moved across the upstairs windows of the old homeplace as a choir of katydids serenaded Baldridge from the creeping darkness. He was struggling to make out the tunnel way now; on several occasions he thought he saw men moving into the front yard, but it was only his imagination. From the blackness to his rear and behind the hickory tree, Baldridge heard a limb crack and leaned to the side, squinting into the darkness. He heard it again. His horse nickered.

"Turner?" he whispered. "Turner?" There was no answer. Pulling himself slowly to his feet, his left leg rigid as a steel rod and tingling from having been dormant so long, he again leaned around the tree and listened. There was no sound now, only the cool breeze carrying the smell of a horse. He limped back in the direction of his mount to quiet him, and was within twenty feet of the animal when he felt a blow to his back just below the shoulder blade. He fell face first, the taste of mulch and dead leaves in his mouth as he rolled over and reached for his knife. His hand had just touched the handle when another blow found his left cheekbone and sent him into a blackness deeper than the surrounding forest.

First he heard the voices, muffled and faint in the beginning; then he felt the dull ache in his head; and finally he opened his eyes. Confused and frightened, he tried to sit up, but his head began to spin and he plopped back to the floor, striking the back of his skull against the hard wood.

"He's comin' to," a man said from nearby. "Go get Mr. Burl."

Through half-opened eyes Baldridge made out the blurry image of a rifle barrel poised not more than a foot from his nose, so he remained still and tried to collect his thoughts.

The woods. Going for his horse. Where was he?

Suddenly he realized who the man had called for. He'd done it. He'd gone and gotten himself caught. He cussed under his breath. He'd gone the whole war without getting captured and now he'd let a dozen or so lowlifes take him. His head throbbed.

Baldridge noticed the rattlesnake boots first, and as he lifted his eyes, he saw Victor Burl standing a few feet away. Well dressed and neatly groomed, he wore a crimson ascot beneath his vest and stood calmly picking at his meticulously manicured nails.

"You just had to stick your nose in this, didn't you, Baldridge?" Burl said.

Baldridge sat up slightly and leaned on his elbow.

"I tried to warn you off. I told you some things are better left alone. Remember? Remember me saying that?"

Counting Burl and the man standing over him with the shotgun, Baldridge saw five men in the room. One of them was Curry. The other two he didn't recognize. He seemed to be lying in a parlor, with a coal-oil lamp flickering on the mantel above the fireplace, and another on a dusty, cobweb-encased end table on the far side of the room. Instinctively he reached for his knife but found only an empty scabbard.

"You'd be a-reachin' for this, now, wouldn't you?" Curry said, offering a look that was about two teeth short of a stupid grin. "This is what he used to cut up Terry," Curry said, holding the Bowie knife up for Burl to see. "Took the boy's ear clean off."

Burl strolled over to a nearby washstand. "Yes, you've been making a nuisance of yourself, Mr. Baldridge." He poured himself a brandy. "And frankly, that surprises me, considering that you presented yourself on the *Paragon* as a gentleman. A gentleman from the South, no less. I'm used to dealing with gentlemen, you see, and since I consider myself to be a gentleman, it alarms me when a man doesn't behave like one."

"Gentlemen don't murder innocent people," Baldridge said, gazing at Burl's glass like a stray dog eyeing a piece of meat. It had been midafternoon when he'd last had a drink and for once his leg wasn't the only thing that hurt. He felt for his flask. It was gone.

Burl took a long, slow drink, then studied the brandy in the yellowish light.

"Oh, I'm sure that's what you call it, Mr. Baldridge. But then, you don't understand."

"Oh, I think I'm beginning to understand," he said, struggling to rise to his feet. The movement spooked the man with the rifle, who jerked the weapon to his shoulder. One of the others pulled his pistol, so Baldridge glanced over at him and held his arms wide from his sides. Tasting blood in the left corner of his mouth, he slowly wiped his cheek, flaking off tiny pieces of dried blood. Amid considerable swelling, he felt a small, clotted cut below his eye.

"It appears that you and these men"—Baldridge surveyed the rough-looking men in the room—"have been sinking steamboats." He looked at Burl and awaited his response.

"Do go on, Mr. Baldridge," Burl said, taking another sip of brandy.

"You're doin' it with those torpedoes—at least, you sank the *Mary Justice* with 'em, and I'd say it was a safe guess that you did the others that way, too."

Burl smiled. "I have to say I'm impressed. As a gambler, I'm afraid I would have bet you wouldn't find us out. I'd have lost, wouldn't I?" He placed his glass on the table. "But I didn't lose, Mr. Baldridge, because I only bet on a sure thing. You're the one who has lost. That is . . . unless I can convince you to join my little group. A man of your talent could be of great help to the cause. Hell, you've served it before. Why not serve it again?"

"The cause I fought for had nothing to do with blowin' up riverboats and killin' innocent people."

"Innocent?" Burl mused. "That's an interesting word. None of us are truly innocent, are we Mr. Baldridge? That's what the Bible says. All have sinned and fallen short of the glory of God. I mean, you yourself are not an innocent man. You're not down here pursuing me out of the goodness of your heart, are you? No, no, I'm sure you're getting paid." Burl shook his head. "But I doubt it's enough to risk your life for, now is it? You see, that's the saddest part of all. You could be making a lot more money working for me—and you could be striking a blow against the Yankees at the same time." Burl glanced down at Baldridge's leg. "After all, didn't you tell me the Yankees gave you that leg?"

"Yes, I was wounded."

"Weren't we all? I mean, more or less? Some of us are still fighting it, though."

"The war is over, Burl."

Burl's face grew angry. "Oh, no. No! As I told you on the boat, the war's still on whether you know it or not," he said, walking over to the window. "Oh, maybe they're not shooting at us," he said, turning back to look at Masey, "but they're killing us just the same. Only difference is now they're doing it with their Freeman's Bureau and their scalawags and their armed bands of niggers and their laws keeping veterans out of government office. You can call it Reconstruction if you want to, but what it amounts to is the destruction of the South. Anything to keep the southern man down. Anything will do."

"And how is all this gonna change anything?"

"They've got to pay. The Yankees have got to pay for what they've done." He stepped within inches of Baldridge's face. "You just don't understand, do you?" His eyes had an otherworldly look. "How many of our innocent men, women, and children died when the Yankees invaded our homes?"

"A lot."

"You're damned right, it was a lot. Thousands—maybe tens of thousands. And not one Federal soldier has been called to account for his atrocities since the war ended. Not one! Look what they did to Henry Wirz, commandant at Andersonville." Burl shook his head. "He did the best he could with what he had and they hanged him for it. All our ports under blockade, no food or medicine to give our own men, much less Yankee prisoners." Burl spun about and pointed his finger at Baldridge. "While in Yankee prisons thousands of our men died of cold, hunger, exposure, and disease—all in the midst of a country rich in food and medical supplies." Burl stood erect and lifted his chin in the air. "Now, you're an intelligent man, so I ask you, Mr. Masey Baldridge . . . who commits the greater injustice? He who has no food and medicine and thus cannot provide it? Or he who has it but refuses to give it?"

"What do you want me to say, Burl?"

"I want to hear the truth!"

"Hell, man, the truth is yes, the Yankees were bastards. Yes, our boys did get a raw deal. And I, too, believe that some Federal soldiers ought to hang for it. But you and me both know it ain't gonna happen. The only thing worse is you killin' innocent people in some crazy notion of revenge."

"Oh, it's not revenge, Mr. Baldridge. No, no! I call it retaliation, because that's the term the Yankees like to use. What they did to us wasn't murder and plunder and robbery. Oh no! It was *retaliation*, and always against a convenient and helpless enemy."

"You're out of your mind."

"Am I? Am I, Mr. Baldridge? I believe not. I think I'm the only person thinking straight around here. You see, I've got to balance the ledger." He stared wide-eyed at Baldridge. "Nobody else is going to do it. All the others are like tired old housewives—weary of fighting off the old man and resigned to letting him have his way with them. But not me. I'll never whore for the Yankees."

"But why the Marine Brigade? Why have you singled them out?"

A faraway look appeared on Burl's face; after several moments he spoke. "You know about Alfred Ellet and his butchers, do you?" He allowed himself a modest smile. "You're a smart man, Baldridge. A smart man."

"There must be hundreds of others you could have chosen, yet you've hunted down these particular—"

"In May of 1963, I was in St. Louis, turning what business deals I could and picking up information for the government in Richmond." He told Baldridge how his wife and two boys were at their home in Austin, Mississippi, the day that two boats from Ellet's Marine Brigade were fired upon by a couple of pieces of artillery and some of Slemmons's Second Arkansas Cavalry a few miles north of town. Ellet returned the following day with his full fleet and put in at Austin, determined to find and destroy whoever had shot at his boats. A fight took place, a pretty heavy little battle, but Slemmons's boys were no match for the combination of Ellet's cavalry and the guns on board his steamers. The Confederates withdrew and disappeared into the Mississippi woodlands, leaving Ellet empty-handed and angry.

"He took it out on the people of Austin," Burl said. "Ellet ordered the buildings burned, but only after shelling the town for half an hour." His voice began to crack. "My wife and my two boys were in our house when the gunboats began firing into the town. They rushed down to the storm cellar and were apparently hiding there when one of those artillery rounds came crashing into the house. Brick and debris fell down on the cellar door, blocking their escape."

Burl bit his lip hard and turned away. He walked over and poured another brandy—a brandy that Baldridge coveted even more than the last. While Burl tried to compose himself, Baldridge took the opportunity to locate the nearest door. The chance of an escape was slim, at least for now; but given the opportunity, he figured a dash for the door was a better risk than waiting around to be shot—a fate that seemed more likely with every passing minute.

"They must've struggled an hour or more," Burl said, his voice still reflecting a certain disbelief. "Then the soldiers came, torching everything in sight. They burned the stores, the churches, and eventually they got to my home." He paused and swallowed hard. "You'll excuse me, Mr. Baldridge. To this day I have trouble thinking about what they must have suffered, much less talking about it." He walked over and stood beside the chair where Baldridge was now sitting.

"Once the Yankees had left, very little of Austin remained. The neighbors found my beautiful house burned to the ground." Burl hesitated. "And beneath the rubble they found my wife and boys." He glanced away, his eyes heavy with tears. "Oh, God, what they must have suffered."

After several pregnant moments, Baldridge spoke.

"What happened to your family is horrible, Burl, but—"

"Do you have any idea what it's like to burn to death?" Burl asked.

"What about the people on the riverboats you've sunk?"

Burl continued as if Baldridge had not spoken. "To choke to death on the smoke of your own home?"

"You've drowned innocent people—people who had nothing to do with—"

Burl was staring vacantly ahead. "To smell the flesh of your own children burning?"

"You still don't have the right to kill other—"

Whirling about, Burl backhanded him across the face.

"How dare you judge me!" Burl pulled a pistol from his belt. "And you call yourself a soldier! You've lost your nerve, Baldridge, and I ought to shoot you right here."

"Who are you trying to kid? You're certainly no soldier," Baldridge said. "And these bums aren't either. You're murderers, that's all you are. No real soldier kills other men in cold blood."

"I'm settling the score, by God! So help me, I'll never rest until every bastard who had anything to do with murdering my family is cold in his grave." Burl smashed the brandy snifter against the wall, kicking up dust and sending shards of glass flying across the room. Baldridge turned away just in time to avoid catching some in his face, but one piece lodged in the bottom of his coat.

"Bring him in here!" Burl ordered as he opened a door and stepped into an adjoining room.

Curry hesitated. "But, Mr. Burl . . ."

"I said, bring him!"

The man with the rifle poked Baldridge to urge him along; accompanied by Curry, they ushered him into the room behind Burl, while the other men remained in the parlor. The room was smoky with the fragrance of eight or nine candles placed along the far wall. Near the candles were photographs affixed to the wall, and something about the room reminded Baldridge of being in church as a child.

"Wait outside," Burl told the man with the rifle. As he disappeared and closed the door behind him, Curry drew his pistol and cocked the hammer.

"Don't do nothin' stupid there, Baldridge," Curry said.

"Look here," Burl said. "See? I'm almost finished." He was pointing at a line of squares on the wall, four above and four below, and as he stepped closer, Baldridge could see that most of the squares contained tintypes. There was a wildness in Burl's eyes now, and an almost panting anticipation in his voice. "I'm almost done. See? Look at them! Look at all those hellbound sons of bitches!"

Baldridge saw on the right the name *E. H. Fairchild,* and just below it two tintype portraits. Beneath one was written "Brooks," and beneath the other "Vernon Marley." The latter, Baldridge recalled from Ferguson's telegram, had been the captain of the *T. H. Thorndike.* To the left of those tintypes was written the word "Baltic," and hanging just below were two other tintype portraits, one bearing the name Falliday, the other labeled "John D. Ballard," the pilot of the *Mercury.*

Baldridge stared in amazement at Burl. "What the hell is all this?"

"The ledger," Burl replied with a strange smile. "It's the balance sheet for what I'm owed by the Yankees."

Baldridge again looked at the wall. He recognized the pilots from the Marine Brigade, but the rest puzzled him. "Who are these other men?"

"Why, the commanders of the boats," Burl said, as if it were blindingly obvious. "The men in charge of the soldiers. The bastards who burned my home to the ground—who murdered my family."

"But . . .which one? Surely you can't believe they all did it."

"It doesn't matter which one. They were all there. They *all* deserve to die." He pointed to one of the portraits. "Take Falliday, for instance. He had a hunting accident up in Ohio about a year ago. A terrible thing. Made all the local papers. Poor man accidentally shot himself . . . five times." He stepped over and pointed out first Ballard, then Brooks. "Ballard . . . well, you know what happened to him—he went down with his ship as a good pilot should. And this Brooks, he commanded the troops on Marley's boat the *Thorndike.* He just up and disappeared one day. Rode out of his law office and just never came back."

That Burl was insane Baldridge was sure, but when he stepped up to get a closer look at this gruesome altar, he felt his stomach seize into a knot. Under the name *John Raine* was a photograph of a man named Hubbard, and just beneath it, instead of a portrait, Baldridge saw a tintype matching the description of the one taken from Henry C. Norman. It showed a riverboat, at night, completely aflame, in its last moments before going under. Beneath it was a name: Edward Smythe.

Baldridge looked at Burl. "Hubbard would have commanded the troops on Ed Smythe's boat."

"Correct."

Burl saw him staring at the photograph. "I want to thank you for recovering my picture," he said sincerely. "My man lost it the night of the mission. A stupid thing to do, losing my only record of the retribution—but he's since paid dearly for his mistake."

"I'll say he did," Curry added with a stupid laugh.

"Where did you get all these tintypes?" Baldridge asked.

"It's really quite simple, Baldridge. My men work all up and down the river. They're photographers, you see. Surely you've encountered someone from Burl Photographic Emporium? I would certainly hope so. But they're much, much more than photographers. They're my eyes and ears. Many of them worked with me during the war, in our little service."

"That would be the torpedo corps."

"My God, man, you've certainly been busy." Burl paused and cocked his head to the left. "I'll bet you've been talking to Zedekiah McDaniel."

"I told you we should have gotten rid of that old fool!" Curry snarled.

Burl smiled. "All in good time, Curry." He looked back at Baldridge. "You see, my photographers find people I'm looking for, they tell me who works where on the river and when the boats are running. They've done quite well . . .except for this last mission. Not only did my man lose the picture you so graciously found for me, but the photographer in St. Louis failed to get me a portrait of Smythe before he left." He turned and looked Baldridge squarely in the face. "Of course, you see how important this particular tintype is to me, being the only record of our effort. Records are important. You must have records to keep the ledger."

As Burl stepped over to a nearby desk, Baldridge looked at the display with disgust. The fourth and final row held no photographs, only empty brackets with the word "*Autocrat*" written above. But as Burl began to speak, it didn't take long to figure what belonged in the picture frames.

"Only two more to go," Burl said in a satisfied tone, as he withdrew a pen from the inkwell. Bending over the desk, he began writing something on two white cards. "Just two more and the scale will be balanced. Although I must admit, this last one is going to be a little more difficult." He glanced over at Baldridge. "But it's the most important of all."

Sprinkling salt across the words he'd penned on the cards, he blew the excess onto the floor and walked over to the display. As he gently slid the first card into the bracket, Baldridge read the name of Alfred W. Ellet.

"This one I'm saving for last. You should always save the best for last. Ellet commanded the whole thing. He bears ultimate responsibility. Isn't that what they teach you as a soldier? You bear responsibility for what your men do . . . or fail to do?"

"You and your men flatter yourselves with the title of soldier," Baldridge said. "You tell me."

"Ellet is supposed to be out in Kansas now," Burl continued, as if the other man had said nothing. "I understand he's a big man with the railroad." He smiled and began to nod slowly. "But make no mistake, Mr. Baldridge. He will pay for his crime. He *will* pay." Burl slid the other card in the lower bracket. "Just like the good Captain Williamson."

The jet-black ink showed the name of Charles L. Williamson in hard contrast against the clean white card. "I guess the river spoiled your little party, didn't it?" Baldridge said.

"How's that?"

"You'll have to wait until spring now, or at least until the water comes up. By then the people I've contacted will have hunted you down and stopped this lunatic operation. And you'll be at the end of a rope, where you belong."

Baldridge was furious when Burl began laughing at him. Surely he must know he couldn't get away with it—especially with Luke Williamson holed up in St. Louis until high water.

"For such an intelligent man, Mr. Baldridge, you surprise me with what you *don't* know." Burl adjusted the card with Luke's name to center it in the bracket. "By this time tomorrow, Captain Williamson will be stopping silt on the bottom of Merengo Bend."

"Luke Williamson is in St. Louis. He'll be there for weeks, maybe months."

Burl walked back over to the desk, picked up a copy of the Natchez *Democrat*, and opened it.

"Today's election day. Did you know that, Mr. Baldridge? Or have you been too busy sneaking around Natchez looking for me to notice?"

"I know what day it is."

"And you didn't vote? How unpatriotic of you! As close as you've gotten to the bluebellies, I'd figure you would want to rush out and cast your vote for that drunken Yankee butcher General Grant." Burl shook his head as he surveyed the front page. "And you say there's no war on? We've got a Yankee general running the country, and trying to get reelected, and still you say there's no war on? You show your ignorance, sir. It says right here that people expect Grant and the Republicans to have a big majority. I figure it'll be thirty, maybe thirty-five thousand, don't you?"

Baldridge was growing tired of this little game. If Burl had something to say, why wouldn't he come out and say it? Out of the corner of his eye he checked Curry, but the man had not lost an ounce of vigilance; to make a move now would be suicide.

"Of course, that's not hard to see," Burl continued.

"Who'd vote for Horace Greeley anyway? He's just another Yankee. Why, he's a member of a temperance society! Did you know that? I'd think that, as a man who likes a drink now and then, you'd cast your vote against Mr. Greeley."

Baldridge wished Burl hadn't mentioned a drink. He had almost put the idea out of his mind, though it was never very far out of reach. His lips were dry and he could feel his hands trembling. He wasn't sure if that was out of fear or from going without for so long. He wished they hadn't found his flask.

"Yankees don't like Greeley either," Burl said, talking as if they were sitting across a table at a gentlemen's club. "One man writes that he knows Grant is an ass, but better an ass in the White House than a mischievous idiot." Baldridge was about to demand that he make a point or shut up, when Burl handed him the paper. "Oh, look at this. Seems the water's not as low as you think."

Baldridge grabbed the paper—it was Monday's edition—and read the headline.

"Race Enters Second Day," it read. The article below described the contest between the *Paragon* and the *Apollo* in their race for New Orleans. There was a wire story saying that the two riverboats had left Memphis within a half hour of each other, with the *Apollo* slightly in the lead.

"You know, Mr. Baldridge, a man in your job really ought to keep up with current events."

"You can't do this, Burl," Baldridge said, tossing the paper at him. It fanned out and floated down to the floor.

"Oh, I can do it, all right. And I think you know that very well. But more important, I *will* do it."

"You're not going to get away with it. No matter what you do to me, others will stop you." Baldridge glanced at Curry, speaking first to him, then to Burl. "I've been following you. I followed you out here with a half-dozen other men. The sheriff's probably here by now. Others are waiting for my signal, and if I don't give it pretty soon, you can damned well bet they'll storm this house."

Baldridge studied Burl's eyes. The bluff was worth a try. In the barn earlier that day, Burl had said he planned to leave at midnight, and though he hadn't seen a watch since he came to, Baldridge figured it had to be getting close. Where in hell were Turner and Jackson?

"You weren't a very good poker player that night on the *Paragon*, Baldridge. I knew when you weren't holding anything then, and you've got no better hand now."

"Listen, Burl—"

"No. There's no more time for talk." Burl started out of the room and motioned for Curry to bring his prisoner. "It's a shame about you. It really is." As he stepped into the parlor, Burl called to some of the other men. "Bring the other one out."

"Oh, shit," Baldridge mumbled as Burl's men led Old Man Jackson in from the front porch. His hands were bound and a rope was stretched across his mouth and between his teeth, tied behind his head like a bridle. The old man was fussing and cussing even with the rope in his mouth, and some of the guards chuckled as he tried to wriggle loose from the bindings. As one of the men removed the rope from around his head, Jackson launched a tirade.

"What in the goddamned hell do you think you're doin', you bunch of murderin', horse-thievin' sacks of shit? Why, I've half a mind to—"

"Quiet, old man!" Burl shouted.

Jackson glanced at Baldridge. "How in the hell did you get yourself into—"

The sound of Burl's revolver stung Baldridge's ears and rattled the window glass, while tiny pieces of plaster crumbled from the wall just above and behind Jackson's head.

"I told you to be quiet," Burl said in a restrained tone, "and I'm not accustomed to having my orders disobeyed." Jackson stood silent, throwing questioning glances at Baldridge, as Burl turned and looked expectantly at one of his men.

"Well?"

"He don't know nothin'. The old coot says he just come down here after the horses we borrowed."

"Borrowed, my ass!" Jackson growled. Burl lifted his revolver again and the old man reconsidered his next comment.

"And the other one?"

"He talked. It took a while, but he finally told us." The man looked confidently at Baldridge. "Ain't nobody else around. Ain't nobody else comin', neither. "Baldridge swallowed hard. With that comment, a man on the front porch pushed the body of Asa Turner through the front door; it timbered like a fresh-cut tree onto the floor not five feet from Baldridge. Turner's body bounced slightly and rolled enough to the side to reveal a clean bullet hole just below the hairline on the right side of his forehead. His glassy eyes evidenced a death stare of disbelief. Baldridge looked at Jackson, who shook his head as if to say, "There was nothing I could do."

Curry began to fidget. "Mr. Burl, it's gettin' late. If you want to leave by midnight, we've got to get rid of these two and get out of here."

"Who's staying behind?" Burl asked.

"Jenkins, Riley, and McGraw," Curry replied.

Burl pulled his timepiece from his pocket and examined it. "Leave Baines behind instead of Riley."

"But, Mr. Burl—"

"Do it. I want Baines to set up the camera."

"Tonight? With all they've got to do after we leave? Mr. Burl, they've got to clean the place up and move the rest of the gear out of the barn, and—"

"They've got all night to do that," Burl said. "I want a picture of Mr. Baldridge and his friend."

Curry was upset. "But Mr. Burl—"

Burl set his jaw. "Don't argue with me!" he said, raising one finger to quiet the man. He looked first at Baldridge, then at Jackson. Straightening his ascot, he spoke quietly. "They're part of it all now. They're part of the balance . . . part of the ledger. I want a record."

"Whatever you say, Mr. Burl." Curry motioned for the man called Baines to set up a camera in the next room. "Lock them downstairs until he's ready."

Burl paused after stepping in front of Baldridge. "And do tie up Mr. Baldridge. He's just rash enough to try to escape before we have the opportunity to make his portrait." Burl tilted his head down and pressed his thumb and index finger on each side of the bridge of his nose. He squeezed his eyes shut like a man who'd had a long day; then he looked up.

"I'm afraid I must go, Mr. Baldridge. I have important work to do before daylight. I'm sorry it has come to this. . . . Perhaps under other circumstances . . ."

"Don't do it, Burl. You can stop right now. Nobody else has to die."

"Don't beg, Baldridge. I figured you'd die like a soldier."

"I'm not talking about me. I'm talking about the *Paragon.*"

"There's nothing more to say. The scales must be balanced. That's all there is to it."

Over Baldridge's continued protests, Burl and his men left the house, and the three men remaining behind ushered their prisoners into a room on the lower floor, adjacent to the entry tunnel Baldridge had observed earlier. His hands tied, Baldridge stood next to Jackson, locked in the darkness of a first-floor room, as both men listened to the sound of the three captors walking around above them. From outside they could hear the wagons moving out; Baldridge pictured them loaded with their deadly cargo and passing down that twisting dirt trail that led back to Pine Ridge Road.

"What in the name of God are these men doing?" Jackson said. "That poor Turner fella said something about them sinking that riverboat you was asking me about. He said they was the ones that stole my horses."

"You're right."

"Oh, I know I'm right about my horses," he said. "I seen one of my mares when they caught me and Turner. One of the sorry rascals was ridin' her. I'd have shot him right on the spot if I could've got to my rifle in time. We never had a chance. They was up on us before we knew it. I doubt that Turner boy would've been much of a hand in a fight anyway, God rest his soul."

"He was a decent man."

"Seemed like it. You figure that's what they gonna do to us?"

"Afraid so."

"I wish I had a fair chance at 'em. I'd show 'em a thing or two. Why, if I had my Spencer back, I'd—" Jackson glanced down in the darkness. He could see that Baldridge's hands, though tied just below his belt, were busy. "Hell, boy, this ain't no time to be a-playin' with yourself! I mean, I know you figure you're gonna die, but goddamn—"

Baldridge laughed. He wasn't sure why, given the situation, but the old man's incessant talk amused him. "Jackson," he said softly, "I'm not playin' with myself."

"Then what in hell—"

"I found a piece of glass in the edge of my coat. It must've stuck there when Burl busted a brandy glass earlier tonight. Now, it's not much, but it's sharp, and I think I can get this rope sawed part of the way through."

"Part of the way? Cut it off! And get me loose, too."

"No. These men aren't stupid. They're damned careful. They'll notice if the rope is gone, or even loose. I want it cut so I can snap it with one jerk."

"How's that gonna help?"

"I'll wait until they get us upstairs. Sometime, when they're making this crazy picture of us, I'll get a chance."

"To do what?"

"To take 'em."

"By yourself?"

"Hell, no! Here," he said, feeling for Jackson's hand and slipping him the glass shard, "work on yours. And hurry up."

A half hour later, Baldridge and Jackson were moved upstairs.

"Do the old man first," Jenkins said. He held a shotgun as Baines lined up Jackson in front of the camera. Baldridge began talking to him, mindful of the position of the third man, McGraw, who held both his pistol and Baines's.

"I know why Burl murders innocent people," Baldridge said, "but what about you men? You're not out for some kind of revenge, are you?"

"Shut the hell up," Baines said, ducking behind the cloth cover of the camera.

"I mean, doesn't it bother you that decent, God-fearing people die when you plant these torpedoes in the river?"

Baines's muffled voice came from beneath the cloth. "I told you to shut up."

"I know you hate the Yankees," Baldridge continued. "Hell, they're not my favorite people either. But there's southerners on that boat you're going to sink."

Jenkins adjusted his grip on the shotgun. "Mr. Burl pays good. Real good. I been with him since right before the war ended. Baines here has been working for him for—"

"Shut up and keep an eye on that old fool!" Baines shouted. "I'm almost ready." His hand emerged from under the blanket and grasped the trigger mechanism on a tiny pan containing a compound of magnesium.

"I don't wanna shut up," Jenkins fired back.

"How many will you use?" Baldridge asked.

"How many what?"

"Torpedoes."

"Quit talkin' to him," Baines said, making the final adjustment on the camera.

"What's it gonna hurt?" McGraw put in. "Hell, he's talkin' to a dead man anyway."

At that comment, Baldridge checked his handiwork by applying slight pressure against each side of the rope binding his hands. Too much force might release the rope, and that would get him shot. But what if he hadn't cut far enough? What if the rope held when he decided to break free? There was no sure way to know until the time came.

"Four. Mr. Burl sets up four torpedoes, just like we did against the gunboats back in the war."

Baines began to count. "On three. One . . . two—"

"Smile, you old bastard," Jenkins shouted, "before you look like that silly fool layin' out there on the front porch!"

"—Three!" The magnesium began to burn, casting a brilliant light for several seconds, while a choking smoke gathered near the ceiling and began to drift downward. "Damn that Burl. I hate doing this indoors," Baines fumed.

As Jenkins pushed Jackson into the corner and ordered Baldridge to take his place in front of the camera, he saw a chance to make his move. He began applying steady, building pressure to the ropes as Baines replaced the flashpan and ducked back under the camera cloth.

"How do you make sure the boat hits one?" Baldridge asked.

"He sure is asking some funny questions for a man that's about to meet his maker," McGraw observed.

"Puts 'em smack dab in the channel," Jenkins said, "forty feet apart in a line. That way, whichever way she steers, she's bound to hit one."

"If the wood don't get 'em first," McGraw said with a laugh.

"The wood?" Baldridge said.

"Just a little insurance," McGraw said. "But you'd know all about that, wouldn't you?"

Jenkins looked suddenly pale. "Baines, did you check the batteries in the wagon?"

Baines leaned from under the cloth cover, obviously frustrated with Jenkins. "Hell yes. I knew you'd up and forget it. Burl would have killed us both."

"I forgot all about it," Jenkins confessed.

"I was supposed to be working the battery for this one," Baines complained. "Instead I'm back here taking these silly pictures." Again he reached for the flash trigger. "On three."

"What do the batteries do?"

"Fires the torpedo in case the boat don't hit it right," Jenkins said. "Smile, dead man!"

"One, two . . ."

On the count of three Baldridge closed his eyes and the magnesium powder ignited. After it had burned for two or three seconds, he jerked with all his might against the ropes, and after a heart-wrenching second when they threatened to remain intact, they snapped and fell to the floor. Instantly he bent forward and charged toward the camera.

"What in hell!" Baines gasped as Baldridge threw both arms around the stand and tackled him, camera and all. They fell backward; the burning magnesium jarred from the flashpan and flew to the rear, striking McGraw across the face and shoulders. As Baldridge tumbled to the floor atop a struggling Baines, he could hear McGraw screaming wildly as he dropped the revolvers and stumbled about the room clawing at his eyes. The burning magnesium had done its work, eating into McGraw's right eye and temporarily blinding Jenkins with its flash. As Jenkins struggled to aim his shotgun at Baldridge, Jackson charged him from behind, causing the shotgun to discharge inches above Baldridge's head.

The struggle had carried Baldridge to within reach of one of the revolvers McGraw had dropped, but Baines grabbed it first and shot at Baldridge's face, narrowly missing his right ear as he grabbed the barrel. That sound was followed by another blast of Jenkins's shotgun. Now Baldridge figured Jackson was dead for sure. Again they rolled on the floor, but this time Baines was on top; and with his bad leg unable to push against the floor, Baldridge couldn't get him off. It was now a question of arm strength and who most had the will to live. Both men's hands shook as they gripped the gun and tried to point the barrel at the other's face. Slowly, much too slowly for Baldridge's liking, the barrel eased toward Baines's nose. Quickly Baldridge pulled his other hand from Baines's collar and slapped down against his gun hand. The force of the blow drove Baines's finger against the trigger and instantly buried a .38-caliber round in his skull. Baines sat up momentarily, wavered first one way and then the other, blinked twice, and slumped to the floor.

Meanwhile, McGraw had stumbled out into the parlor.

When Baldridge got up, he was relieved to see Old Man Jackson standing over the still-writing body of Jenkins, whose chest was now little more than a mass of pulsating crimson. Seeing the agony of the mortally wounded man, Baldridge picked up the second revolver that McGraw had dropped, gave Jackson a knowing glance, and tossed the weapon to him. A few moments later, as he came upon McGraw feeling his way along the wall in the parlor, he heard a shot from the other room—and then silence.

It wasn't hard for Baldridge and Jackson to get McGraw to talk. Terrorized by the loss of the sight in his right eye, and still suffering from the burn of the magnesium powder, he was brought around by their promise of medical help if he cooperated. He told them that Burl planned to intercept the *Paragon* at Merengo Bend, some eight miles west of Natchez along Cowpens Point. With the water so low, it was the deepest spot for miles, still registering almost eighty feet. The men would plant the torpedoes on the west side of the bend, where most steamboats hugged the outside of the channel to gain speed. Setting the charges for both electrical and contact detonation, Burl was taking no chances that the *Paragon* would get by. When asked how he knew the *Apollo* wouldn't reach the bend first, McGraw said that Burl's men had taken over the woodyard near Rosedale Landing from old man King, and with eight of his own men working the loading, they would see to it the *Apollo* was delayed.

While Baldridge was getting McGraw to talk, Jackson located his Spencer and the seven-shot Smith & Wesson revolver he'd brought along. But there was no sign of a Bowie knife. The old man hung on to McGraw's pistol for himself and gave the Smith & Wesson, Baines's revolver, and the shotgun to Baldridge. After he rounded up three horses, one of which was the mare they'd stolen from him, Jackson, Baldridge, and a firmly lashed-up McGraw set off for Natchez.

The moon was three-quarters full and helped to light the way on the ride into town. According to a watch Jackson had lifted from McGraw, it was almost two-thirty in the morning by the time they reached the sheriff's office. They banged on the front door of the jail succeeding only in getting cussed out by the prisoners they awoke; finally Baldridge discovered a low, brick building adjoining the rear of the jail. Several knocks eventually produced a sleepy-eyed Sheriff Powell, closely followed by his rather chunky wife still in her nightclothes. At a quarter to three in the morning, the sight of a man he'd thrown in jail for drunkenness two days earlier, another man who'd threatened to kill him if he ever saw him again, and some scruffy-looking fellow clawing at his face and whining about wanting a doctor didn't exactly present the sheriff with the most believable story. He probably would have arrested the lot of them if they hadn't been so well armed. Pushing his way into the dwelling and sending Mrs. Powell scurrying for a robe, Baldridge was determined to be heard. He forced the man to sit at his dining table and wouldn't allow him to leave the room for fear he'd come back armed. While Mrs. Powell treated McGraw's face with cool, wet cloths, Baldridge told the sheriff what he'd discovered about Burl. He could tell the lawman doubted the story at first, but when Jackson mentioned that Burl and his men had been holed up in the deserted Concord mansion, he seemed to suddenly grow more interested. An old Negro hired man who worked for a planter not far from Concord had been telling stories around town about how the old house was haunted. He'd claimed to have seen lights in the mansion, which had been deserted for years. The sheriff had dismissed him as an old colored fellow trying to get attention; but now, hearing Baldridge and Jackson's story, he began to take notice. Still, he hesitated when Baldridge demanded he gather some men to help him stop Burl.

"I don't know," the sheriff said tentatively. "I mean, this whole thing sounds pretty crazy, what with talk about torpedoes and ex–Confederate soldiers . . "

"I never said they were soldiers," Baldridge corrected him. "In fact, I told you they *weren't* soldiers; but they're damned sure killers."

"How many men would it take?"

"As many as you can get," Jackson said.

"Raising a posse this time of night won't be easy. I doubt I could get more than eight or ten men, and by the time we got saddled up and rode out to Merengo Bend—hell, that's almost ten miles—why, it'd be three, maybe four hours."

"We don't have three or four hours," Baldridge said. "Burl left Concord around midnight. He's already got a three hour head start. He'll be out there waitin' for that riverboat."

"I just don't know."

"You don't know?" Baldridge shouted. "What the hell is there not to know? Listen, if I've lied to you, then you can put me in this jail till I rot. Jackson too." Old Man Jackson frowned; that was something he hadn't agreed to. "But if you don't go out there, and the *Paragon* hits one of Burl's goddamned torpedoes, then you're gonna have the death of a lot of people on your hands. And when I get through telling the good people of Natchez that you had a chance to stop it and didn't do it because you wouldn't drag your ass out of bed . . . well, I doubt you'll be living here much longer."

"All right. All right. I'll get some men together."

"Now me and Jackson are gettin' out of here. We'll ride on ahead and see if we can hold 'em up. Maybe we'll get lucky. Maybe the *Paragon* will be delayed." Baldridge shook his head. "But with Luke Williamson in charge, I doubt it."

Powell looked at Jackson. "We're talking about Cowpens Point, right?"

"To the Snakeshead," Jackson added, "that sandbar that hooks out into the channel."

Baldridge walked over to McGraw, who sat sniveling with his face buried in the wet towels. Grabbing him by the collar, he jerked him up from his chair, sending the towels tumbling into the floor.

"Is that right? Are they setting up the torpedoes off this Snakeshead?"

"I need a doctor," McGraw whined. "Please . . . please . . ."

"Goddamn you, you better not be lying to me!" Baldridge said, balling his fist and drawing back. "Or I'll come back here and rip out that other eye."

"I'm not. I swear! Merengo Bend," McGraw began to sob. "That's where they're doin' it."

"Snakeshead?"

"Yes, yes." His hands were quivering. "Just get me a doctor. Please!"

Fortunately the horse Jackson had found for Baldridge back at Concord was faster than the nag he'd rented, but the notion of having to pay for the one Burl's men had taken kept bothering him as he rode for Merengo Bend. Ferguson would be furious, but he wouldn't be as mad as he'd be broke if the *Paragon* went down. On the way into town, Baldridge had learned from McGraw that Burl had some twenty-two men in his employ, counting the six photographers who worked up and down the river. Burl usually kept most of them close to Natchez, and with the fresh opportunity to go after Williamson and the *Paragon* coming on such short notice, he had gathered all of them together for the mission. At least a dozen were men he'd worked with during the war; the rest were criminals and drifters Burl had come across traveling the river, men who'd cut a throat for a plug of tobacco. The idea of bottling them up out on Cowpens Point so the sheriff could apprehend them all at once excited Masey. He just hoped the sheriff would come through with that posse; these weren't men who were likely to give up without a fight.

Old Man Jackson picked up some fresh wagon tracks as they began descending the high ground just north of Natchez and west of the town cemetery. They followed the road north along an old levee for about a mile, around a huckleberry grove, then broke due west paralleling the river. Burl's party appeared to have stopped for a while at Moses Woodyard, now abandoned during the off season, then pressed on west through some marshy ground that would have been impassable had the water been up to normal. A mile from the

Snakeshead sandbar the road gave out, and the broken limbs and bent saplings of a willow grove testified to Burl's determination to rendezvous with the *Paragon*. As they pushed into the grove, the smell of damp bark weighed heavy on the pre-dawn air and sent Baldridge's thoughts back to that day in Alabama when he rode out on picket. It was as if he were there again, watching the line of trees ahead for signs of a Yankee patrol, listening for a horse or the rattle of a rifle sling. He jerked his head quickly to the left, just as he had the day he felt the fiery lead piercing his leg, but this time there was no sound of a rifle. Still, he gripped the saddle horn, momentarily terrified, fearing that any moment he would plunge to the earth as he'd done that day, grasping his knee and writhing in a pain that was to harass him for a lifetime. A willow branch slapped him across the upper lip; he shook off the memories and tried to concentrate on Jackson up ahead. He would rather have been in the lead, but the old man knew his way around these bottoms, and the last thing they needed to do now was get lost. About twenty minutes after they left the road, Baldridge noticed off to his left that the eastern sky was beginning to glow as a gentle breeze fanned the willow branches. Jackson suddenly stopped and motioned Baldridge forward.

"I thought I heard something," he whispered.

"Which way?"

"Over there." Jackson pointed southwest.

"How far are we from the bend?"

"It's over thataway about a quarter of a mile. I ain't been down here in four or five years, but seems I remember a clump of cottonwoods just over there, running along a neck of land that turns into the sandbar."

"The Snakeshead?"

"That's what they call it." Jackson pointed again, toward the sandbar. "A slough used to come up this side of the bar, but I don't know if it still does with the water this low."

"Is this neck the only dry land out there?"

"If there's still water in the slough."

Baldridge strained to make out the cottonwoods Jackson had described, but he couldn't see through the undergrowth. If Burl had taken his wagons out on that sandbar, Baldridge figured he might be able to cut him off.

"How wide is that neck of land?"

"A quarter of a mile." Jackson looked up. "Too much for a couple of men to cover, if that's what you're thinking."

"That's exactly what I'm thinking. If we block their route off the sandbar . . ."

"There's too many of 'em," Jackson said. "Besides, we can't see all the land to cover it."

"We've got to try. It's the only way to hold them until the sheriff gets here."

"What about the boat that's comin'?"

"If we raise enough hell behind them, maybe we can distract them and warn the *Paragon* at the same time. It's the only chance we've got."

The two men moved toward the Snakeshead. Upon reaching the stand of cottonwoods Jackson had mentioned, they dismounted and left their horses concealed. They proceeded out into the switch willows and new growth of hardwood trees until they reached the water's edge; then they moved south along the sandbar until they spotted Burl's men. The sun had broken above the trees and was illuminating the far bank when Baldridge saw the rowboat off the westernmost point of the sandbar, not more than a thousand feet from the Louisiana side. Burl's men were working feverishly with ropes and poles, apparently positioning one of the torpedoes.

"We've got to stop them," Baldridge said. "Can you hit those men from here?"

Jackson rose slightly and peered through the vines. "Too far."

They eased closer to the point; Baldridge again asked the old man if he could hit the boatmen with his Spencer.

"It's a reach, but I can try it."

Instructing Jackson to give him two minutes before firing, and armed with revolver and double-barreled shotgun, Baldridge pushed farther south through the switch willows until he reached a spot from which he could see the rest of Burl's men. There were six wagons, two of which were double-teamed, lined up some twenty feet from the edge of the river. Burl appeared to be carrying on a conversation on the far side of one of the wagons. Two other men stood near the last wagon, guarding the path they had taken down to the water. Including the two out in the river, Baldridge counted ten men.

The sharp report of Jackson's Spencer, followed quickly by a second shot, sent Burl's men running for cover. Baldridge's right hand was trembling as he lifted the revolver to open fire. Maybe it was the whiskey, or lack of it, causing him to shake; but the fact that he had not discharged a firearm since the day he was wounded in 1865 weighed upon his mind. The Smith & Wesson felt at once frightening and oddly comfortable in his hand, like an old friend returned after a long time away. His first shot was off target, but it spat some splinters from a wagon, sending Burl crawling back beneath it. Immediately Burl's men returned fire, wildly at first, but as the rounds whizzed closer to his head and cracked the willow limbs around him, Baldridge backed into the under-growth to find a new position. Crouched low, he was working his way around the perimeter of Burl's position when he stopped to listen. Seconds later, he heard someone moving through the brush; then he saw a dark green shirt bending the willow limbs not five feet away.

"Fool!" he mumbled to himself at the brazen way the man was wandering around. When he finally saw Baldridge it was too late. Before he could turn to fire, Baldridge had dropped him with a chest shot. Then he heard someone splash through a shallow marsh hole a short distance behind the first man. Waiting silently for three or four seconds, he saw the brim of a gray hat peeking through the limbs and vines. Laying his hand over the hammer to muffle the sound, he cocked the Smith & Wesson; taking aim about a foot below the edge of the hat, he fired one shot, then dove to his right. He ducked his head into his arms and was awaiting the return fire when his wrist began to sting. Blood oozed from a tiny red line where some briars had caught him as he rolled. No return fire came. Instead, he heard someone running away.

"They've killed Marcus, Mr. Burl," someone shouted wildly, "and Neil . . . they got him, too!"

Baldridge rose enough to get a glimpse of a man backing his way toward the wagons, his face betraying the terror of one who'd never taken fire. But as he lifted his weapon for a shot, Baldridge again heard the crack of Jackson's Spencer. The man stood up, his back rigid, his arms extended before him, and fell dead in the grass. If Baldridge had counted right, that left Burl with seven men—maybe fewer, if Jackson had gotten the ones in the boat.

"Burl! Victor Burl!" Baldridge shouted, his voice drawing fire as he again changed position. "Burl, give it up!" The rounds played near him, so he found a depression and hugged it closely.

"Baldridge!" Burl called back. "I guess I shouldn't be surprised."

A round sawed off a tiny water oak near him and sent it crashing onto Baldridge's head. A bug crawled across his neck.

As the firing died down, Burl spoke again. "It's too late, Baldridge. Everything's set. The *Paragon* will be here soon, and then I'll record its demise in the ledger."

Baldridge rolled over and pointed his weapon as the vines to his right parted, lowering the hammer when he recognized Jackson. The old man sported a broad grin.

"Got two of 'em," he whispered, glancing in the direction of Burl's voice. "One in the boat and another one trying to find me along the bank." Jackson laughed softly and patted his Spencer. "He found me all right."

Five left, Baldridge thought.

"Did you hear me, Baldridge? I said it's too late," Burl shouted. "They're all set. It's just a matter of time." The firing had stopped now. "It's got to happen, you know. It's justice. That's all. Justice, pure and simple. Think about it."

Burl's voice held a tone of self-satisfaction. "He'll hug the outside of the bend. Luke Williamson always does that. I must've ridden with him six or eight times over the years." Burl paused, apparently awaiting a response. "My boys do good work, you know. It'll be over fast. He'll come up even with the tip of the point and then . . . well, and then he won't be there anymore."

"Where in the hell's the sheriff and that posse?" Baldridge whispered.

"Ain't no tellin'," the old man said. "They're liable to not even show."

Baldridge stood up slowly near some switch willows.

"You can't get away with this, Burl," he shouted, ducking to await a volley of fire that never came. He cautiously stood up again. " 'Cause I got the sheriff and some men from Natchez out here with me. We've got you cut off. You can't get away."

"I told you, you're no good at bluffing, Baldridge," Burl shouted back.

"I'm serious, Burl. We're coming after you if you don't—"

"You got two, maybe three guns, that's all. If you had more you'd already have come. It's you who'd better give it up, Baldridge. I'm content to just sit right here and watch this steamboat blow sky-high. Then, after the wreckage washes downstream, we'll come and get you."

The sun warmed the back of Baldridge's neck during the next few moments of silence. Finally the calm was broken by the distant squall of a steam whistle. Both men looked north, then at one another.

"That'd be two, maybe three miles away," Jackson said.

"Go get my horse," Baldridge said.

"What for?"

"I'm ridin' down there."

"Mister, you can't go—"

"Just get my horse, Jackson. I got no choice." The steamboat whistle sounded again. "I ain't askin' *you* to go. But I can't just sit here and let that boat hit those torpedoes."

"If they weren't on the far side of the river, I say we could maybe warn 'em off."

"You can try it," Baldridge said. "Bring my horse and then you can ride for the shoreline."

In a few moments Jackson returned with Baldridge's horse; keeping watch while the other man mounted, he spoke quietly to him.

"I never thought I'd say it, but I'd almost be glad to have some of those armed coloreds from the Freeman's Bureau around here."

"Right now I'd settle for that sorry-ass sheriff," Baldridge said.

Jackson mounted up and looked momentarily at Baldridge as he checked the load in the shotgun.

"Here," the old man said, tossing him the other revolver. "You're gonna need it more than I will."

"You've got to stop the boat in case . . ." Tucking the extra weapon in his belt, Baldridge held the Smith & Wesson in his right hand, lifted the rein and placed it between his teeth, and then cocked both triggers on the shotgun lying across his lap and took it in his left hand. With a nod, he spurred his mount and started toward the tip of Snakeshead sandbar at a gallop. As the memories of past charges flashed through his mind, he wished for the security of some old comrades on his right and left, and the smell of their gunpowder, and the sound of the rebel yell that always made his blood boil. Instead there was only the painfully solitary sound of his own horse slapping past the willow branches and sloshing through the isolated pools of standing water. Any moment he would break into the clearing near Burl's wagons, so he squeezed his legs tight around the saddle to keep a well-placed round from unhorsing him.

Once out of the undergrowth, he took by surprise the two men whom he had originally seen guarding the wagons. One of them managed to get off an errant shot before Baldridge closed the distance to the first wagon, but before the other could fire, he lowered the shotgun and squeezed the first trigger. The blast jerked him sideways in the saddle and spooked his horse, which balked and reared. But Baldridge's shot had been close enough to nearly take the arm off one of the men. The other was running in the direction of the wagon where Burl had been standing earlier.

Two more of Burl's men emerged from the edge of the willows, some thirty yards away and in the direction of the river. They began firing at Baldridge, who had managed to gain enough control of his frightened horse to maneuver it behind the last wagon. A shot ricocheted off the metal wheel rim, betraying another of Burl's men firing from the adjacent wagon. Baldridge dispatched three rounds from his pistol at the man, then fired until the chamber was empty at the two rushing toward him from the willows. The hot barrel burned his belly as he thrust the empty weapon in his belt and drew the second revolver. Then, riding toward the next wagon, he began firing, sending Burl's man between the wheels for cover. Panicked, the man fired wildly from between the spokes as Baldridge spat lead at the wheel. One shot shattered the spoke and a second drove the man backward on to the sandy ground, his body twisting as he cried out.

Spurring his horse forward toward the wagon where he'd seen Burl, Baldridge ignored the shots coming from the two men chasing him. When he found no one there, he looked toward the southeast tip of the sandbar, where a man was pushing a rowboat into the water. It had to be Burl. He wanted to fire, but the two men pursuing him were making it too hot to remain exposed, so he rode behind a third wagon and tried to return fire. He was leaning over in the saddle, using the high sides of the wagon for cover, getting off an occasional shot and trying to get an angle on the man he figured to be Burl. He wanted to ride for him, but that would be suicide; the other two men had him pinned down. As he struggled to keep his terrified horse behind the wagon, a piece of the sideboard, carried away by a bullet, seemed to explode near his right leg. Taking a round in his good leg would just complete the set, he thought. With only two rounds left in his revolver, and knowing the *Paragon* was drawing nearer by the second, Baldridge began to regret having so brashly ridden into this hornet's nest. Burl's men were loading and firing at leisure now, almost like hunters shooting at a trapped squirrel. His back ached from leaning down, and he expected his horse to take a round at any moment, perhaps toppling over on him, or leaving him unmounted at best.

Suddenly there was rifle fire—not from one weapon but from several—erratic at first, then swelling into a general clamor from the direction of the willows. The two men had stopped shooting at him now, and were directing their fire north. That could only mean that Powell had arrived with his men; taking advantage of the distraction, Baldridge rode for the tip of the sandbar. But when he arrived the rowboat was well out into the channel and heading downriver. He fired a shot at the figure desperately rowing away, but missed. Dismounting, he held the revolver in his right hand, and supporting it with his left, he prepared to take his last shot. He squeezed off the round and saw the man slump and tumble over the side of the boat. The craft continued downriver.

The firing behind him abruptly stopped as Burl's men surrendered to the posse's overwhelming numbers. Jumping on his horse, Baldridge raced up the sandbar, where he immediately recognized Curry as one of two men standing under guard, their hands behind their heads, backed up against a wagon. As he came to a halt, Jackson handed him the Bowie knife Curry had taken from him.

"I couldn't stop the boat," Jackson said, "so when I ran into the sheriff, I figured the next best thing was to help you out."

Baldridge gave the old man a nod to say it was all right, then turned to Powell. "Sheriff, these men are responsible for the murder of Asa Turner and the wreck of the steamboat *Mary Justice*."

"He's crazy as hell," Curry protested. "He come riding in here shooting at us and all we did was shoot back."

"Where are the torpedoes, Curry?" Baldridge asked.

"Torpedoes? I don't know nothin' about no torpedoes."

With the *Paragon* less than a mile distant and bearing down upon Merengo Bend, Baldridge was growing desperate.

"Goddamn it, Curry," he shouted as he leaped from his horse, his bad leg nearly giving way as he landed. Stumbling toward Curry, he lifted his knife, and was almost upon the man when Powell and two of his men stepped in.

"Hold it there," the sheriff said, pulling Baldridge's knife hand away. "I can't let you kill this man."

Baldridge was furious. "He knows where they are. I know he does!" He tried to pull free, but the deputies held him tightly. "I'll get it out of him."

The sheriff stepped between them. "Now hold it right there."

Curry kept taunting him. "I told you he was crazy, Sheriff. Why, he's killed at least four men. Nearly killed us, too."

When Baldridge backed away the deputies released him and he sheathed his blade. Some twenty yards away was a second rowboat. He recalled what Jenkins had said—how the torpedoes would be in a line, four of them stretched forty feet apart. From what Zedekiah McDaniel had told him, he had no doubt that the explosives were rigged both for electrical and impact detonation. Finding the batteries wouldn't stop the blast; but batteries meant wires, and wires might lead him to the torpedoes. While the sheriff and his men continued to question Curry and his accomplice, Baldridge hustled along the bank until he came upon a freshly dug pit containing two hidden batteries. From the batteries to the edge of the river ran two thin platinum wires. He dashed back over to Curry.

"You don't know anything about torpedoes, huh?"

"No. I never even heard of any such—"

"Then you won't mind a little boat ride." Baldridge turned to the sheriff. "I found the wires leading from the batteries. They're just down by the water's edge. Give me two of your deputies to watch Curry and let him come with me."

"I ain't goin' out in no river with you," Curry said.

"I don't know about this," Powell mumbled.

"For God's sake, man, it's our only chance. The men on that boat can't hear us if we try to warn 'em. If we don't get to those torpedoes before the *Paragon* does, people will die!"

The sheriff motioned for two men to accompany him.

"Sheriff, you ain't got no right sendin' me out with this here crazy man. He's a killer!" Curry protested.

While the deputies pushed the rowboat into the river, Baldridge laced one of the wires into an eyelet on the front of the craft; as they rowed, the wire rose out of the water some two or three feet in front of the boat, guiding them toward the sunken explosives. Still Curry refused to admit they were there, but Baldridge could tell he was getting nervous. They were halfway across the river and well into the channel, still following the trail of the wire, when the *Paragon* appeared from the north, growing larger in the distance as she swept along the outside of the bend less than three quarters of a mile away and closing fast

"Where are they, Curry?" Baldridge asked.

Curry refused to answer, but stared wide-eyed at the water in front of the boat. The two deputies working the oars were struggling to hold the boat as they rowed across the current. They were within fifteen hundred feet of the Louisiana shore and due west of the tip of Snakeshead sandbar, the very area Burl had described earlier as he taunted Baldridge from behind the wagons. They had to be close. Curry was sweating now as the *Paragon* rushed toward them, his anxious gaze alternating rapidly between the steamboat and the water nearby.

Suddenly Baldridge sat back on the seat near the bow.

"Okay, Curry. What the hell, we'll just wait right here. Hold her steady there, boys," he said to the deputies. "We'll have us a real good view of the action."

When Curry reached for the edge of the boat to jump over, Baldridge grabbed the back of his shirt and jerked him to the floor. He slapped his blade to the frightened man's throat and pressed it until the skin was indented. The deputies eyed each other nervously, but neither interfered.

"Oh, no. You can't be leaving us now. We'll wait this one out together. What're you so scared of, Curry? You said it yourself. 'There ain't no torpedoes out here!' "

Curry grabbed for the side of the boat again, settling down only after Baldridge increased the pressure from his blade.

"Over there," he said, pointing out the right front of the boat. "But I ain't sure where, 'cause I didn't set 'em. But they're probably right out there. Now please, get us out of here!"

"Keep an eye on him," Baldridge told the deputies as he shoved Curry down at their feet. Removing his boots and his jacket, and placing the two revolvers on the seat of the rowboat, he wrapped the jacket around his left hand, grasped his knife in his right, and slipped over the edge of the craft and into the water. The muscles in his legs seized as the November-chilled water engulfed him. Then, sliding his jacket-wrapped hand down the thin wire, Baldridge dove. He worked his way down at an angle, going no more than four or five feet below the surface, when his left hand slid into something solid. At once he froze, expecting an explosion from the force of the blow, but none came. Darting upward, he broke the surface and took a deep breath, then dove back down in the same motion. Although his bad leg would scarcely bend in the cold water, Baldridge kicked his right one hard and pressed his arms against the current in a breast-stroke. This time he eased up to a glass demijohn, shielded with wicker and loaded with powder. Unable to see more than a foot, he gently felt his way around it and over the exposed friction primers, eventually discovering the taut rope that anchored the torpedo to the bottom. And though his lungs now ached for oxygen, he sawed at the rope with his Bowie knife, eventually severing it and sending the torpedo floating harmlessly to the surface. Baldridge was not far behind.

"There's one of them," he called to the deputies in the

boat as he gasped for air. Again he dove and began looking for the next device. Since they were wired in series, the thin platinum led him to the next torpedo, which he quickly dispatched to the surface as he had the first. This time when he surfaced, he looked in horror at the *Paragon* cruising directly toward him and showing no signs of slowing, despite the clamor of the deputies from the rowboat nearby. The boat might pass safely through the gap he'd created in Burl's trap, but she might as easily veer off just enough to strike one of the remaining torpedoes. He had no choice. He had to get the others. The third one he found quickly and diving to just beneath it, managed to sever the anchoring rope. Then holding on to the end of the rope, he let the rising torpedo pull his nearly exhausted body to the surface. He quickly released it to keep from banging his head into the friction primers, then turned to see the progress of the *Paragon*, now so close he could hear the deckhands cursing him for swimming in front of an oncoming steamer. The whistle squalled a warning, yet the *Paragon* showed no sign of slowing. His legs were stiffening from the cold water and his lungs burned as he rolled over in a desperate dive to reach the last torpedo before the *Paragon* came rushing over him. As he descended into the dark, muddy water, he could hear the thrashing of the paddle wheel as it pressed relentlessly forward. If he didn't reach that mine, he and the boat would be blown to pieces. If he did reach it, he might still be overrun, chewed up by the paddle wheel.

$\triangledown$

14

Wednesday morning, November 6

LUKE WILLIAMSON HURRIED down the steps from the texas as several of the deckhands rushed past the stairs toward the bow.

"Man in the water!" Jacob Lusk had called only moments before, and Luke, hearing the call from inside the dining hall, ran at once for the lower deck. All he needed now was some passenger taking a dive over the railing and drowning on him.

"Where is he?" Luke demanded as he emerged on the deck.

"Right yonder, Cap'n." Jacob pointed directly ahead.

"It's not a passenger, then?"

"No sir. I reckon he come from that boat over there."

Luke saw a rowboat with three men aboard off to the left about a hundred yards away. Two of them were wildly waving their hands and shouting, but he couldn't make out what they were saying.

Glancing back at the figure in the water, Luke noticed he was swimming cross-current. As he disappeared underwater, Luke climbed on a flour barrel to try to see him again. He turned to Jacob.

"What in hell would a man be doing in this cold water?"

"I don't know, Cap'n, but he sho' better get out of the way."

"There he is," one of the deckhands called. "He's come up again. Looks like he had ahold of a buoy, Captain, but he let it loose."

Thinking the man was sure to move out of their path,

Luke hesitated to have Martin slow the boat. They were within fifty yards of the swimmer and closing fast, and still the man appeared to be bobbing and diving like a coot chasing minnows.

"Cap'n, something's wrong," Jacob said, studying the men in the rowboat. "They're tryin' to tell us something."

Luke shook his head. "They're tryin' to tell us we're going to run over this fool in the water, but I can see that for myself."

"No sir, I don't think that's it."

Lifting his hand in the air and turning toward the pilothouse, Luke shouted to the pilot: "Slow her to one half!" He looked back at Jacob. "Well, what is it, Jacob?"

"I don't know, Cap'n, but something ain't right. Seems like they're telling us to stop."

The nose of the *Paragon* was within twenty-five yards of the swimmer now, but as he again disappeared beneath the surface, Luke hesitated to order her left or right, for fear the man would pop up in the chosen path.

"All stop!" Luke shouted. "Reverse 'em!"

"All stop! Reverse engines!" a senior hand echoed from the hurricane deck.

The *Paragon* coasted several feet before the momentum of the paddle wheel stopped, allowing Ham to throw the lever engaging the wheel in the opposite direction. Already the craft had drifted well into the area where Luke had last seen the swimmer. He cussed the man loudly and stormed toward the lifting spars, fearing the very worst.

"Stop engines!" Luke commanded. All available hands were peering over the sides, searching the water for some sign of the swimmer, when someone shouted from near midship.

"There goes a buoy!"

Luke noticed the top half of what appeared to be a light brown, oval object floating with them on the current eight or ten feet from the *Paragon*.

"Man in the water!" shouted another crewman, and Luke saw a figure bobbing with the waves.

"Get that son of a bitch aboard!" Luke ordered, and under

Jacob's immediate supervision, the roustabouts drew the man in, using a long rescue pole fitted with a hook on the end. After they lifted his dripping body from the water and laid him out on the deck, Luke heard Jacob calling him.

"Cap'n! Cap'n, come quick!" When Luke arrived Jacob stared up at him in astonishment. "It's that fella from Memphis. That insurance fella."

Although coughing, heaving, and spitting water on to the deck, Masey Baldridge was trying to speak.

"Williamson," he grunted. "Williamson . . ." He lifted his hand weakly and Jacob Lusk supported his head. Still choking, he forced out the word: "Tor . . . tor . . . torpedoes."

It had been years since Luke had heard that word, but it frightened him just as it had during the war. His eyes went immediately to the object pacing the *Paragon* on the current.

"Slow reverse," he called to the pilothouse. "Hold her steady as she is. No drift!"

A crowd was gathering on the hurricane deck as gradually the paddle wheel began to rotate backward, holding the big riverboat in position with respect to the bank. Luke watched the oval object, carried along by the current, distance itself from the *Paragon.* The men in the rowboat had now come alongside the steamer and were being helped aboard. With Jacob Lusk's assistance, Baldridge had drawn himself up on his good leg and was leaning on a lashing knob. Luke ordered the men to find blankets and towels and had Jacob lead him to the first available cabin. Once inside, and having begun to breathe easier, Baldridge quickly told Luke of the trap Victor Burl had set for him.

"Victor Burl? The gambler?" Luke asked.

"The man's a lunatic, Williamson. He'll stop at nothing to sink this boat." Interrupted by a coughing fit, he added, "He's the one who sank the *Mary Justice.*"

"Are you sure? What about VanGeer?"

"VanGeer had nothing to do with it. He may want you out of business, but from what I can tell, he's not a murderer."

"But why?"

That was going to take some explaining; Baldridge was about to try when one of the roustabouts came up to the cabin and announced that the *Apollo* was rounding the bend and closing fast.

"Where are the rest of the torpedoes?" Luke asked.

"Floating downriver, I suppose. There were four of 'em and I cut 'em all loose."

"Get him dried off and give him some hot coffee. Then bring him up to the pilothouse," Luke ordered. "Jacob, come with me."

"There's something else—" Baldridge shouted, but Luke and Jacob were already out the door and headed for the upper deck.

"I want lookouts stationed on the texas," Luke ordered. "If they see anything floating that looks round, or almost round, like a big glass jar, they're to sing out. Got it?"

"Yes, sir. Lookin' for something round."

"And have Steven get the passengers inside again."

"Again, Cap'n?"

"Again."

"Yes, sir."

From the pilothouse Luke Williamson took his Henry rifle and a pair of binoculars; then he climbed on the roof above the pilothouse and sat cross-legged, watching the water off the bow.

"Take her ahead slow," he shouted through the window below, and the *Paragon* began to move under power. As she pushed slowly forward, the *Apollo* was coming up on the left, nearer to mid-channel but less than a hundred yards away. Driving ahead at full speed, Creed Haskins's boat soon overtook the *Paragon*, and then was passing her amid the cheers of her passengers. Lifting the binoculars to his face, Luke could see Haskins standing near the deck rail on the starboard side. He appeared momentarily puzzled as his craft eased past the *Paragon*, but then he placed his hands on his hips in a position reminiscent of John Paul Jones, and seemed to delight in overtaking his rival.

"Ahead full speed," Luke called out, and the *Paragon*, though now slightly behind, ceased to lose distance to the *Apollo*. The two boats hadn't gone three hundred yards when one of the deckhands on the texas identified an object floating up ahead. Aiming his binoculars off the port bow, Luke saw the sun glint off the neck of one of the torpedoes Baldridge had cut loose. It bobbed in the water, eased along by the current. Just beyond it, Luke spotted a second one, drifting less than a hundred yards off the bow of the *Apollo*; given the crosscurrents of Merengo Bend, it was likely to float squarely in the ship's path. The celebrating passengers and crew of the *Apollo* rushed unaware toward their death as Luke shouldered the Henry rifle and took aim. His first shot missed the torpedo, but sent the passengers on the *Apollo* screaming and running for cover.

"They must really think I'm crazy now," Luke told himself, squeezing off a second round. The sound of the rifle was overwhelmed by the blast in the distance—a blast that showered the crew and passengers of the *Apollo* with muddy river water. Irate roustabouts cursed from the deck of the rival ship as Creed Haskins stared toward the *Paragon* in disbelief. His passengers ran for their cabins, while Luke's passengers watched in amazement from inside the dining hall. Luke's third shot detonated the second torpedo, the one closest to the *Apollo*, forcing her pilot to react with a sharp left turn that sent her driving toward the shallow water below the Snakeshead sandbar. The *Paragon* now passed the *Apollo*, as Haskins's boat sought to regain the channel.

"Got another one, Cap'n," Jacob shouted from the lower deck. Spotting the torpedo some fifty yards off the right front bow, Luke ordered a hard left turn much like the *Apollo*'s. As the boat swung around, Luke got off two shots, the second one detonating the torpedo and sending a spray of water skyward. The blast shook the boat. After locating the fourth demijohn, caught on a snag closer to the shore, Luke successfully targeted it as well, then stopped the *Paragon*'s engines and allowed her to drift momentarily. He called

Steven Tibedeau up to the roof, gave him a quick explanation of what had happened, and dispatched him to brief the bewildered passengers. Then he let out a long, slow breath.

For the next few minutes he sat alone on the roof of the pilothouse, his Henry still lying across his lap, contemplating how close he'd come to losing it all. He owed a lot to Baldridge, and an apology was probably the first order of business. But by now, the *Apollo* had recovered and was steaming around the inside of the bend and nearing the *Paragon*. As she came up alongside, Luke saw Creed Haskins standing atop his pilothouse as well. The passengers were just beginning to emerge from inside both ships, all muttering about what had happened. The *Apollo* stopped her engines and drifted alongside the *Paragon* for several moments, the deckhands of the two riverboats eyeing one another defiantly while the two captains stared at each other from atop their perches. Finally, Creed Haskins called across the water.

"Were those meant for you or for me?"

"I don't guess it really matters, does it?"

The crowd began to quiet as they endeavored to hear the shouted conversation.

"I'd just kinda like to know," Haskins said nervously.

"Well, they must've been meant for me," Luke said, "because anybody with any sense would know I was going to get here first."

"Now, you know that's a damned lie," Haskins said, glancing downriver. "Are there any more?"

"I think that's all of them."

"I guess this is one I owe you," Haskins shouted, "but I still think you're crazy as hell."

Luke nodded. "You could repay me by pulling out of the race."

"I'll see you in hell first," Haskins said with a tip of his hat. "Engines ahead full!" he called to his pilot. "Look me up when you get to New Orleans. I'll buy you a drink. I'll be waiting for you in the Fontainebleue."

"Engines ahead full!" Luke shouted down to Martin; then he called back to Haskins: "I'll have a table reserved."

Less than twenty minutes later, Luke was four miles north of Natchez, trailing the *Apollo* by some two hundred yards, when Jacob brought Masey Baldridge up to the hurricane deck.

"Cap'n, Mr. Baldridge here says we got problems," Jacob said.

"More torpedoes?"

"No. It's the wood," Baldridge said. "You've got to stop using it. I'm pretty sure Burl has rigged it."

"Stop using the wood? Are you crazy? How can I run without wood?"

"You'll just have to take on more."

"And where am I going to do that?" Luke asked. "It's fifty miles to the next woodyard, if it's even open this time of year. And how am I supposed to get there? Drift with the current?"

"It's too dangerous, Luke. I'm telling you, Burl's not a man to—"

"So what's wrong with the wood?"

"Burl and his men have this way of loading up a piece of cordwood. An old naval officer told me about it. They rout out the middle of a shank of wood and place a sawed-off rifle barrel inside, then tamp the end so no one can tell it's been messed with."

"And you think he's done that to us?"

"It's possible. Where'd you take on wood last?"

"King's, where I always load."

Baldridge took Luke by the shoulders. "You gotta stop the boat."

"I *can't* stop the boat. It's going to be hard enough to keep up with Haskins as it is. Especially if you're not even sure there's anything wrong with the wood."

"Then at least search it. Have a man you trust examine every piece. You're looking for an end that shows signs of being altered, grains that are misaligned, anything that would arouse suspicion."

"Cap'n, they was actin' awful strange back at the wood-yard," Jacob added. "Ike wouldn't even look me in the face. I thought something was wrong even then."

"Why didn't you say anything?"

"What could I say? Anyway, we ain't had time for—"

"It doesn't matter, Jacob," Luke said. "Get Steven. He's got the best eye for cordwood. Have him walk the stack and visually inspect every piece. You go with him. Let's hope Baldridge is wrong about this one."

"And have your firemen watch for a piece that's heavier than the rest," Baldridge reminded Luke as he started down the steps. "That barrel of powder has got to be heavy."

"Yes, sir."

When Jacob left, Baldridge told Luke the rest of the story about Burl and his obsession with Ellet's Marine Brigade. The captain shook his head in disbelief.

"Baldridge, I don't even remember such a fight. We were always putting in to shore and chasing guerrillas."

"And firing artillery into towns?"

He shook his head again, and took a seat in a deck chair. "Oh, we threw some shells . . . but I had no idea . . . I never realized . . ."

"Where did you think those rounds were going?"

"I *knew* where they were going," Luke said defensively. "They were going at bushwhackers. Do you know how many soldiers I saw die at the hands of bushwhackers?"

"But everybody in a town is not a bushwhacker."

Luke studied Baldridge in silence before speaking. "Damn it, man, you sound like you agree with this maniac!"

"Agree with him? No. No, I don't agree with what he's done. Wrong was done on both sides and people like Burl are just prolonging the pain. That's why I've got to know I got him."

"I thought you said you shot him. You saw him go down."

"I said I *think* I got him. A gambler like him runs a good bluff. I'm not going to be satisfied until I see the body."

"Where are you going to look?"

"If he got out of that boat alive, I've got a pretty good idea where he's headed, and when you put me ashore in Natchez—"

"Put you ashore? You've got to be kidding! I can't—"

"Luke, you've got two deputies and one of Burl's men down below. You have to put them ashore at Natchez. Burl's still got a half dozen men working the river between here and St. Louis. If those men aren't found, they could cause trouble yet."

"And how do you plan to find them?"

"The one who got his eye put out is in jail in Natchez. What he doesn't tell, I suspect the sheriff can eventually get out of Curry. But they've got to get ashore soon or else Burl's men will scatter like dandelion seed."

Luke slammed his foot into the railing. "How in hell am I supposed to win a race if I'm having to stop at every port between Memphis and New Orleans?" The two men stared at one another for several seconds; then Luke spoke. "All right. I'll put you ashore. I reckon you did save my boat."

"And your hide, too."

Luke grinned. "But you'd better haul ass when I touch that dock, because I'm not waiting around."

"Agreed."

As the *Paragon* swept around the bend, trailing the *Apollo* on the approach to Natchez, a crowd of local citizens had lined the bluff to cheer on the competing riverboats. Since neither boat was supposed to stop, the spectators were surprised to see the *Paragon* veer from the channel and approach the docks near Natchez-Under-the-Hill. Baldridge, the two deputies, and Curry, his hands bound behind him, had gathered along the port deck. Luke Williamson was talking to Baldridge about Victor Burl when Steven Tibedeau, sweat-soaked and out of breath, came running up to the captain. Jacob was close behind.

"Captain, Jacob and I have checked all the wood on this boat and we can't find anything that looks suspicious," Steven said, trying to catch his breath.

"You saw every piece?" Luke asked.

"Well, as best we could. We went down both sides of every cord and all through the holding area. I saw the ends of each piece and I couldn't tell that a one of them had been altered. Just looked like normal firewood to me."

Jacob interrupted. "And me and the firemen checked all the wood piled up near the boiler, Cap'n. Even took the sticks right of their hands before they threw 'em in. None of it was messed with, and there wasn't no heavy pieces like Mr. Baldridge said."

Luke looked at Baldridge, who stared down at the deck in thought. "I know Burl's done something. I'm sure of it," he said.

"And you're sure you saw every piece that you took on at King's Woodyard?" Baldridge asked.

"Yes, sir," Jacob said. "We stacked it all separate—that way we know how much we're using."

"No chance it could have gotten mixed in with what you had before?"

"No, sir. Steven here, he don't allow no foolishness when it comes to takin' on fuel."

Baldridge glanced up at the second deck. "Where's that boy going?"

Luke looked up and saw Anabel's son carrying an armload of firewood.

"Hold up, there!" Luke shouted.

The boy halted and looked over the rail. When he realized the captain was addressing him, his eyes widened.

"Did you call me, sir?"

"Where are you going with that wood?"

"To the k-k-kitchen, sir?" It was more a question than an answer as the boy stammered. "My . . . uh . . . the cook, she says she needed another load, sir."

Jacob, his face terrified, turned to Luke.

"*Another* load? Anabel! The kitchen!"

Both men went tearing across the deck, but Jacob reached the stairs first. Luke was close behind him as they rushed for the kitchen at the rear of the boat. Two passengers were slammed against the wall and one hit the floor as Jacob's broad shoulders cleared a way along the second deck. Luke stepped over the startled, angry passengers and was close behind his first mate. As he dashed inside the kitchen behind Jacob, he saw Anabel near the stove. In the corner he saw the half-filled wood box, and then looked on in horror as Anabel, her back to the door, stood holding two pieces of wood near the open grate of the stove.

She had poked the first piece into the fire and was about to follow it with the second when Jacob cried out in his deep voice, "No!" He ran across the room, knocking over a chopping block and sending pots and pans flying. Anabel was looking back to see what the commotion was about, her hand still reaching to drop the cordwood into the stove, when Jacob dove at her. His right hand caught her forearm and drove it down only an instant before the edge of the wood entered the flames. His momentum carried him into the base of the stove and took Anabel's feet from under her. She lay on the floor, momentarily dazed, until Luke came over to help her up, then looked up at him in puzzlement as Jacob examined the wood on the floor. The piece looked all right, so he took a set of tongs, pulled the already smoldering first piece from the fire, and tossed it on the floor. He could find no evidence of tampering, so he immediately went over to the wood box. Luke had helped Anabel to her feet, and was trying to explain what they were doing when Jacob called to him.

"I got it! I got it!" Wheeling about, he held up an ordinary-looking piece of cordwood, then proceeded to pick up the cutting table and find a butcher knife. "This has got to be it, Cap'n. It's way too heavy." He examined the end. "See here? See how these grains is off? Just like that Mr. Baldridge said." Jacob grinned. "Just like he said they'd be." Prying gently at the end with the butcher knife, Jacob slowly worked loose a wooden plug, and tilting the piece of firewood, produced a long, cylindrical tube tamped at both ends with tar.

Luke glanced out the door and let out a sigh of relief, as Jacob came over to Anabel. Throwing her arms around him, she began to weep on his shoulder; and the first mate, still holding the loaded cylinder in his hand, lifted both arms and hugged her tightly.

"It's all right now, Anabel. It's all right," he said, patting her back. Jacob looked at Luke. "I'll go through the rest of that wood box, Cap'n, and make sure ain't no more of these things around."

"You do that," Luke said. He could feel the boat beginning to slow, so he rushed down to the foredeck, where Baldridge and the others stood. "Jacob found it in the wood box in the kitchen."

"Thank God," Baldridge said.

"Thank *you*," Luke countered, extending his hand as the engines stopped and the *Paragon* drifted closer to the landing. Baldridge turned and motioned for the deputies and Curry to step off first as soon as they hove to the dock. Luke still had hold of his hand. "You saved a lot of lives, Baldridge. If there's anything I can ever do for you, anything at all . . ."

"There is one thing you can do," Baldridge said with a smile. "You can get to New Orleans first. I'd hate to think I went through all this just so Mid-South Insurance could lose a good customer." With that, he and the others stepped on to the dock as the *Paragon* bumped it gently, then eased away, her paddle wheel again churning the brown water as she pulled for the channel in pursuit of the *Apollo*.

$\triangledown$

15

Wednesday afternoon, November 6

THE LIVERY STABLE owner wouldn't accept a promissory note for the horse Baldridge had lost, and he belligerently demanded to be paid in cash for the animal. After charging Baldridge twice what the nag was worth, the proprietor was still reluctant to rent Baldridge another horse. But having been scalded, shot at, and half drowned in the past week, Baldridge wasn't in the mood to be trifled with. His tone of voice, his constant caress of the revolver handles protruding from his belt, and the sight of the Bowie knife occasionally winking from under his coat convinced the owner that he could trust this customer with a second loaner.

Baldridge had ridden just past the edge of town when he realized he'd been in such a hurry that he'd forgotten to pick up the bottle he'd been promising himself since before daylight that morning. A shot of whiskey would do more for him than anything else he could think of, except for maybe the sight of Victor Burl dead. That would close the matter as far as he was concerned. He was proud of what he'd accomplished. Curry and McGraw would probably hang, or go to jail at the least; and if Sheriff Powell moved fast enough, Burl's men at King's Woodyard and elsewhere could be rounded up. But he kept seeing Burl slipping that white name card into his hideous display while he talked so coldly about killing innocent people, all the while filing those damned nails and looking as unaffected as if he were about to draw four to an ace in a poker game. A dozen times in his mind Baldridge had seen that rowboat in the distance and heard the pistol discharge and watched the figure tumble into the Mississippi. Surely he'd gotten him that morning. Burl was probably dead and floating in some backwater slough downriver.

A pudgey gray squirrel was jumping down the steps to the front door of Concord as Baldridge approached cautiously along the trail. Sitting up, the squirrel stared defiantly at the horse for two or three seconds, as though deciding whether to charge right over and whip its ass, but then dashed across the yard and up one of the broad oaks nearby. Baldridge listened at the edge of the woods for several minutes but could detect no one around, so he rode up to the house and dismounted. Drawing a revolver, he entered the tunnel on the first floor and went into the house, beginning a room-by-room search. In the parlor he came upon the body of Asa Turner, and glancing around the room for security, he knelt down beside the corpse. It was a shame about Turner; Baldridge couldn't help feeling responsible for what had happened. Through the door into the room where the camera had been set up, he could see the head and torso of Jenkins, the wood beneath him stained dark even a foot from his body. Peering inside, he found that room, too, to be quiet and empty. On the floor beside the camera stand, of which one leg had been broken during the scuffle, was the body of Baines. Baldridge had sworn not only to give up guns after the war, but also never to take another life. But those vows had gone the way of his sobriety, and the only thing that really surprised him was how quickly he'd gotten used to killing again.

He cleared the rest of the rooms on the second floor and at last entered the place where Burl had built his altar. The tintypes were all in place, just as he'd seen them the night before, and with the sun casting an angular light through an unshielded window, the hard shadows and unbroken tranquility created an eerie sensation in the room. The mansion was a place of death—not only for Turner and Jenkins and

Baines, and all those whose pictures lined the wall, but for Baldridge, too. His dreams of leaving the war behind, of overcoming the pain, of getting on with a new life that didn't involve killing and suffering, were gone. He realized just how much he'd been kidding himself all these years, drifting from one two-bit job to another, half trying, getting fired— he'd been a loser. There was only one thing he could do and do well, and it involved a gun and a knife and seeing people die. And as he stood there thinking about what he'd been through and the sad shape of his life, he allowed as how his skills might not count for too much on the big scale of things, but they were better than nothing. Hadn't he, after all, saved a boatload of people? Hadn't he stopped a madman?

Satisfied that the house was empty and there was no sign of Burl or any of his men, Baldridge removed the tintypes and the name tags from the wall and bundled them in a velvet desk cloth to hand over to the sheriff. Then he walked out to the barn and surveyed the inside. An empty wagon sat near the door, its team having been confiscated by Baldridge and Jackson for their escape. There were still four kegs of powder along the north wall, and two glass demijohns sat empty beside the long worktable. A spool of platinum wire, a roll of cotton rope—it was all to have been loaded up and removed by Burl's trail party, and it was more than enough evidence to hang McGraw and Curry. Still, it would have been better to have found Burl, to see him either behind bars or dead.

When he returned to Natchez, Baldridge discovered that Sheriff Powell and his men, along with old Jackson, had made it back from the Snakeshead about half an hour earlier. The man they'd captured with Curry joined him and McGraw in a cell, and on Baldridge's direction Powell dispatched four deputies to Concord to confiscate the evidence and to set up a watch in case any stragglers from Burl's gang happened to drop in. After filling the sheriff in on some of the details of Burl's operation, and handing over the tintypes he'd taken from Concord, Baldridge found Jackson out watering his horse beside the jail.

"Mr. Jackson!"

"Well," he said, looking rather surprised, "I wasn't sure if you'd gone down for the third time or not." He shook Baldridge's hand. "From where we was standin' on the sandbar, the last we seen of you was when you jumped out of the rowboat." He rolled his head toward the office. "All the way back the sheriff figured you for a goner, but I told him I didn't think so. You're a fella with a lot of pluck."

"I'm a fella with a lot of aches and pains right now," Baldridge admitted.

"Me, too. I can't remember when I've ridden as far and hightailed it as much as I have these past few days," Jackson said with a grin. "But I mean it when I say that it took some nuts to ride into Burl's men out there on that sandbar."

"But I'd be dancin' with ol'Rigor Mortis without you to help me," Baldridge replied, "and I don't forget things like that."

"You're all right, young fella."

Baldridge pulled his money pouch from his pocket. It was still damp from the river.

"I was going to the hotel to change clothes," he began, counting what was left of Ferguson's money, "but I'd like to at least buy you supper. I think there's enough here."

Jackson scratched his head. "That sounds like a right fine idea."

Baldridge stretched out his last three bills in his left hand, running each of them between his fingers to wring out the water. "Reckon they'll take river money?"

"Hell, they better. River money built this town."

It was just after eleven o'clock when Baldridge awoke Thursday morning. The dinner with Jackson had led to a few drinks afterward; and then, courtesy of a couple of men who'd accompanied the sheriff to the Snakeshead, he was treated to several more rounds in his honor. He ended up telling the story of the gunfight more times than he could remember, to more people than he cared to, but the whiskey kept coming right along with the questions and he'd felt duty bound to answer the call of both.

His plan was to drop by the sheriff's office that morning to answer any last-minute questions, move on to the telegraph office and wire Ferguson about what had happened, and then drop off his mount at the livery. With the river showing no signs of rising, there was no telling when Luke Williamson would return north; and while he liked Natchez, it was definitely time to go home. Down to his last few dollars, he figured he'd better check out of the Pollock House, pay for the horse, and get a train ticket to Memphis before he was broke. On the way across town he picked up a copy of that day's Natchez *Democrat*, which declared President Grant and the Republican party's overwhelming victory in Tuesday's election. The old warhorse had won Mississippi by 35,000 votes and garnered for the Republicans five out of six congressional seats. It was a good thing Burl wasn't around to see this, Baldridge thought. He would have been crazy enough to go after Grant himself. Baldridge scanned the rest of the front page and was delighted as another wire story caught his attention.

VICTORY FOR THE *PARAGON*!

NEW ORLEANS, LA., In a close, and sometimes desperate, race from St. Louis, Missouri, two of the river's most elegant steamers came into New Orleans today amid the cheers and music of a brave early-morning crowd of onlookers. Some two hundred citizens saw Captain Luke Williamson, owner and operator of the *Paragon*, toss his mooring lines on to the dock at Front Street some twelve minutes before Captain Creed Haskins of the *Apollo*. Passengers aboard both boats on this historic run told of an exciting and often harrowing series of obstacles that both pilots overcame to reach our fair city. While Captain Haskins is to be commended for his daring effort, Captain Luke Williamson's stunning victory, under the most adverse and daunting of water and weather conditions, makes his *Paragon* the premier player in both the cargo and passenger markets.

Stopping in at Gurney's Corner, Baldridge thanked Henry C. Norman for his help, and even shelled out some of Ferguson's dwindling cash for a portrait to be mailed to him in Memphis. While at the sheriff's office, he learned that a fisherman on the Louisiana side of the river, near Vidalia, had discovered a corpse floating facedown and caught on a snag about twenty feet from shore. The alligator gars had apparently gotten to some of the flesh, but the fisherman had offered a detailed description of the dead man and his clothes. A tall man, probably in his late forties, wearing what was left of an expensive-looking gray suit, he bore a Masonic ring on the left hand, and the head evidenced a gunshot wound. On its feet were a pair of brogans. Pending the arrival of papers found in the clothes, Sheriff Powell was certain the body was that of Victor Burl.

With Burl's body surfacing to settle the matter, Baldridge should have been busy accepting congratulations for such an accurate head shot. Instead, after hearing the man's description, he reached inside his coat pocket for the message he'd drafted to send to Ferguson in Memphis; and taking a seat at the sheriff's desk, he began scribbling. He figured he better try to get some more money out of Ferguson and postpone buying that train ticket. After all, Victor Burl wouldn't be caught dead in work boots.